LOCAL ARTIST

"A compelling mystery told with an extraordinary insight into the heights and depths of human nature. Paul Trembling has a gift for making heroes out of ordinary people."

Fiona Veitch Smith, author of *The Death Beat*

PAUL TREMBLING

LOCAL ARTIST

PERFECTING THE ART OF MURDER

LION FICTION

Published by Lion Fiction
an imprint of
Lion Hudson IP Ltd
Wilkinson House, Jordan Hill Road
Oxford OX2 8DR, England
www.lionhudson.com/fiction

ISBN 978 1 78264 259 6
e-ISBN 978 1 78264 260 2

First edition 2017

Acknowledgments
Cover photo © Philip Askew / Trevillion Images

A catalogue record for this book is available from the British Library

Printed and bound in the UK, October 2017, LH26

For my boys – Tom, Matt, and Andy. Thanks for all the support and encouragement. Each one of you is an artist: you have painted love into my life.

DAY 1: LOLLYGAGGING

A phone call at four in the morning is rarely a good thing. Especially not from the police.

I fumbled through the clutter on my bedside table, found my mobile, and jabbed my finger at the screen, more or less at random, until the noise stopped.

"What?" I muttered.

"Hello? Is that Sandra? Sandra Deeson?"

"Um."

"Sandra, this is June Henshaw. Sergeant Henshaw. From Central Police Station?"

"Um. Yes. June." I knew her slightly.

"Sorry to bother you at this time, but we've got your name and number as keyholder for the library on Bromwell Street?"

My brain fog started to clear. "Yes. Yes, that's right. Has something happened?"

"We're not sure, but an officer has discovered an insecurity at the library. We need to gain access to find out what's happened. Would you be able to come down and meet us there?"

"Yes. Of course. I'll be…" I paused, trying to focus my thoughts. It could take an hour to get to work in rush hour traffic, but at this time the roads should be much quieter. "Half an hour."

"That's great. Thank you, Sandra. I'll meet you there."

Graham had rolled over in bed and was peering in my direction. "Who was that?" he muttered.

"June Henshaw."

"Rob's girlfriend?"

"Yes, but she's got her police hat on. Helmet on. Whatever. Something's happened at the library. I need to go and open up for them."

"Want me to come with you?" He was already half out of bed.

"No, love; no need for that. I just need to drive down there and open the doors. And you're supposed to be avoiding stress, remember?"

"Nothing stressful about a phone call from the police at this time of the morning."

"My call, my stress. Really, love, you don't need to bother yourself. Go back to sleep. I'll be back for breakfast."

He gave me a long, if still bleary, look. "OK. If you're sure. Call me if you need an emergency flask of coffee rushing to the scene, or anything like that."

I nodded. "It'll be fine."

I fumbled for some clothes, made my way downstairs. The dog raised his head and wagged a hopeful tail.

"You go back to sleep as well, Brodie."

Nevertheless, he got out of his basket and followed me to the shoe cupboard, to make sure I wasn't sneaking out in walking boots. I slipped on my trainers, and he wandered grumpily back again.

Clear skies, cold night. I wished I'd had time to make a coffee, but I'd just have to manage without. No time to do anything with my hair, either. Being pale blonde disguises the grey quite well, but without grooming, it sticks out at ridiculous angles. I pulled a woolly hat over my head, found my keys, and went out.

Even without the coffee, the sharpness of the night air began to wake me up, and the empty roads gave me opportunity to think.

DAY 1: LOLLYGAGGING

And the first coherent thought that came to me was: "Why didn't the alarm go off?" If there had been an intruder in the library, I should have been woken up by the company that monitored the alarm, not the police.

I'd locked up myself last night. Hadn't I? I was sure I was the last one to leave. I'd been helping the art club set up for their exhibition. It was supposed to open this morning… they'd been fussing over their displays, arguing over who got the best positions. Closing time was six, but it had been nearly eight before I'd managed to usher the last of them out.

The ring road was a fifty-mile-an-hour limit, but I felt no guilt at doing sixty. Maybe sixty-five, but I was responding to a police emergency, wasn't I? And in any case, there was no other traffic to speak of. One set of headlights passed on the other side of the dual carriageway, some huge artic lumbering through the night, but I had the rest of the road to myself.

I was sure I'd set the alarm. It made a horrendous high-pitched warbling sound when you did, to let you know you had ten seconds to get out of the building. Since the panel was right next to the exit, that wasn't a problem, but it still made me panic slightly. And it was impossible to forget to do it.

Wasn't it? If I'd failed to set the alarm and there had been a break-in…

Worrying about that, I nearly failed to stop at the red lights as I came off the ring road. Not a residential area, fortunately, or the screech of rubber on road might have woken someone. Why were the lights red at that time? There was nothing else moving.

Having enjoyed their little joke with me, the lights reluctantly allowed me to go on my way. Down through the industrial estate and out onto Lock Road.

No, I must have set the alarm. So that meant nobody had actually got in, then. Perhaps just some drunk causing damage to the door or a window. Years ago, when we were more lax about security, someone had left a fire escape door open. We'd come in

9

next morning and found an inebriated gentleman sleeping it off in the reference section. He was very apologetic when he woke up and realized where he was. Didn't remember how he'd got there.

That must be it, I thought. No actual burglary. Panic over.

All the same, it still made my stomach churn when I finally turned onto Bromwell Street and saw two police cars pulled up in front of the library.

As I parked behind them, a police officer got out and walked towards me. I wouldn't have recognized June if I hadn't been expecting her: in fleece and stab vest she looked stocky, and the blonde hair which normally framed her face was pulled back into a ponytail.

"No blue lights?" I asked.

"On the off chance that someone is still inside, we didn't want to alert them. Of course, they're probably long gone, if anyone was there at all. Still, we need to be sure, so thanks for coming out, Sandra."

"Well, I didn't want you kicking the door in!" I meant it as a joke, but tiredness made it come out sharper than I intended. I forced a smile. "Not that you would, of course."

"We try to avoid it wherever possible." June showed no sign of offence, but of course she was used to dealing with much worse than grumpy middle-aged librarians. "In this case, we're not even sure that there has been any illegal entry, so we weren't about to cause any unnecessary damage."

The word "damage" drew my eyes to the library itself, wondering just what harm might have been done.

About a hundred and fifty years ago, a local businessman had been inspired to build a great edifice of learning and enlightenment. And self-importance; it was to be named the Arthur Diogenes Bromwell Institute of Culture. However, his lofty vision came into conflict with his natural inclination to save a bob or two wherever he could. The result was a single-storey red-brick building, high windows facing the street, blank walls along the back, and a massively oversized front entrance, all columns, brass plaques, and Latin inscriptions. The double doors were ten feet high, oak and stained glass. In short it was a fine example of Victorian Monstrosity. Various mismatched additions accumulated over the years as needs dictated and funds enabled, improving functionality but doing nothing for appearance.

It was hard to see details in the dim street lighting, but everything looked as solid, secure, and ugly as normal. I raised an eyebrow in June's direction.

"It's round the back," she explained, and led the way. "We got a call from a member of the public about an hour ago, telling us something was happening here. PC Newbold" – she indicated the young copper who had joined her – "came to have a look round, and he found an open window."

We came to the narrow alley between the library on one side and a block of flats on the other. June shone a torch down it. "Mike, you stay and watch the front, just in case someone tries to do a runner. Are you OK with this, Sandra?"

"Of course. I doubt if anyone's actually got in, or the alarm would have been activated."

"You're probably right, and if anyone *was* here I expect they made off when Mike showed up. But there might be somebody lurking around at the back, so stay behind me and if anything kicks off, don't get involved, OK?"

We walked down the alley, the only illumination coming from June's torch. I told myself to stop feeling so nervous. I'd come this way every working day for twenty years, after all. Just not at night with the police.

The red Victorian brickwork gave way to the grey blocks of the Children's Section, a 1950s addition. "Was it someone from the flats who reported it?" I asked.

"We don't know. Anonymous call from the TK down the road. Telephone kiosk, that is. Long gone by the time we got here. But I'm not sure how much of the library you can see from the flats; there are no windows directly overlooking it."

We came to the end of the Children's Section, followed the path round the back, and came out on a scrappy bit of lawn. Ahead of us was the toilet block, built in the late eighties to replace the original facilities.

"Just there." June shone her torch, indicating a transom window sticking out rebelliously when it should have been flush with the wall.

"Ladies' loo. Is that big enough for someone to get in?"

June shrugged. "You don't get many fat burglars. You'd be surprised at the holes they can wiggle through. Could it have been left open by accident?"

I thought back. "I locked up, but it was quite late, and I didn't check everywhere. One of my staff had done that earlier, but I suppose it's possible that someone came in and opened a window afterwards. The art club were here all evening – though I don't know why they'd open a window."

"The windows aren't alarmed?"

"Not here. There are sensors in all the rooms, though, and the corridor."

She looked more closely at the window. "No sign of any forced entry. Screwdrivers or crowbars leave marks, especially in UPVC like this. OK, let's go inside. Which door do we use?"

"Round here." I led the way to the bottom end of the toilet block. "The main entrance is bolted from the inside, the back door is easier."

I fumbled with my keys. The door had both a Yale and a solid mortise lock. I opened them both, and paused with my fingers on the handle.

"The alarm panel's on the wall just next to the door. The delay is quite short, so I'll go straight in and turn it off. Then you can go ahead and look round – OK?"

June nodded. I pushed the handle down and the door in. Strip lights automatically began flickering into life as I stepped through, turned sharp right, and put my hand out to the keypad.

It wasn't there.

For a moment I stood and waved my hands in empty space, glancing round in bemusement. Was I in the wrong place? Was this even the right door?

Then I registered the holes in the wall where the screws had been, plaster dust leaking out and a bent Rawlplug showing. I glanced down, and saw the shattered plastic box with broken wires trailing out of it.

"June…" I began, but she was already through the door behind me. "Wait outside please, Sandra." She keyed her radio. "November Delta one-five to HQ. Confirmed break at Bromwell Library."

"Ten-four. Do you need back-up?"

"No sign of anyone still here at present, but if November Charlie three-six has finished booking her prisoner in, you can send her over."

"Three-six. Got that, Sarge. On my way."

"Thanks. November Charlie four-two, receiving?"

"Four-two. Do you want me to join you, Sarge?" Mike's voice.

"Not yet. Cover the front till Sara arrives, then come round the back. I'm going to stay here till then."

"Roger that."

June stepped back out through the door. "Do you want to go and wait at the car?"

I thought of finding my way back through the alley, which would be pitch-black without June's torch. Of course, I could ask her to escort me, but then if there was anyone still in the building, that would give them an opportunity to escape.

I shook my head. "No, I'm fine. I expect you'll want me to see if anything's missing when you go in?"

"Once we've checked it's clear. This shouldn't take long. Sara – PC Middleton – is only about ten minutes away."

It was a very long ten minutes. We waited in silence, June carefully scanning all the other windows visible and listening intently. But the silence was unbroken except by the buzz from one of the fluorescent tubes and the occasional message coming over June's radio. I had to restrain myself from jumping every time I heard it crackle.

A good thing Graham hadn't come, I decided. This was definitely tense, and I could imagine how he'd fret if he was sitting in the car waiting for me. Not doctor's orders at all.

My phone pinged, another pluck on my overstretched nerves. I fumbled for it, my chain of thought leading me to expect Graham, checking up on me.

"Message?" asked June. "From the alarm company?"

I located the phone, deep in the most inaccessible pocket, unzipped several layers, and finally managed to pull it out.

"No. Just my 'Daily Eloquence'."

"Daily *what*?"

"It's an app I've got. It sends me an 'Eloquent Word for the Day' every morning. Usually something obscure. The game is that I've then got to use it in conversation sometime that day, and post it online. There's a sort of points system for the best use of the word, and you get a prize if you come out top over the month – a dictionary, usually!"

"That sounds like…" June obviously didn't want to say what she thought, but couldn't quite bring herself to say something polite and meaningless.

"Sounds weird, I know! Don't worry, Graham tells me that every day. I tell him, 'No, it sounds eldritch!'"

I gave her a hopeful look, but June just raised an eyebrow. Someday, that's going to get a laugh.

"Never mind. I'm a word-nerd, that's all."

"OK. So what's today's word?"

I glanced at the screen again. "Lollygagging."

"Lolly–gagging? Choking on a lollipop?"

"No. It's an American word, I think. It means 'to spend time aimlessly, to dawdle or be idle, to procrastinate or avoid work'."

"As in lying around, doing nothing? I can think of a few people

I could apply that to! But not this morning, I hope… that sounds like Sara arriving."

"November Charlie three-six, State 6 at the library."

A few moments later, PC Newbold appeared. With firm instructions for me to stay there until told otherwise, the two officers pulled on disposable gloves and went inside.

The silly conversation over words had relieved some of the tension, but standing round on my own brought it back. I always had suffered from an excess of imagination, and my mind, running in neutral, quickly began to offer increasingly bizarre scenarios for what they might find. When I reached "terrorist incident" I decided that enough was enough. I had to do something before I progressed to "alien wormholes". And I'd been wondering about that open window. I knew it was the ladies' loo, but which part did it actually open into?

I crept forward, ready to turn and run if anyone not the fuzz came out of the main library. The ladies and gents had both been checked by the coppers on their way in, I'd seen them do that, so at least I knew that no one was hiding in there. Therefore it was safe to proceed that far at least – or so I told myself.

There were three doors along the corridor, all on the right: cleaner's store nearest the exit, then the ladies, then the gents. The store was locked, as it should be. I progressed a few more steps, and eased open the door to the ladies.

The lights flickered on automatically as I stepped in, showing the sinks directly in front of me, a row of cubicles running off to the left. The windows over the sinks were firmly closed, which didn't surprise me. With taps, basins, and soap dispensers in the way, they were awkward to get at and probably hadn't been opened since they were installed.

I went to the first cubicle and – remembering just in time that this was a crime scene – pushed it open with my elbow. I had read enough detective novels in my time to know not to leave my fingerprints on the door handles.

Sure enough, the window above the toilet was wide open.

These windows would be easy to reach if you stood on the toilet seat. Anyone climbing in would probably have trod there as well. I peered at the plastic lid, trying to make out any footprints, but the position of the strip lights put it in shadow. I stepped forward for a closer look, and the door swung shut behind me with a bang that made my heart lurch.

"Sandra?" I heard June call. "Are you all right?"

"Yes, I'm OK, no problems!" I reached for the handle, stopped myself, and pulled at the top of the door, hoping that the intruder hadn't followed the same thought process.

The door was stuck. I remembered then that we'd had trouble with this particular door before. Last winter an old lady had been stuck in here for twenty minutes before someone heard her banging. They'd supposedly fixed the problem – but not completely, it seemed. I heaved on it and it came free suddenly; I nearly fell back onto the toilet seat but managed to hold myself upright on the door. I regained my balance and scampered out, nearly running into June.

"I told you to stay by the door!" she said sharply.

"Yes, sorry, I was just, er, checking for any damage. I didn't touch any handles, though."

She shook her head. "My CSI colleagues tell me that they rarely get anything useful from handles anyway. Too small, too well used. What *did* you touch?"

So much for detective novels. "Just the top of the door."

I pointed, and she ran a professional eye over the relevant area. "I'll mention that to CSI. You'd better come through and have a look in the main library. We haven't found anyone, but there's a bit of a mess, and some locked doors we'd like you to check."

I followed on, abashed.

The lights in the main room weren't on sensors as they were in the newer areas. The coppers had been using their torches, but with a nod from June, I switched everything on, and saw what June had called "a bit of a mess".

DAY 1: LOLLYGAGGING

The main reception desk had been trashed. Every drawer was out, contents emptied over the floor, the files pulled out of the cupboards behind and tossed around, computer screens smashed and hanging from their leads.

June gave me a moment to take it in, and gently restrained me from stepping too close. "There might be footwear marks on the paper," she explained. "Was there anything of value kept here?"

I shook my head. "No, not really. Just paperwork, records, forms – junk, a lot of it. Some of those files are decades old! Pre-computerization – we've never got round to archiving everything."

"Do you have any cash on the premises?"

"A bit. Payment for events, and so on… Oh! I just remembered! The art club charge their members to display in the exhibition – just a small amount, but some paid in cash. Might have been a hundred pounds in notes or coins. And the library has a petty cash tin as well. But that's all kept in a safe in my office."

"We'd better check that."

I led the way through the aisles to the Children's Section – the only two-storey part of the building. A door labelled "Staff Only" led up to an office and a staff room. It was securely locked and apparently undamaged. Nevertheless, June inspected it carefully before I unlocked it, and she led the way upstairs.

"All clear," she called back down to Mike. No damage, no one lurking in the shadows, safe untouched.

"Just one more area to check, then."

We went back down the stairs and across to the other side of the library.

At one time there had been a little alcove here, which had been kept free of books to provide space for readings, workshops, and exhibitions. Now there was a rather grand set of sliding doors where the wall had been: pale wood, nicely grained and polished, surmounted by a neat brass plaque announcing it to be "The Laney Grey Memorial Wing". Very fitting – our famous local poet had been a regular user of the alcove before her tragic death. She would have loved the new room, though she'd have poked fun at the idea of a "memorial wing".

"Just finished last month. This art exhibition is the first major event we've had here," I said.

June nodded, and moved closer to the door. "Was this here before, Sandra?" She pointed to a small mark just above the handle.

I looked at it and frowned. On closer inspection, the mark was a rounded indentation in the wood. "I don't think so. I don't remember seeing it before. Of course, it's all still quite new…"

"There's another one. Two more, in fact." June indicated two places, one higher up than the first one, the other further down. "Could be tool marks. But they're only on one side. If someone had pushed a screwdriver in and tried to lever the doors open, you'd expect to see marks on both sides."

I shook my head. "I suppose they might have been there before. I just haven't noticed them. Might have been something done when they were made. A local company donated them free, so we weren't going to be overly critical."

"I'll have a closer look with the doors open." June tugged on the handle with her gloved hand. "Still seems secure, so I doubt if anyone got in. Burglars don't usually lock up behind themselves!"

"Actually, they wouldn't have to," I said. "These doors are on an automatic system. They detect movement in and out. After thirty minutes, if nobody goes through, they close and lock themselves. It's a security feature, to stop them being left open by accident. Of course, you can lock them open permanently, but you need to put in a different code."

June raised an eyebrow. "Very sophisticated!"

"Yes – a bit over the top for a library, but I think the manufacturers were getting the maximum publicity out of it. They made a big thing about all the features; we've been in trade magazines all over the world, apparently."

"Who knew the codes?"

"All the library staff, of course. The manufacturers, I suppose. I can't think of anyone else who would have had them."

PC Newbold spoke up. "Have you seen this, Sarge?" He was pointing his torch into the corner, where the beam highlighted a small, pale object.

"Cigarette end? Good spot, Mike. You don't have anyone smoking in here, do you, Sandra?"

I shook my head firmly. "Of course not!"

"Good! Could be our burglar, then." She crouched down for a closer look, and sniffed. "No sign of burning on the carpet, no smell of smoke. But it hasn't been stubbed out, either. Burned down to the filter. Curious."

"Might have been walked in on someone's shoe?" Mike suggested.

"Doesn't look crushed." June stood up again. "We'll leave it for CSI to collect and send in for DNA. I'll try to get them to come as soon as possible, Sandra, to minimize the disruption, but they don't start until eight, so I'm afraid you'll probably have to stay closed for the morning at least."

"That'll be a disappointment for the art club, but I'm sure they'll understand. We can rearrange things, I suppose."

"Thanks, that would be helpful. We'd better check the exhibition, just to be thorough. How do we get in?"

I flipped open a discreet panel next to the doors, revealing a keypad. "This looks OK. Shall I go ahead and open it?"

"Let me do it." June stepped over. "I don't think they can get fingerprints off this surface, but no harm in being careful." She poised a gloved finger over the numbers. "What's the code?"

"Five-three-nine-one."

June punched in the numbers as I spoke them. The lock disengaged with a distinct click and the doors slid smoothly open, the lights coming on as they did so.

PC Newbold swore, softly but distinctly.

In order to maximize display space, the new wing had been

designed without windows. Instead, the curving roof was all toughened glass, to give the biggest possible amount of natural light – with discreet artificial illumination to give the same effect at night.

The lighting had been another contribution from a local company, and it worked perfectly. Every display stand, every painting and collage and sculpture, was brilliantly illuminated, with no shadows to hide anyone's work. Even the empty display directly in front of the door was bright and distinct.

As was the man lying sprawled face down on the floor in a pool of red.

DAY 2 : SPRUNT

There was a noise. Not a loud noise. A rhythmic creaking noise that, inexplicably, filled me with dread.

There was a door. I didn't want to go through. I didn't want to know what was making that noise. But my hand was on it, pushing on the door, and the noise was terribly loud, filling my head...

I woke up with a gasp, a strangled shriek.

Graham was there, his hands strong and reassuring as he held me. "Sandy? It's OK, love. It's OK."

I held on to him. "Graham. Graham – it was horrible – this man..."

He nodded. "Yes, I know. They told me." He shook his head. "They should never have let you go in there!"

"They didn't know. The door was locked and..." I lost my train of thought, dream-door and real-door jumbled together in my head. I took a deep breath, and tried to take a firm grip on myself. "Did I faint? I can't remember how I got here."

"I don't think you fainted, but you were pretty out of it. Shock. They called an ambulance, but decided you didn't need the hospital and brought you home. Gave you a sedative."

"Yes. I remember the ambulance."

There had been blue lights. They took me out in a wheelchair, I thought. And before that, I remembered sitting on the floor in the library. Sobbing and gasping for breath. Mike Newbold had been with me. He took his fleece off and put it round my shoulders and was telling me everything was all right, though he didn't look good himself. I'd heard June on the radio, calling for an ambulance for me, asking for the Duty DI.

But the memories were confused. I couldn't grasp how one thing had led to another, and every thought of the library came back to the doors sliding open, and the terrible thing behind them...

I gritted my teeth, and focused on the here and now.

"What time is it?"

He indicated the digital clock next to the bed. "Just after midnight."

"What? I've been asleep all day? What sort of sedative did they give me?"

"Nothing too strong. I think you just needed to sleep."

"But there's things I have to do! The library – I have to tell everyone we'll be closed – I need to ring Marilyn at County Hall. And the art exhibition!"

I was sitting up in bed, looking around wildly for my phone, for clothes, but Graham held me again, gently but firmly. "Calm down. It's all sorted. Everyone who needs to know, knows. The rest can wait. You just need to rest."

"Rest? I've been resting all day!" But his calmness helped to reassure me, and I settled back.

"That's better." Graham nodded and stood up. "I'll get you a cup of tea, shall I?"

He'd been sitting on the bed, but looking round I saw that an armchair had been put in place of the bedside table, and that he was fully dressed under his dressing gown. And very dishevelled. "Graham – you didn't sleep in that chair, did you?"

He shrugged. "Didn't want to disturb you. And I didn't mean to sleep. I was sitting here, watching you, and sort of drifted off."

I gripped his hand. "Thanks for being here."

"Where else would I be? Now, do you want that tea? Or would you rather go back to sleep for a bit longer?"

I thought about it. Actually, I did feel tired, but not sleepy tired, more drained of energy. And also in need of the loo.

"No, no more sleep. Not just yet. My mind's buzzing. I'm going to get up, I think. I'll have that cup of tea downstairs. You should get into bed and have some proper sleep yourself."

He shook his head. "Later. I'll go and put the kettle on."

I joined him in the kitchen a few minutes later. Bright lights, gleaming crockery, warm pine cupboards, and furniture that almost matched. I took comfort from domestic familiarity as Graham bustled around, making his manipulation of kettle, teapot, and two mugs into an episode of *MasterChef*.

"There you are. Do you want anything to eat with it?" He put the mugs down on the table and went looking for the biscuit tin.

"Not for me, thanks." Thinking of food made my stomach churn. Reaction to the sedative, I decided. "Thanks for the tea." I sipped gently, appreciating the warmth.

"No problem." He settled down with his mug and a handful of bourbons. "Do you want to talk about it?"

I shook my head. "No."

He nodded, and dunked a biscuit.

"How much did they tell you?" I asked.

"Just that it was a murder. And a nasty one."

"Yes. Very." I sipped some more. Not wanting to think about it. Not able to avoid it. "There was so much blood…"

He reached out and gripped my hand. "Oh, no! That bad? And you walked into it without warning? No wonder you were in shock."

"Yes. And I'd just been thinking what a pain it was to have a burglary, especially just before our first major exhibition in the new wing, and then… and then…"

He came round the table, hugged me. "OK. OK. You don't have to talk about it."

But having started, I found it hard to stop.

"The doors slid open and he was just lying there… I knew he was dead. Well, I didn't check his pulse or anything, but with all the blood – this huge pool of it, and he was lying face down in the thickest part of it…"

The image filled my mind, I couldn't get away from it. Graham held me tight. "OK. It's OK now."

I took a deep breath. "Sorry. It's just difficult to think about anything else. Have you heard anything on the news? Did they identify the… body yet?"

"Very little on the news at all." He went back to his side of the table, and stirred his tea with another bourbon. "Just a bare-bones statement – police called to an incident at the library, body of a man discovered, investigations ongoing, etc. I made a few calls, talked to Gary Easton, and to Ray at *The Echo*, but they don't know any more than that. They've promised not to send anyone round, as long as I keep them informed. Usual quid pro quo."

"Good thing you've kept in touch."

"Well, thirty years as a local hack isn't something you just walk away from entirely, is it? Of course, if the nationals get interested I won't be able to do much about that – or even local TV. I hear they had a camera down at the library this morning, so they've got some good contacts!"

I picked up a biscuit myself, nibbled absent-mindedly, put it down, drank some more tea. "I expect they'll be wanting to talk to me at some point. The police, that is. Or did they do that already? I can't remember giving a statement or anything like that."

"I don't think you did. Someone rang up while you were asleep – Detective Inspector Macrae, I think he said. Asking how you were, and no rush but please let him know if you would be able to answer a few questions. Usual stuff, but at least he was polite about it. I told him you'd talk to him when you were ready and not before."

"I'll have to deal with it sooner or later, Graham. Can't hide from these things, you know. It only makes them worse."

"I know." He gave me a wary glance. "But I've been thinking – this might bring back memories from that other incident…"

"It's *nothing* like that at all!" I snapped.

"OK. Sorry to mention it," he said, giving my hand a placatory pat. But the vehemence of my response had obviously surprised him. It had surprised me, for that matter.

"Well, I suppose there are similarities," I admitted. "But this was different. Very different." I decided not to mention the dream.

"All right, then."

We sat in silence for a while. My mind was racing, going over every detail of the events: Graham's, on the other hand, was obviously slowing down. His eyelids were drooping and he was struggling not to yawn.

"Go to bed," I ordered.

"I don't want to leave you alone."

"And I don't want you getting exhausted. You're still recovering from serious heart disease, remember? You only had the stents in last month. Getting any chest pains?"

He tried to hide a guilty look. "Not really pains; just a little tightness."

"Well, get yourself off to bed. I know you're worried about me, but I don't need to be worrying about you as well! And I need a bit of time to get my head round things. I think I'll start writing a statement. It'll help later on when this Macrae man comes to talk."

"If you're sure…"

I nodded, and smiled. "Sure. I'm going into the office, anyway, and I don't need you hovering around distracting me. So you might as well go to bed. Before you finish off all the biscuits."

"Oh, all right then. But you will get me if you need me, won't you?"

Suitably reassured, Graham finally took himself off, and I went into the converted garage that we'd made into an office and study area. I switched on the laptop, and focused on getting myself in the right mindset.

A long time ago, when I was trying out a career in journalism, I learned the trick of detaching myself from my emotions and focusing on the facts. I had an editor who was very strong on that. "I don't want to know about how you feel," he used to say. "I want to know what happened, whom it happened to, and how *they* feel. But you are not part of the story. Keep yourself out of it."

It's not a bad skill to learn. Especially useful now. I didn't suppress or deny my shock and horror, but I put them firmly to one side and concentrated on what had happened. From the time when June had called me, to the discovery of the body.

I edited out the extraneous details. The DI wouldn't be interested in lollygagging, for example. Nor did he need vivid descriptions. Just the bare facts.

Writing it down helped, as I had known it would. Words do that for me. Putting things into clear, well-ordered text brings them under control, puts them into perspective. I can deal with words.

Someone once said to me, when they found out that I was a librarian, "You must love books then." It's not quite true. I love *some* books, especially poetry. I like many books; there are a few that I've hated.

But what I love is words.

By the time I had finished my statement, printed off a copy, and signed it, my appetite had returned. I went to the kitchen, made cheese on toast, and took it back into the office to do a final read through of the hard copy. I started yawning as I did so. Ridiculous, I told myself, since I'd been asleep all day. I'd get up and make some coffee in a moment. But for now, the padded office chair was very comfortable. I lay back in it and closed my eyes for a while.

I'd slipped my mobile into my dressing gown pocket. Its sudden vibration jerked me out of a doze.

The Word for the Day. Why did it always come in at three in the morning? Who on earth – who in what time zone on earth! – would do that?

The word was "Sprunt", meaning "to germinate, to bring to life, to leap or make a sudden movement". Or in Scotland, "to chase girls around the haystacks after dark". Interesting, but I could see no immediate way of using it. It certainly wouldn't fit into my statement.

I was yawning again. Not wanting to disturb Graham by going back to bed, I went into the living room and lay down on the couch. I probably wouldn't go back to sleep, I thought, but I should probably try to rest for a while.

My eyes closed for a moment. When they opened again sunshine was slipping through the gaps in the curtains.

Daylight already? I rubbed my eyes and peered at the clock, which had suddenly jumped past 7 a.m. I sat up and searched through my head, but thankfully there were no dreams or memories of dreams. Just the memories of reality, which were bad enough, but even they were at a safer distance now.

I made coffee and stood in the kitchen to drink it, watching the morning light on the hill behind our house. It looked inviting. It promised a gentle peace, the freshness of a new day. I dressed, put on the walking boots, and took Brodie out to enjoy it with me.

We have the great privilege of living on the outskirts of town, with open countryside at the end of our street. Within a few minutes Brodie and I were on the footpath, winding through trees, skirting fields, and climbing gently to low hills where the first hints of autumn were showing in distant woods.

Early morning sunshine has an especially intense quality to it. It stabbed between leaves, poured over rocky outcrops, challenging all the living world to get up, get going, and face the new day. It washed over me, wiping away the darkness and the ugliness of what had been concealed there.

Brodie bounded ahead, dropped behind, caught up, and wandered off on little side expeditions of his own, sniffing, marking territory, and contentedly living in the moment. I watched him, wondering (not for the first time) what it was like to always be in the "now". No future to worry about, no past to overshadow, just the present tense.

It occurred to me that this would be a good time and place for prayer. And – God knows! – I had enough to pray about.

But I wasn't really in the habit of talking to God. Hadn't been for a long time now.

Perhaps this was when I needed to reopen that channel?

My mobile rang, closing off the moment. Graham's ringtone.

"Are you OK?" he asked, trying to sound casual.

"Yes. I'm OK," I confirmed. Better, at any rate, thanks to Brodie and the countryside.

"Good. I've got DI Macrae on the landline. He was asking after you and would you be up to a visit this morning?"

I glanced at my watch, noted that it wasn't long past eight o'clock. "He starts early, does Mr Macrae. Well, I suppose he does have a murder investigation under way."

"Shall I put him off till later?"

"No. I'm heading back now anyway. Ask him to come round after nine. Unless he's planning on a bit of sprunting."

"What?"

"No, ignore that last bit. It's too late for that, now the sun's up. And besides, he's got a Scottish name, he might understand."

"I certainly don't. I'll just tell him nine o'clock, then."

Graham hung up. I stood still for a moment, once more allowing the sunlight and peace to touch me, closed my eyes in a silent prayer of thanks, then called Brodie and headed back down the path.

*

Detective Inspector Macrae arrived at nine on the dot. June Henshaw was with him, in civvies. I shut Brodie in the kitchen (to his annoyance, as he loves meeting people), while Graham got them sat down in the living room, with tea and biscuits.

Macrae both looked and sounded as Scottish as his name – slight, wiry, and sandy-haired, with an intense look in his eye, slightly at odds with the gentle burr of his voice.

"Mrs Deeson. Thanks for letting us come and visit. I appreciate you've had something of a shock, but I'm sure you'll understand that we need to progress this inquiry as quickly as possible."

"Of course. I'm over the worst of it, I think."

"You'll perhaps be wondering what a Scotsman is doing down here?" Macrae smiled gently – obviously making small talk to settle the atmosphere, but doing a good job of it. "I'm on an attachment with your local force, they being a bit short-handed in the CID department recently. And I understand you know Sergeant Henshaw? She's helping me out on this investigation."

"Yes, of course. Hello, June. Thanks for getting me home safely yesterday. I was a bit out of it, I think."

She nodded. "You were, but that wasn't surprising under the circumstances. I was shaken up myself!"

I turned my attention back to Macrae. "I've written out a statement about what happened. I hope that helps."

He took the paper from me, but barely gave it a glance before passing it over to June. "Aye, that's very useful, Mrs Deeson. Thank you. But we've pretty much got those events clarified. What I need your assistance with is in what led up to this tragic situation."

Graham picked up at once on my puzzled and slightly worried expression. "I don't think Sandra can help you with that, Inspector. She doesn't know anything about it apart from what she saw the night before last."

Macrae placated him with a gentle smile. "That may well be the case, Mr Deeson. But you'll understand that we need to get as full a picture as possible. At this stage of the investigation, we can't be sure what is or isn't relevant."

He turned back to me. "For example, I understand that in the evening prior to the incident you were working quite late at the library?"

"Yes. I was helping the art club set up for their exhibition."

"And that would be the Templeton Art Club?"

"Oh. Yes, but everyone just calls it 'the art club'. There isn't another one locally."

"And you were the last to leave?"

"That's right. I think it was all secure then, though I must admit that I didn't check the bathroom window, so that could have been left open." I wondered if that was going to be an issue, and gave June a worried look. Her face, however, was giving nothing away.

"Tell me, Mrs Deeson – were there any problems with the art club at all?"

Not a question I'd been expecting, and it threw me a bit. "Problems? What do you mean?"

"Did any difficulties arise whilst they were setting up? Any disagreements, arguments?"

"Oh. Well, there was some discussion over who got what position for their paintings. Most of it was quite good-natured, though."

Macrae homed in on the slight ambiguity. "Most of it?"

"Um. OK, there was quite a heated argument at one point. That was between the chairman and the club secretary."

"The chairman being Mr Claude Ferrers-Manton, and the secretary, Mr Jonathan Carr?"

"That's right. But although it was quite heated, as I said, I don't think there was any suggestion of violence."

The DI nodded in gentle agreement. "You're probably right, Mrs Deeson. But perhaps you could just go over what happened anyway?"

"Yes, OK. Er – if you could give me a moment to think about it. With all that's happened since…"

"Certainly. Take all the time you need." He picked up his cup, took a few short sips, and cradled it in his hands while he waited for me.

I sat back, stared at the ceiling, and tried to recreate the scene. The two of them had been standing just inside the exhibition – in exactly the same place where the body had been, I realized with a chill. Ferrers-Manton was short and rather rotund, going red in the face with indignation. He'd been wearing a long black leather coat, which looked ridiculous on such a little man. And a wide-brimmed black hat, which I'd never seen him take off, even inside. Perhaps he thought it made him look more artistic.

Carr, on the other hand, was tall, dark, impeccably dressed in a grey suit, all very urbane and cultured. Quite calm but not giving an inch.

"They were arguing about the display stand directly in front of the doors," I said. "It's the prime location, the first pictures anyone would see as they came in. Ferrers-Manton thought that, as chairman, he should be able to put his paintings there. But Carr was telling him that the stand was reserved for someone else's work."

"For Mr Carr's own paintings?"

"No. At least, he didn't say so. In fact, I don't think that Carr is an artist himself."

"Really?" Macrae raised an eyebrow. "And yet he's secretary of this rather prestigious art club?"

"I know. It does seem strange. But from what I understand, he's some relation to Sir Arthur Templeton, the patron of the art club. Nephew, I think."

"Ah. So that's where the club gets its name, then."

"That's right." I paused for a sip of tea, which was getting cold, but it helped lubricate my mouth. "It used to be just the 'Northdene Art Club', I think. Northdene being the area it was based in. It was rather a small affair in those days, I understand, and essentially moribund. Carr arranged for his uncle to lend his name and patronage – Sir Arthur was born somewhere round here and was quite a well-known artist in his day. The club picked up after that and has become quite a big thing."

"I see. So Carr, despite not being an artist himself, has a lot of influence in the club. That would explain why he was able to overrule the chairman."

"Yes. That seems to be how it works."

"And who was the stand reserved for?"

I shook my head. "Carr wouldn't say. I think that that was what was making Ferrers-Manton angry as much as anything. He was demanding to know who had more right to it than him, but all Carr would tell him was that it was a top artist whose inclusion would hugely increase the club's standing in the art world. Then he was asking where this person's paintings were, claiming that he should be the one to decide if they were good enough for the exhibition. Carr told him that they would be arriving later, and said, in so many words, that Ferrers-Manton didn't know enough about art to make that judgment. He was all very cool and calm about it, but the chairman was spitting nails by this time, going red-faced and shouting loud enough for the whole room to hear."

"Saying what?"

"Oh, something about how Carr wasn't even an artist, it was only due to his uncle's influence that he was secretary, he had no right to make judgments about other people's work when he didn't produce anything himself… and so on."

"Did you get involved?"

"No. I was about to, but fortunately Emily stepped in. Emily Coombe, that is. She's one of my staff at the library, and also a member of the art club, so she was probably in the best position to intervene. At any rate, she managed to get Ferrers-Manton to calm down and stop shouting. I'm not sure what she said, but I made an excuse to take Carr away and talk to him about something innocuous, and then Ferrers-Manton left. Still a bit huffy, I gather, but that was as far as it went."

Macrae had finished his tea, put the cup down, and selected a bourbon. "*Miss* Coombe, would that be? Not married?" When I nodded, he continued. "What can you tell me about her?"

Again, I found myself wrong-footed by the shift in focus. "Emily? Well, she's what we call a Library Assistant. Nice girl, very efficient, but quiet. She's been with us about two years, I think, but I can't say I really know her well. She hardly ever talks about herself.

The only thing I can say for certain is that she's quite passionate about art. She'll talk about that readily enough. In fact, she had a lot to do with organizing this exhibition. The art club normally hire somewhere in the town centre, but with our new wing opening, she persuaded them that the library would be a good place to use."

"I take it that she would have had a key? And the alarm codes?"

"Yes, all our staff have those."

"How many would that be?"

"Well, we have five full-time staff at the moment, and three part-time. The cleaners have access as well, and there's a caretaker who covers all the libraries in this area for general maintenance and so on."

"And all these people would also have the code for the door to the exhibition?"

"That's right."

"Do you know if the keys or the code have ever been given to anyone else?"

"Not as far as I know. There is a set of master keys at head office, of course – County Hall, that is. But there's a strong policy on security, and I can't think that any of my staff would go against that."

Macrae had been playing with the bourbon, rolling it around in his fingers. Now he broke it in half, but still didn't eat any of it. "What happened after Miss Coombe broke up the argument?"

This tactic of suddenly changing the line of questioning was certainly effective in keeping me on my toes. It would have made it particularly difficult to keep track of a lie, so it was fortunate that I only had truth to tell.

"As I said, Ferrers-Manton left. I talked to Carr about organizing some refreshments, and Emily… I'm not sure what she did then. I didn't see her for a while. But people started leaving, and she was standing by the door, seeing them out. Carr left as well. I said goodnight to Emily – thanked her for sorting out the argument – then she left through the front door. I locked up and left through the back, putting the alarm on as I did so."

"Does Miss Coombe have a boyfriend? A partner?"

I shook my head. "No. I shouldn't think so. Well, not that I know of."

"Why wouldn't you think so?"

"OK, I suppose that's a bit of an assumption," I admitted. "It's just that she isn't very… sociable, I suppose. Not outgoing. And, to be honest, not what you'd call pretty."

"Plain, then? Not attractive?"

"Well, yes. I mean, she has a pleasant face, and I always thought she could do more for herself if she wanted, but she's never seemed to give much thought to her dress or appearance."

Macrae finally took a nibble from his biscuit. "We have an address for her of Flat 5, 62 Market Way. Do you know if that's correct?"

"I think so. I'd have to check the records at the library, but I'm pretty sure it's Market Way, anyhow."

"Did she have any other properties that you know of?"

"No, I don't think so." I was finding all this interest in Emily very strange, and gave June a glance which tried to convey my puzzlement, but she made no response.

"Any family?" He finished the biscuit while I thought about it.

"As far as I can remember, her next of kin is listed as a sister who lives somewhere abroad. I'd have to check her records to be sure, but you should be able to get the details from County Hall. I believe that her parents passed away some time ago. I don't know about anyone else."

"Can I ask if you have a contact number for her here with you?"

"Er – yes, I have her mobile number in my phone. I don't know if she has a landline at her flat."

"That's no problem, Mrs Deeson. Would you mind telling us what that is, to compare with the number we have?"

"Of course." I dug my mobile out and started scrolling through my contacts. As I did so, I finally realized why there might be so much interest in Emily.

"Has something happened to her?" I blurted out.

"We've no reason to believe that," Macrae said. His tone was professionally reassuring, but something in his face belied his words. "It's just that we haven't been able to make contact with Miss Coombe as yet. Under the circumstances, we're keen to do that as soon as possible, of course."

"Of course." I handed my phone over. Macrae opened a notebook and checked the number against what he had written down.

"Aye, well, it's the right number. A pity. It would have been a lot easier if we only had a misplaced digit to contend with."

He handed my phone back to me. "Could I ask you to call Miss Coombe yourself, please? It may be that she's blocking calls from unknown numbers, but perhaps she'll talk to someone she knows."

I nodded, and pressed dial.

It was very quiet in our living room. Apart from distant traffic noises, the only sound was the gentle "burr-burr" of the ringtone.

It rang six times, while we all stared at the phone. Then it stopped, and I felt a moment of relief as a voice spoke. But I quickly realized that it was just the voicemail message.

"Emily, it's Sandra. Please get in touch as soon as you can. Please!" I said, almost desperately, as if the tone of my voice could increase the chances of a reply. I broke the connection and looked up at the others.

"Well, it was worth trying. Thank you for that, Mrs Deeson. If you do hear from her, please let us know as soon as possible." Macrae wiped a few biscuit crumbs from his fingers, and stood up. "We're all but finished for the moment, but I was just wondering… did Miss Coombe ever say anything about any particular artist that she was interested in?"

Once again, he had confused me. "Artists? Well, she talked about all the usual names, and a lot more that I don't know… She liked the Impressionists, I think…"

Macrae shook his head, smiling slightly. "I doubt if they would help our investigation. My apologies. I meant a modern artist that she might have known personally."

"No. I don't recall her mentioning anything like that. But I don't see…"

Lightbulb moment. Sudden understanding flooded my brain.

"The body! You're thinking that the body might have been this mysterious artist that Carr was talking about!"

"It's one of the possibilities that we are considering," Macrae acknowledged with a poker face.

Graham had been sitting quietly to one side, not interfering but not missing a word, either. And making connections along the way.

"You haven't identified him, then," he said quietly.

"Not as yet," Macrae admitted. "The investigation is ongoing."

"And Carr hasn't said who this artist is?"

Macrae gave Graham a speculative look, clearly wondering how much to tell him. In my experience, the default police position is to say as little as possible – for good reason, to be sure – but the Scottish detective surprised me.

"Mr Carr doesn't know the name. Apparently, Miss Coombe came to him some time ago with the idea to hold the exhibition at the library, and she also hinted that she had contact with a very talented new artist who would be willing to include some of his work. She refused to reveal his name, but did show Carr some examples of his work. He didn't recognize them, but described them as 'extraordinary'."

"They must have been, to justify reserving the prime spots for his work without even knowing who it was," I said.

"Just so. And you'll understand from that just how important it is that we find Miss Coombe as soon as possible. So if you hear anything from her – or if you remember anything that might be useful – call me directly. At any time."

He left a card on the table. Graham showed them both out, while I sat and thought about it all.

What I thought about mostly was that huge pool of blood spreading out from under the body. Particularly from under his head.

Graham came back in, having given Brodie his liberty.

"I know why they haven't identified the body," I told him.

He sat next to me and put his arm round my shoulders. "You shouldn't have to be thinking about the body," he said with regret.

Brodie, not wanting to be left out, came over and put his head on my lap. I scratched behind his ears. "It can't be avoided. We've got to deal with this. And especially if Emily's involved. I just hope she's OK."

Graham nodded. So did Brodie, though probably because I'd stopped scratching. "So why haven't they identified him, then?"

"There was so much blood. It wasn't a small wound. And it was mostly round his head. His face – he was face down, so I couldn't see it – but I think that that was where the blood was coming from."

"So you're thinking that his injuries must have made him unrecognizable?"

"Yes." I was trying to consider the thought without dwelling on the details. "Of course, they'd have checked DNA and fingerprints, but if he'd never been arrested for anything, he wouldn't be on the database. And dental records…"

"Probably not," Graham jumped in, to cut off that train of thought before I could think about it too much. "And obviously they would have checked his pockets, so we can assume that there was nothing in them to help."

"I wonder if he was a smoker?"

"How does that come into it?"

I explained about the cigarette end that Mike Newbold had spotted. "If it was his, then it probably doesn't help much. But if it was someone else's – it wouldn't have been any of the staff; I certainly didn't see any of the art club smoking – I'd have stopped them if I had – so it would have to be the killer's!"

"Let's hope so. They need to get the person responsible, and quickly!"

"They need to find Emily," I answered. "I just hope she's – she's not…"

There was no need to finish the sentence. We both knew what I meant.

*

I spent the rest of the day mostly on the phone. First, contacting all my staff, reassuring them at length that I was OK, and asking them if they knew anything about Emily. None of them did, and in any case the police had already spoken to them on the subject.

Then I had a long conversation with my boss at County Hall – Marilyn James, the Area Librarian – with similar reassurances and an edited update on events. She too had been asked about Emily, but beyond confirming what was in the personnel records, had no information to offer.

Most people would probably put family first on the list, but in our case there's no point in making it a priority. After a lot of thought, I fired up the PC, went online, and left a message for Sam.

We don't have any direct contact with him. No telephone number, no email address, no social media. Just a website where we can leave messages. Sometimes he gets back to us, sometimes not. Sometimes he tells us where he is and what he's doing. There's actually more chance that he'll respond to Graham than to me, but I still keep trying.

Experience told me to keep it short and to the point. "Hi, Sam. We've had some drama here – a murder in the library! Bit of a shock. Hope you're all well. Love, Mum."

Not a fraction of what I wanted to say. "How are you? Where are you? What are you doing? Are you working? Are you with anyone? Do you have friends, a girlfriend?"

When will you come home?

Last we heard he'd been backpacking round Australia, but

that had been months ago. He could be anywhere by now. With anyone. Or on his own.

I logged off the website and deleted the train of thought. It couldn't help.

There were plenty of other people I needed to talk to. Friends, many of them local, who had heard one version or another of the story and wanted to hear everything else. Catching up with all the messages in various media formats took a surprising amount of time, so it wasn't until early evening that I finally made the call that I had been wanting to make all day.

I had June's personal number in my mobile from some time ago, when she and Rob had been involved in a Laney Grey memorial event. I hadn't had occasion to use it since, and I was hesitant about it now. It was imposing on a rather casual friendship, I knew, and trying to get information out of a police officer by unofficial channels could even be illegal. But I'd heard nothing from official channels all day, and I couldn't suppress my worry any longer.

She answered at once, sounding tired but hopeful.

"Sandra? Hi. Have you heard from Emily?"

Which pretty much answered my question.

"No. Actually, that was what I was going to ask you about. Apologies for bothering you, but I'm getting really worried for her."

"Of course. I understand. But no, we haven't heard anything. Her flat has been searched, but no clues. Don't spread that around, please."

"I won't. Thanks. I know I shouldn't be calling you like this."

"As long as you understand that there are limits on what I can say. In fact, the DI is very keen on keeping open all possible channels of information, formal or informal. It's his way of working – not everyone likes it, but you can't argue with his track record."

"A bit of a high-flyer?"

"Sort of. Not so much in terms of looking for promotion. I understand he could easily have been a DCI by now, if he'd wanted, but he doesn't want to get sucked into management and taken further away from actually investigating cases. I think that's probably why he came down here."

"After all that happened with Laney?"

"Yes. The fallout was pretty brutal in local CID – lot of transfers, some early retirements, and so on. They desperately needed someone with a bit of class to come in, restore morale, and generally get their act together for them. And along comes Jimmy Macrae, riding to our rescue like the Seventh Cavalry. Or the Highland Guards, perhaps? Whatever. He had a really impressive clean-up rate in Edinburgh, and he hasn't slowed down any since he got here. Trust me, you couldn't ask for a better copper on this one, and if anyone's going to find Emily, it'll be him."

"Thanks, June. That's reassuring. But... Jimmy? Really?"

"His first name's actually David. But the day he arrived, while he's being shown around, some idiot greets him with 'Hey you, Jimmy!' in the worst Glaswegian accent you can imagine. A bit of a test, really. But Macrae just turned it round, came back with 'See you, yer Sassenach.' Which got him off on the right foot with the lads, but ever since he's been 'Jimmy', at least in the station."

We shared a chuckle. "Don't answer this if it's out of order, June, but any idea when we'll get the library back?"

"I think CSI have pretty much finished. They've had a full team on it right through the night. Macrae authorized the overtime himself, said he'd cover it out of his budget if necessary. He really gets things moving! You should be able to go back in sometime tomorrow, though the exhibition room itself might be sealed off a little longer. I'll call you as soon as I know for definite."

"Thanks for that. Just a minute, though – I'm losing track of time. It's Sunday tomorrow, isn't it?"

"Just another working day for me!"

"Oh. Well, it shouldn't be for us. All the same, it would be good if we could get there and start clearing up so that we can open on Monday."

"It's possible, but I'll let you know. I'll say goodnight now, if you don't mind – I've had a long day and it's an early start tomorrow. Jimmy keeps his people busy!"

DAY 3 : POLTROON

Sunday morning for us usually means church, but I couldn't face it. It wasn't the prospect of meeting with God that put me off, but of meeting with God's people. Some of them would be thrilled by the opportunity to fuss over me, others would want the full story with all the details – "so that we can pray for you", of course. And their motives would be (mostly) good, but their intense desire to show proper concern would be overwhelming.

So in a show of cowardice, I sent Graham down on his own. I gave the excuse that I was expecting a phone call from June about lifting the crime scene on the library, a half-truth that added to my guilt without deceiving him in the slightest. Nevertheless, he gave me a hug, a kiss, and a knowing grin before setting off into a gloomy grey drizzle of a morning, while I stayed behind to prepare lunch and contemplate the Word for the Day.

Which, as it happened, was "Poltroon". Defined as "a wretched coward, a craven" and apparently one of the favourite insults of the nineteenth century. It didn't help to know that. However, my guilt was slightly assuaged by the fact that June did indeed call.

"Yes, you can go back into the main part of the library any

time you like. CSI are still working in the Memorial Wing, but I've checked with them and you can start sorting out the rest of it."

"That's great! We should be able to open again tomorrow!"

There was a slight but significant hesitation. "Perhaps it would be best not to be too ambitious on that point, Sandra. The examination process can be a bit, ah, messy. All those powders and chemicals, you see. Perhaps you'd better have a look before you make any plans?"

"Oh. OK. Well, thanks anyway, June. I don't suppose you've heard anything from Emily?"

"No. Sorry. I'll keep you updated as much as I can."

She hung up. After some thought on the matter, I phoned Yvonne.

"Hi. How are you? Have you heard anything about Emily?" She rattled off the questions as soon as she picked up.

"Hi, fine, and no, not yet," I answered, and carried on quickly before she could throw any more queries my way. "Are you free this afternoon, Yvonne? Only I've been told that we can go back into the library, but that it might need some cleaning up before we can open again. I'm going down to make an assessment – I'd be glad of your company."

"Of course. Now? Or later?"

We agreed on one-thirty. I finished the conversation, and sent up a silent but heartfelt prayer of thanks for friends. Officially, Yvonne was a Leading Library Assistant, and my second in command at Bromwell Street. But we've known each other for fifteen years, and she's never let me or anyone else down in all that time. Reliability on that level is beyond value.

Graham wasn't keen on me going back, and would have insisted on coming with me if I hadn't been able to assure him that Yvonne would be there to hold my hand. I told him to stay at home and recover from his stressful morning at church, where he'd had to explain to everyone that my absence was not due to my being comatose with shock.

*

The library looked a lot better in the daylight, especially as the sun had forced its way through the clouds and was busily touching up all the colours. It also helped to see Yvonne waiting to greet me – which she did with a hug as soon as I was out of the car. Yvonne is a big lady, and when she hugs, you notice it. Slightly breathless, I untangled myself and promised her that I was OK, and yes it had been a terrible shock, but I was coping with it, thank you.

We walked up to the front door together. A PCSO was on scene preservation duty at the front door. With her was a tall woman in a white forensic suit.

"Afternoon," she said. "You'll be from the library? Alison Kepple. CSI. Sergeant Henshaw told me you'd be coming, asked me to show you what we've done."

I introduced myself and Yvonne, we signed ourselves into the scene with the PCSO, and followed the CSI inside.

"Stay on the stepping plates, please." Square metal panels, about a foot across and raised a few inches off the floor with little legs, marked out a path from the main door. "We've finished everything in here, but we've used chemicals on the floor to show any blood traces, and it would probably be best not to get it on your shoes or clothing."

"I've heard that that stuff is carcinogenic," Yvonne said, staring suspiciously at the carpet. "And it's left stains!"

"The hazard sheet says nothing about 'carcinogenic'," Kepple told us. "But it can be an irritant, and yes, sorry, there are a few stains."

We reached the reception desk. The paperwork and other items that had been scattered over the floor had been moved up off of it and piled onto every available surface, apparently at random.

"I'm afraid we had to clear the floor," the CSI explained apologetically. "Some of the items that were there we recovered for lab treatment. Other items and surfaces – here and around that

44

open window in the toilet – have been dusted for fingerprints. Messy, I'm afraid, but that should clean off with some neat detergent. Washing-up liquid's good."

"Is it toxic?" I asked, before Yvonne did.

"No. Well, you wouldn't want to breathe the powder, but the building's been well ventilated, so that shouldn't be a danger."

"What about in there?" Yvonne nodded towards the Memorial Wing.

"We've still got a bit of work to do. The paintings have all been removed – they're stacked in the Children's Section – and they can go back to their owners. But inside the room itself we've used superglue."

"Superglue? Was something broken?"

Kepple grinned. "No – not by us, anyway! But if you heat superglue the vapour sticks to fingerprints, shows up all sorts of detail that you can't get with powder."

"Found anything?"

"Oh yes. Fingerprints everywhere. Superglue is sometimes *too* effective! Everyone who's ever touched a surface in there has left a mark, probably right back to the original manufacturers. That's why it takes so long – each one has got to be diagrammed and photographed. We should be finished today, though."

"This superglue – how do we get that off?" Yvonne asked suspiciously.

"Acetone's good. You get it in nail polish remover."

"For an entire room?" I raised an eyebrow. "And wouldn't the acetone itself stain things?"

"Well, perhaps. You may need to do a bit of redecorating." She unzipped the forensic suit, fumbled inside for a moment, and produced a business card. "Or you could try these people. Specialist cleaning service. They're very good, I hear."

"But pricey, I expect," said Yvonne. "Shouldn't the police pay for this?"

Kepple shook her head. "Sorry. Our budget is for the

investigation. We don't have anything for the cleaning up. The price of crime."

"OK. I'll ring Marilyn in the morning, and if she's good with it I'll get a quote. We might have insurance to cover it – she'll know. In the meantime, I don't suppose there's much more we can do here. Sorry to drag you out for no purpose, Yvonne."

"No problem. I didn't have anything else planned! I'll go and see what state those paintings are in – we can at least get them back to the owners. The art club will want to reschedule their exhibition, though probably not here!"

She headed off towards the Children's Section.

Kepple was zipping up her suit. "Actually, while you're here, can I ask you about something? If you don't mind just having a glance through into the Memorial Wing, that is?"

I took a deep breath. I'd have to do this sooner or later. "Not at all. Do I need to put on a suit?"

"Technically, you should, but at this stage of the examination there are no cross-contamination issues. If you put on a mask and don't touch anything it'll cover the health and safety. You only need to glance through the door, anyway."

She handed me a disposable mask and led the way over to the doors, while I forced myself to saunter along behind her as if my heart rate hadn't shot up and my knees weren't trying to knock together even while I walked.

"Don't be such a poltroon!" I told myself.

"Pardon?" asked Kepple. My mutterings had fortunately been disguised by the mask.

"Nothing, nothing at all," I assured her brightly, not wanting to get into a long explanation about "The Eloquent Word for the Day".

She punched in the code, and I was nearly dazzled by a brilliant flash as the doors slid open. Peering in, I saw another CSI adjusting a camera on a tripod. Dozens of little arrows had been stuck all over the walls, and the camera seemed to be pointing directly at one of them from only a foot or so away.

"As you see, the superglue worked. We're only looking at marks around this end of the room – there's no indication that anything happened beyond that point – and only at marks with some clear detail visible. Even so, that's a lot of marks."

The other CSI glanced in our direction, grunted something inaudible, and went back to his work.

"Excuse him. He doesn't like to be interrupted, so I won't even try introductions."

"Do all those arrows indicate fingerprints?" I asked.

"We usually refer to them as 'skin ridge impressions'," Kepple explained. "Could be fingerprints, palm prints, or partials."

"They can't all be the murderer's, surely?"

"Oh, no. Most of them will be marks left by legitimate users. We're lucky that this is a fairly new building: under the right conditions, fingerprints can last for years, and superglue is very good at bringing them out! Has anyone talked to you yet about eliminations?"

I shook my head.

"OK. At some point we're going to need elimination prints from all your staff at least. But that's not what I wanted to ask you about just now. You see that bracket over there?"

"Yes. It should have a fire extinguisher in it. Where's it gone?"

"That's the question. Can you confirm that it was there when you were last in here?"

"I don't know about when I was *last* in here," I answered, forcing myself to stay calm. "That was when we discovered the body, and I certainly wasn't looking at extinguishers. But it was definitely there on Monday – we had a regular check of all the extinguishers, and everything was OK."

"Thanks, that's all I needed." She shepherded me back into the main library, apparently unaware of the trauma she'd potentially put me through. "Just drop the mask into that yellow bag, there, and we'll dispose of it."

"Glad to be of help," I said, trying to be sincere not sarcastic.

I put her down as not deliberately insensitive, just very focused on her job. And I needed to get over it.

"Oh, and some mail came. I put it all on the desk in the upstairs office. On top of the big envelope."

"Thanks." It occurred to me that I didn't remember any big envelope. "Just a minute – what envelope?"

Kepple had hit the button to close the doors again, and answered me through the narrowing gap. "Big brown envelope. Or package, or something. It was on your desk when we went up there."

The door finished shutting before I could ask anything else. Easier, in any case, to go and look for myself.

On the way, I passed Yvonne, who was sorting through piles of paintings and trying to arrange them by artist.

"Are they OK?"

"Some of them are quite good. Others… not to my taste."

"No, I meant is there any damage?"

"Not that I can see. I think that this one's meant to look damaged." She held up a framed canvas that had been carefully covered with loose strips of cloth and some ornamental tassels. "Does this mean anything to you?"

"Well – it's an interesting combination of textures and colours. Perhaps that's what was intended?"

Yvonne snorted. She has very conservative tastes when it comes to art. "I wouldn't hang it on my wall, that's for sure!"

Our discussion was interrupted by the sound of raised voices from the main entrance. We exchanged raised eyebrows, and I went to see what was happening.

Jonathan Carr was at the door, arguing with the PCSO. "What do you mean, the 'scene is still being preserved'? You've let the library staff in – that's Sandra Deeson's car parked outside if I'm not mistaken!"

The PCSO, a short and slightly built young woman, tried to answer, but Carr talked right over her.

"I'm secretary of the Templeton Art Club, and I have the right and the responsibility to ensure that our members' artwork is being properly preserved and that every effort is being made to return it as soon as possible! I have been in touch with senior officers and they have assured me that I would have the full cooperation of the police – which is not what I am getting from you now!"

Carr was perhaps a few years older than me, though you had to get close to notice it. His dark and wavy hair showed no traces of grey and he was normally the epitome of smooth and cultured. But now an uglier side was showing as he leaned over the PCSO in an intimidating manner. His lips were pulled back in what was almost a snarl.

All credit to her, she stood her ground and, after several attempts, finally managed to get a word in. "I'm sorry, sir, but I have had no instructions to let anyone in except for police personnel and library staff. If you'll give me a moment, I'll contact my sergeant and if she's OK with it, then you can have access!"

"Contact your sergeant? Young woman, I am a personal friend of your chief constable! I think that outranks a mere sergeant!"

It's amazing how many friends chief constables have, especially among people who are trying to get something out of the police. But things had gone far enough.

"Perhaps I can help?" I stepped up next to the PCSO as I spoke.

Carr blinked, and a remarkable transformation took place: the angry bully was instantaneously transfigured into a polite and civilized gentleman being harassed by obdurate officialdom.

"Sandra!" he exclaimed. "What a pleasure to see you! And how fortunate! Perhaps you could explain to this officer who I am and why I need to come in and examine our paintings?"

I looked at the PCSO. "He won't need to go into the area where the CSIs are working. If I promise to escort him to the paintings and out again, will that be OK?"

Wheels turned inside the girl's head. Passing on responsibility to someone else is always an attractive option, especially when the alternative is to be the subject of another diatribe.

"He'll have to sign in," she said firmly. "And I'll have to inform Sergeant Henshaw."

"Of course. That'll be fine, won't it, Jonathan?" We'd never been on first-name terms before, but I certainly wasn't going to let him patronize me.

He flashed his teeth at me. "Of course, Sandra." Ignoring the well-worn ballpoint offered by the PCSO, he produced a stylish and expensive piece of silver and enamel jewellery that incorporated a pen, signed the log with an unnecessary flourish, and strode majestically into the library.

He ignored the stepping plates. Mindful of the warning about possible chemical contamination, I said nothing. Damage to his shiny leather footwear would be fitting recompense for his manners, I thought.

"The paintings are all in the Children's Section." I indicated the way. But he stopped in front of the reception desk and shook his head slowly.

"What a terrible mess! These people have no respect for property, do they?"

"The property isn't important. We can sort that out easily enough. But somebody died, and they're irreplaceable."

Carr turned his attention to me, putting on a concerned expression.

"Of course. I heard that you actually discovered the body. What a terrible shock for you! I don't know how you can even bear to come back in the building!"

I shrugged. "It wasn't pleasant. But I'm coping with it."

"Clearly you are. But shouldn't you be taking some time off?"

He was doing his best to sound sympathetic, but to me it seemed a little forced. "No, I'm better off with something to do."

"Well, I think you're being very brave. And I understand that this person is still unidentified? Unidentifiable, perhaps?"

An image flickered across my mind – body, face down, pool of blood. I pushed it away.

"I think the police are still working on that."

"So do they have no clues at all? Have they mentioned anything?"

"Not to me. And at the moment we're more concerned about Emily. Emily Coombe, that is – she's a member of your art club. She seems to have disappeared."

"Oh dear! That's sad news. Miss Coombe was so very helpful in organizing our exhibition, and so enthusiastic about art. I do hope that she's all right."

"We all do," I agreed.

"Has there been any word of her at all? Any sightings, any ideas where she might be?"

"Not as yet. Not that I've been told, anyway."

"But surely one of her friends or colleagues here must know if she had somewhere she might go? To hide, perhaps?" The sympathy was still on his face, but his eyes were intent.

I frowned. "Why would she hide?"

He shrugged dismissively. "Oh, I don't know. Just a figure of speech."

"Well, in any case, no one knows anything like that." I didn't like Carr, and I didn't like his manner. The sooner he did whatever he wanted to do and left us to get on, the better. "The paintings are over here – the police had to move them for their forensic work…"

I started moving towards the Children's Section again, but Carr went the other way.

"So this was where it happened?" He indicated the closed doors of the Laney Grey Wing.

"Yes. You can't go in. CSI are still working there."

"Hmm. Yes. I see. Very substantial doors, aren't they? Much more than you'd expect in a library. And that keypad – is that the only way to open them?"

"Yes," I answered shortly. I was finding his interest in the murder scene ghoulish.

"Well. Well well." He glanced round, taking it all in. "Quite a classic mystery, isn't it? A locked room, a body in the library…"

"I believe you came to see the art club paintings?" I was struggling to keep my tone polite.

"Of course." He turned away from the door, and strode briskly back across the library to where Yvonne was still sorting the artwork.

"You've met my assistant, Yvonne?"

Carr gave a perfunctory nod in her direction, and turned his attention to the paintings. "Is everything here?"

"As far as we know. Yvonne was just checking them." Yvonne was giving Carr a stony look in response to his casual dismissal of her. He ignored it.

"Very well. If there's anything damaged or missing, it will be up to the artist to sort out any liabilities between the library and the police. However, the art club will expect a full refund of our booking fee. I'll inform our members that they can come and collect their work."

With that, and without waiting for a reply, he turned and strode out again.

With the look that Yvonne sent after him, he was lucky to make it out alive. "That man is a slimy stain on the surface of the earth," she muttered. "And what did he want anyway? All that fuss to get in and he barely bothers to look at the paintings!"

I shrugged. "I don't know. He was more interested in the murder than the paintings. Probably just wanted an excuse to see the scene. Never mind. Forget him. I meant to ask you before he interrupted – do you remember seeing a large brown envelope on my desk before all this happened?"

"No. But there could be anything on your desk, Sandy, and no one would know about it. Entire undiscovered tribes could be living on there!"

"Yes, OK, thanks. You said all that before. I'll just go and look."

It was an old issue between us. Yvonne thought that my comfortable clutter was inefficient. However, I agree with

Einstein: "If a cluttered desk is the sign of a cluttered mind, of what, then, is an empty desk the sign?" I'd printed that quotation off, framed it, and put it on my desk for Yvonne's benefit. It's still there, somewhere.

Admittedly, it was hard to see any one specific item at a glance. The computer monitor poked up from behind a collection of brightly coloured folders, and at the other end of the desk the telephone was clearly visible on top of the directory, just next to the three-tier letter tray, each tier cheerfully stuffed with paperwork. In between... the keyboard was somewhere in there, and after a moment I identified the pile of mail that Kepple had mentioned. It was indeed on top of a large brown envelope. Very large – A2 size. Big enough to be hard to miss, even on my desk.

Had it been there on the night of the murder? I didn't remember seeing it, but I hadn't looked at my desk. I'd only come into the office to check on the safe. I probably glanced at my desk in passing, but I couldn't say for sure if the envelope had been there then.

It certainly couldn't have been there the last time I went on the PC, since it was half covering the keyboard. And that would have been during the afternoon before the art club people arrived to start setting up. Someone might have dropped it on my desk while I was busy with that. But who? Only the library staff should have access to the office – but the door might have been open, so someone could have come in.

I dumped the pile of mail on the chair, and picked up the envelope. There was only one thing written on the outside. My name. Not even my full name.

"SANDY DEESON" it said. Block capitals in blue ink. Carefully written. Informal, someone who was comfortable calling me "Sandy", not "Sandra" or "Mrs Deeson". Someone who labelled things with neat capitals.

You couldn't really tell handwriting from block capitals. But I did know someone who tended to label things like that, with neat capitals.

Emily. Emily had done that.

I held the envelope carefully, feeling the weight of it. Not especially heavy, but it was very stiff. Cardboard-backed, and heavy-duty paper.

I fumbled round my desk for a letter opener, and carefully slit it open.

The contents were tightly fitted, hard to pull out. As I tugged at them a small bit of paper came loose and fluttered to the floor. I picked it up.

"Dear Sandy, This is a personal gift for you. You'll understand why when you've seen the exhibition paintings. We plan to donate prints from them to the library, once things have quietened down a bit! But we thought that this would be appropriate for you to have. Emily."

Clearly her handwriting, on a large yellow Post-it note. Cramped, to fit in the space. But hers.

I was shaking slightly. I took a deep breath. Then pulled out the remaining contents of the envelope.

It was a painting, in a cardboard mount.

Much of it was executed in shades of grey, so the eye was drawn at first to the small section of bright colour. A flower, a potted plant, stood in a shaft of brilliant golden light, leaves and petals upturned to drink it in. Some sort of orchid, I thought. Or perhaps something that never existed outside of the artist's mind. If so, they had a powerful imagination and a technical skill to match. Each petal was a brilliant swirl of colour – predominantly a rich, deep red, shading to brighter crimson at the edges, but laced with intricate patterns in white and yellow. The leaves below were done in similar detail, the veins making a tracery of green shades on the green background.

But even as I absorbed the beauty of the flower, I was becoming aware of the rest of the picture. There were other flowers there. A row of them – or perhaps a circle, as they seemed to curve in towards the edge of the picture, as if the point of view was the centre of a ring of potted orchids.

But no sunlight fell on these, and no bright petals glowed. These were all dead or dying. Leaves drooping, petals falling, stalks withered and sagging. Here and there a trace of colour showed what beauty could have been there – a line of dark blue, a hint of purple. But everything else was grey. The plants were grey, the pots were grey. The stone flags on which they stood were grey and worn, and behind them were shadows and darkness, with just the hint here and there of thick wooden beams in dark grey and black, of crumbling old bricks and peeling paint.

There was a window, boarded up, except for one broken slat through which that one light beam came. Touching that one flower, and giving it life. While everything around it was death and decay.

It was powerful, and clearly symbolic – but symbolic of what?

I had the feeling that I should know. That there was something here that I should be recognizing.

I looked at the note again. *"You'll understand when you see the exhibition paintings."*

What paintings? None of those I'd seen seemed to bear any relation to this one. Did she mean the four that had had the best places reserved for them? The places left for the unnamed artist?

I looked again at the picture, searching for a signature or at least an initial, but nothing stood out.

Footsteps on the stairs, then Yvonne came in, already talking. "Finally got that lot into some sort of order. You'd think they could have taken some care to keep them together when they took them out, but no, just dumped any old place! No damage that I can see though, so the artists – if that's what they are! – can come and collect their masterpieces any time." She stared warily at what I was holding. "Now don't tell me that there's more of them up here! Surely they could have at least put them into one room?"

"There's just this one. And it's not part of the exhibition. It's from Emily."

"Emily!" Yvonne came over for a closer look. "That doesn't

55

look like Emily's work. I've seen her paintings – there were some in the exhibition. She did watercolour landscapes. Quite nice, but nothing like that."

"No, it's not her work. But she left it here, for me."

"For you?"

I showed Yvonne the note. She raised an eyebrow, then took the picture from me and held it so the light caught it. "Well, I'm no expert, but this looks pretty good to me. Some sort of mixed media, do you think?"

"Yes. Acrylics for the colour, and charcoal or pencil for the rest, perhaps."

"And what about these prints for the library? Anything else in the envelope?"

I picked up the envelope again and peered inside, but it was empty apart from a faint smell. Distinctive. Something that I might have come across before sometime, but I couldn't place it.

"What are you going to do with it?"

"I suppose I'd better tell the police. It might help them find Emily."

I pulled out my mobile to call June, then on impulse switched to the camera setting and took a couple of pictures of the painting. And one of the note, for good measure.

June was very interested to hear that we had something from Emily, less pleased that we had opened and handled the evidence.

"You should have called us as soon as you realized it was from her!" she admonished. "Put it down somewhere and don't touch it again! I'm on my way over."

I made suitable apologies, and put everything back on the desk. Yvonne and I stood there and regarded the painting from a safe distance.

"Why a gift to you particularly?" Yvonne wondered aloud.

I shrugged, shook my head.

"Is there some connection? You haven't taken up orchid growing, have you?"

"No. My gardening skills are just as they always were – basic. I can do a bit of weeding or trim a hedge, but nothing fancy."

"So what's the connection?"

I shrugged again. I didn't want to think about it. Something about the picture was disturbing, and I didn't want to go there.

I turned away and headed back down to the library. "Anyway, we'd better leave it alone until June gets here," I shouted back over my shoulder. "We're in enough trouble already!"

"Where do you get 'we'?" asked Yvonne, chasing after me. "You're the one who opened it!"

I made a bit of work for myself, putting returned books back into place and making a start on tidying the reception desk. Fortunately, June wasn't long, and wasn't alone either – DI Macrae was with her.

"I'm sorry about opening it. I wasn't thinking." I got my apology in quickly before June could say anything, but Macrae just waved it off.

"It's no' a problem, really. I can't expect you to be thinking like a police officer, now, can I?"

June said nothing, but gave me a look, which I carefully ignored. "It's up in the office," I said, and led the way.

Macrae had put on some disposable gloves, and, after a glance at the painting, picked the note up. "Do you use this sort of Post-it in the library?" he asked.

"Yes. But who doesn't?"

"A good point," he acknowledged. "And blue pen?"

"Ah – well, actually, we only have black in the office supplies. I think it goes back to a time when photocopiers didn't reproduce blue ink very well. Of course, anyone could use their own pen."

"Oh, certainly. But it inclines me to think that this was written somewhere else and brought here."

I remembered the faint smell of the envelope, and made a connection. "In a studio! An artist's studio!"

Macrae raised an eyebrow.

"There's a smell in the envelope," I explained. "It reminded me of an artist's studio that I went to once. I think that they told me it was turpentine and linseed oil."

"Very good, Mrs Deeson!" Macrae picked up the envelope and had a small sniff himself. "Yes, I think you're right. But there's a wee problem here. That sort of smell comes with oil painting – and this is done in acrylics."

"So the artist works in oils as well? Nothing unusual in that, especially if they like to do mixed media."

"Indeed, that's so." He put the envelope down and looked at the painting itself. "So, why do you think Emily gave this to you?"

"I've no idea."

"It's not one of her own?"

"No. She only worked in watercolours, as far as I know. And frankly, she was never this good."

"But she thought that this had a connection with you."

"Apparently. I don't know what, though." I didn't want to know what. "Perhaps there would be a clue in these other paintings she mentions."

"Aye, that's likely. We certainly would like to look at those. Perhaps if we can find this studio, we may find the other pictures."

He looked at the painting again, scrutinizing it carefully. "Interesting that there's no signature. You know, I've learned recently of another artist who didn't sign his work. Sir Arthur Templeton."

"Really? I didn't know that."

"Oh, aye. He was quite famous – or infamous, perhaps – for that little quirk, amongst others. Apparently he once said, 'If an artist is any good, their work will be recognized. If they aren't any good, their signature won't help it.'"

"Sounds like he had a good opinion of himself," said Yvonne.

"Arrogant, many people called him. But he had a lot of reason to be, back in the day. He didn't get that knighthood for nothing, you know. He had commissions from virtually everyone in the British

58

Establishment, it seemed, and many more besides. Back in the eighties, you weren't anyone unless you had a Templeton painting on your wall." He shook his head, frowning. "Then he suddenly packed it in, left the country, and wasn't heard of again for years. He never gave an explanation, so it's still a bit of a mystery."

I was impressed by his knowledge. "Do you have an interest in art, DI Macrae?"

He gave me a warm smile. "Oh, David, please. I'm no' much for formality. And as for the art, and Sir Arthur, it's just the way I like to approach a case like this. I get together as much information as I can – not just the obvious stuff, you understand, but all the background as well. Then I look for patterns, for the links, the connections. That's where the answers are often enough." He retained his smile, but gave me a searching look. "So if there's any more information you can give us, Sandra – anything at all?"

I shook my head, feeling at once flattered by his familiarity and threatened by his probing questions.

"Sorry, no. If I think of anything, I'll let you know."

"Aye, do that please. June – have a word with CSI, please. While they're still here, they can get these items photographed, packaged, and off to the lab ASAP."

"They won't damage the painting, will they?" I asked.

He nodded. "There should be no need for that. June, be sure to tell them, chemical treatment on the note, the envelope, and the mount, but visual examination only on the painting itself."

June nodded and went back down to find the CSIs. David turned back to me.

"Thank you again for bringing this to our attention. I'll see that you get the painting back in due course."

I glanced at it again. I wasn't sure that I wanted it back. It still made me uncomfortable.

"I just hope that it helps."

"Oh, it's helped already." He picked up the note again. "You see this word she uses? This 'we' she mentions? In the context of that picture, that's strong evidence that she was working with this mysterious artist. I'd suspected that, of course, but now we've confirmation."

"And the timing as well!" I repeated my thoughts on when the envelope could have been left.

David nodded in approval. "You see? You know more than you think! I was wondering about that very thing myself, and now you've helped me out again."

June came back in. "I've had a word with Alison. She's just getting some evidence bags from her van, and she'll be straight up. She'll get elimination prints from you two as well," she added with a stern look at Yvonne and myself. "But I'm afraid we'll have to consider this office part of the crime scene again – so if you don't mind?" She indicated the door.

David Macrae was sniffing at the envelope again. "You know, Sir Arthur mostly painted in oils. I wonder if he has a studio?"

"He hasn't painted in years!" said Yvonne.

"He hasn't *exhibited* in years," the DI corrected. "That doesn't mean that he's not painting. Perhaps we'll go and ask him. Thank you again, ladies," he added, giving us our cue to leave. He and June followed us down the stairs, and left by the front door.

"Hmm – the DI's a bit dishy, don't you think?" Yvonne gave me a little nudge as the doors shut behind them.

"He seems very on the ball," I answered non-committally. Yvonne watches too many soaps and likes to create her own storylines using the people around her.

"Yes, but he liked you! Didn't you see that smile he gave you? And 'David, please'!"

"Don't be fooled. It's just his way of putting people at ease so he can get more information out of them. Let's do some work, shall we? I'll ask the CSI when she wants to take our elimination prints – you phone the art club chairman, tell him what Carr said about getting the paintings moved. We might get something moving quicker that way."

DAY 3: POLTROON

It took Alison Kepple a while to get round to taking our fingerprints, since her priority was obviously dealing with the new evidence in the office. So it was getting on for evening when I finally got home, fully expecting a telling-off from Graham for working so long on a Sunday.

Instead, he greeted me with a broad grin.

"Sam's been in touch!"

My heart leaped. "Sam! Really! He answered my message?"

"Well, I'd left him a message as well. But he's replied to both of us! *Both* of us, Sandy!"

I stood there in the doorway, keys still in my hand and tears in my eyes. Sam had barely spoken to me in three years. Not since he'd left home. Not much before then, either. Even his messages to Graham hardly mentioned me.

"What… what does he say? Is it still on the PC? Show me! Show me, please!"

"I've printed it off."

Graham was waving a sheet of paper in my face. I snatched it away from him, and peered at the print, but couldn't make the words out, my vision was too blurry. I rubbed frantically at my eyes, but the tears were still coming. I thrust it back at him.

"You read it."

"OK. It starts, 'Hi, Dad. Hi, Mum.'"

"He said that! He said 'Hi Mum'?"

"Yes, that's just as he sent it. Hot off the printer. The message only came in half an hour ago. I was just about to phone you…"

"Yes, yes, but what else does he say?"

We were still standing in the hallway, with the door open, but there was no question of waiting until we'd sat down and got comfortable.

"He says, 'Hi, Dad. Hi, Mum. Got your messages. Wow, does sound like you had a nasty experience, Mum. Hope you're getting over it OK. Don't let it get to you! Seriously, don't. Watch out for her, Dad, you know how she gets. I'm in Thailand at the moment.

Wonderful country, lovely people. Might stay here a while. Take care, Sam.'"

I had him read it again. Then I took the sheet of paper from him, and held it tightly, scanning the words again and again.

He led me gently into the lounge, sat me down, and went to put the kettle on – before thinking better of it and pouring me a large glass of wine.

I sat and held it, taking occasional sips, and not letting go of the paper.

"He spoke to me, Graham! He talked to me!"

"I know, Sandy." He hugged me, still beaming.

"That's the first time in..."

"I know."

We sat together, savouring the moment.

"That's the longest message we've had from him in... I don't know. Years, maybe?"

"Something like that."

Graham had had more contact than me. Sam hadn't had an issue with his dad, except where Graham had supported me. I'd been the problem. It was me who had destroyed our relationship with our son. But now he was talking to me again.

"So he's left Australia, then."

Graham chuckled. "If he's in Thailand, I suppose he must have done."

"Whereabouts, do you think?"

"Goodness knows. It's a big place. Probably somewhere remote, knowing Sam."

"But not too remote to get in touch."

"The internet covers a lot of places."

Underneath the euphoria, the relief, a fear was rising. An old enemy. I tried to push it down, but it forced its way out anyway.

"Thailand... it's not a safe place, is it? I mean, there've been stories."

I felt Graham go tense. "Sam's good at looking after himself,

Sandy. He's been knocking around the world for three years now, and he was always pretty streetwise. He's fine."

"Yes. Of course. He is." I tried to force myself to relax. "Does he know anyone there, do you suppose? I mean, does he have any friends?"

"Of course he has friends. Sam's great at making friends – you know that. Five minutes on a bus or in a bar, and he's everyone's best friend ever."

"Yes. He's like that, isn't he?"

There was a pause.

"But – he can't have been there long, that's all. I mean, we know he was in Australia not long ago, and he's been travelling, so he won't know people well…"

"Sandy…"

"It's just that if something happened to him – and no one knew him – does he have identification? Would they know who to contact?"

My breathing had become shallow and rapid. Graham held my hands, spoke urgently. "Of course he has identification. He's got a passport, remember? And probably other documents."

"But they could be stolen! And if he was mugged, if he was injured or killed and left in some place where he wasn't found, not found for weeks or months, so he couldn't be identified…"

"Sandy! Don't do this, please! Not now! Just leave it!"

"I'm sorry. I'm sorry, Graham – but I can't leave it!" I was starting to shout. "You don't understand, you never understand. Something might happen to him and no one would know who he was and his body would never be claimed; it would just be left there, left swinging…"

I stopped abruptly, suddenly realizing what I'd said, suddenly seeing the tears in Graham's eyes.

"I knew this would happen," he said, and sounded so broken and despondent that I began to cry again myself. Not from joy this time. From guilt, because I had done this. "I knew this thing at the library would bring it all back again. How couldn't it? Coming across a body like that, and an unidentified one at that."

I closed my eyes and nodded. "You're right. I didn't want to admit it. Especially not to myself. But... I had that dream again last night. The noise... And the picture..."

"What picture?"

"The picture... Oh! Of course, the picture!" I began a frantic search through my pockets for my phone.

"I don't understand, Sandy. What picture are you talking about?"

"The one at the library!" I tried to explain. I couldn't find my phone in any of my pockets. Had I left it behind? I started searching again. "Emily left me a picture – a painting! I only found it today."

The phone wasn't in a pocket. I'd put it in my handbag. I pressed buttons, my fingers shaking so much that I kept pressing the wrong ones. "Incorrect Password," the screen told me.

"What does the picture have to do with it?" Graham was struggling to stay calm himself, but my agitation was scaring him. I closed my eyes, took a deep breath, and then started again, taking care to press each key properly.

"I'll show you." The password was accepted and the phone opened up its secrets. I went into the photo albums, opened up the most recent pictures. The first one that came up – the last one I'd taken – was Emily's note. "Look, this was with the picture."

Graham squinted to read it. "OK. So – the painting?"

"Here." I scrolled across to the image I'd recorded. Even on the small screen, the brilliant colours of the flower in the sunbeam stood out.

"Flowers? I don't get it, Sandy. What is it about a painting of flowers?"

"No, not the flowers!" The words tumbled out of me. I was understanding more even as I spoke. "That's what I was looking at first, the flowers, but I knew there was something else there, only I couldn't see it, I didn't want to see it, I didn't want to be reminded, but my subconscious knew all along!"

Graham, more perplexed than ever, could only stare at the picture and then back at me.

"It's the background, Graham! The place where the flowers are!"

"You can hardly see the background. It's all in shadows."

"Yes! Yes, exactly! That's just how it was! All shadows, and dark old beams and peeling paint – it was just like that, even the boarded window, though there wasn't a hole in it then!"

I reached over and grabbed his hand, desperate to make him understand. "I know that place, Graham! I've been there! That was where I found the body – thirty years ago!"

DAY 4: SCINTILLA

Of course, I should have told David Macrae. Or June. But in all honesty, it didn't even occur to me until the following morning.

That evening Graham and I had talked it over, trying to work out the implications. What was the connection? How could Emily have a picture of that place, of all places? Clearly, it was no coincidence that she had left it for me. But the meaning behind it escaped us.

I went to bed early, exhausted by the emotion of the day. Even so, I'd been reluctant to sleep for fear of the dream. That soft and terrible creaking noise had haunted me for years, coming back in times of stress or worry. But I'd thought it long over and gone. It was a huge relief when I woke up and realized that I'd slept through without any dreams at all – or none that I remembered.

Graham was up early. He was supposed to be out that day: though officially retired, he still did a bit of freelance work, and had arranged to interview an ex-England rugby player about a new youth team that he was sponsoring. He was all for cancelling it and staying with me, but I wouldn't hear of it.

"There's no need," I assured him. "I'm feeling a lot better now it's all out."

That was the truth. Recognizing the location of the painting had

had a cathartic effect, draining off a huge amount of excess emotion and leaving me with a clearer head. I could even contemplate the thought of Sam being out in Thailand with only a faint trace of worry – no more than any mother would feel, I told myself.

Not totally convinced, Graham set off, leaving strict instructions that I was to call him immediately if necessary and at lunchtime in any case. I settled down to do some work. Online research first, regarding the cleaning up of crime scenes and the possible cost implications.

As I'd suspected, there were several companies offering specialist crime scene clean-up services, apart from the one recommended by the CSI. Some even offered a twenty-four-hour emergency call-out service. All of them included chilling lists of the possible dangers from inadequately cleaned crime scenes, especially those involving blood spillage.

"Even a small amount of blood can release airborne pathogens..."

There wasn't a small amount of blood involved here, I thought with a shudder, and I was glad that Alison Kepple had given me a mask when I looked into the Memorial Wing.

Armed with this information, I contacted Marilyn at County Hall, and persuaded her that this wasn't something we could leave to the normal cleaners. I painted a lurid picture of our regular library visitors being wiped out by hepatitis B or worse, and she agreed that I should get some quotes for the work to be done as soon as the scene was released.

Which, as it turned out, was going to be a little longer than expected. A call from a constable at the station informed me that DI Macrae sent his regards and apologized for not being in touch personally, but he was keeping the library sealed pending lab results from the envelope, note, and painting, in case they led to further work needing to be done.

I could have mentioned my revelation about the picture then. But I didn't. Better, I thought, to wait until I could speak to Macrae in person.

I had a sandwich and sat thinking about things. About recent events, and events long past.

Brodie wandered over to have a fuss made of him.

"Brodie," I asked as I scratched behind his ears, "how do you fancy a little trip out?"

He signalled his agreement with a vigorous wag of his tail. Actually, I knew that it was a pretty safe bet. Brodie's a brindle Staffie, past the first flush of youth and getting grey round the muzzle, but still ready for an adventure, any time but mealtimes.

Ten minutes later, he was in the back of my Fiesta, barking happily at the world in general as we headed into the heart of the English countryside. Green fields, little woods, sleepy villages each with an ancient church and a pub or two.

Narrow lanes, slow tractors, and missing signposts. I thought I knew the way, so I hadn't bothered with the satnav. But it had been a very long time. After crawling along behind something large and agricultural for several miles, I came to a crossroads with no signs and realized that I hadn't a clue where I was.

And no idea, really, why I was even doing this. What could I possibly learn from revisiting a place I'd been trying to forget most of my adult life?

I sat at the crossroads, looking out at high green hedges and overhanging trees, feeling lost and afraid and alone. I got out my phone to call Graham, but there was no signal. Perhaps just as well. It would be a bit hard to explain what I was doing, since I hardly knew myself. He wouldn't be happy about it, that was for sure. He'd told me thirty years ago to forget it, and I'd told him I would. My being here was proof that I'd lied. To myself as much as to him, but it would hurt him.

There was a satnav on my phone, though I'd never used it. I started flicking through icons, trying to find it. Perhaps it could get me home.

I was still puzzling over the technology when a horn sounded behind me. I dropped the phone and fumbled in the footwell for it while simultaneously trying to look around. I failed at both, and the horn sounded again, closer and louder, and I sat up and looked properly, to see an immense tractor rumbling down the lane towards me.

Panicked, I tried to get into gear and move out of the way but only succeeded in stalling the engine and rolling forward just far enough to block the crossroads in all directions.

There was a squeal of brakes and another blast of the horn as the tractor came to a halt just behind me. Too close behind for my liking. A red-faced man leaned out of the cab and made waving motions at me.

I started the car again, but still had no idea which way to go. There was a long sustained blare on the horn. Brodie, not wanting to be left out, was adding his bark to the noise, and my panic was replaced by a sudden flare of irritation. Whatever happened to countryside hospitality? I got out of the car and walked back to the tractor.

"What do you think you're doing?" the driver shouted down at me over the noise of his engine. "This isn't a car park!"

Actually, he said a bit more than that, using words I considered inappropriate. I smiled sweetly back and put on my best helpless female voice.

"I'm *terribly* sorry, but I'm quite lost. I wonder if you could help me?"

He frowned. "Where do you want to go?"

That was a good question. I hesitated, his frown deepened. "Back to town, please," I said quickly, before he could start swearing again.

"Turn right. Three miles, left at the T-junction and that'll bring you to Coren Hall Village. It's signposted from there."

That name was familiar. "Coren Hall? Isn't that where that orphans' school used to be?"

He shrugged. Didn't know, didn't care. He was younger than me, wouldn't remember that far back. "Just move your f… car. I've got work to do."

"Of course. Thank you so much." I gave him another smile, sauntered back to the car, and took the time to pick up my phone and wave at him before driving off. Childish, and not really very satisfying.

The directions were accurate, at any rate. The junction put me on a better road and in sight of a rather grand house perched on the top of a hill.

"I know that place!" I told Brodie. "It's Coren Hall! Used to be a private school, and an orphanage."

He put his head up, looked round, then lay down again. The excitement with the tractor had tired him out, and he'd decided to rest until the next interesting thing came into his life. Ancient history didn't do it for him.

Nevertheless, lacking other companionship, I continued to tell him all about it. Dogs are good for that sort of thing.

"I used to walk all round here. Got a bus out to Frayhampton then walked back. Lot of footpaths to follow. I mostly went along the top of the ridge, for the view, but it could be a bit windy up there."

Which was why I'd taken a different route the last time I'd walked here. A storm had been forecast, but wasn't due until evening, so I had plenty of time, I'd thought. I could do a brisk five or six miles and be in the Dog and Duck on the outskirts of town before it arrived.

A bright day, though. A lot of clouds, but they were racing across the sky, driven by the approaching storm front. The high paths would have been a struggle. So instead I went down into the valley, followed the river route.

"Trouble was, Brodie, I didn't know that path, and it just faded out on me. Left me in the middle of a field with barbed wire on one side, a bog on the other, and the woods in front. Of course, I should have gone back. But the storm was coming in faster than I'd expected. I thought I'd have some shelter under the trees."

DAY 4: SCINTILLA

And besides, I always hated going back. My stubborn streak showed itself: I'd set out to walk this way and so I would continue to walk this way, path or no path.

"Of course, I soon got totally lost. I wish I'd had you with me to sniff a path out! But I just wandered round, tripping over things, getting scratched on brambles and branches, until the storm hit. Then I couldn't even see where I was going."

It had gone very dark; the wind had increased and was making an incredibly loud noise as it thrashed the branches. Then the rain started, wind-driven and hammering down, a solid deluge of water forcing its way through the leaves and branches and through my coat as well. I was soaked and cold and wet and frightened. And annoyed with myself for being frightened; annoyed that I'd got myself into this.

"Then there was thunder and lightning… I've never heard it so loud, Brodie. I was really scared. You would have been as well! With good reason – all those wet trees, and the lightning seemed non-stop. I expected to be fried at any moment."

I slowed down for a sharp bend, and Brodie whined.

"No, I couldn't phone for help," I explained. "Didn't have mobile phones back then. Well, I didn't, anyway."

The country road continued along its winding way ahead, but a sign announced "Coren Hall Village" off to the left, down a much newer looking section of road.

"I don't remember that. Let's take a look, shall we?"

A few minutes later we were passing some rather magnificent residences. Large, in extensive grounds, and none more than a few years old. I could practically smell the fresh paint.

"This certainly wasn't here before, though I had heard something about a new development out this way. Looks very upmarket, doesn't it?"

Brodie declined to comment. I drove on. More houses, some side streets – smaller residences, packed a bit closer together, but still looking new, and not cheap.

"Someone made some money out of this lot," I observed. "You'd need a lot of dog biscuits to buy one of those kennels!"

We came to a traditional village green, clearly designed from scratch to be so. The road circled genteelly round the manicured central lawn with its newly planted trees and extensive car parking area, flanked by village hall, post office, and supermarket – all in keeping with the style of the place.

A signpost indicated that the main road back to town was straight ahead. Left was Coren Hall Hotel and Health Spa. Right, past the village green, was the Farmer's Rest public house. And a public footpath.

I hesitated, then pulled into the car park.

"I did promise you a walk, didn't I?"

Brodie confirmed that I had indeed made that commitment. So, with lead clipped on we set out to explore.

From the far end of the village green the footpath ran off to the right, while the road to the Farmer's Rest curved away to the left. A line of trees had been planted along the road. Fast-growing conifers: the estate was new, but already the pub was almost hidden. I could just make out the line of the rooftop. I stopped and stared at it, while Brodie did his best to drag me down the path.

"Have a bit of patience," I admonished. "That rooftop looks familiar."

Patience was not in Brodie's vocabulary, nor his nature. He heaved on the lead again, whining.

"OK, OK. I'm coming."

We set off down the path. It was a nice path, well gravelled and with neat wooden steps on the steeper bits. Overhead and on either side the foliage was sprinkled with autumn gold; the gravel was carpeted with red and yellow. I sniffed the rich scent of autumn woodland. Brodie, with far more interesting smells to investigate, strained at the lead, and since the path seemed deserted I let him have his freedom. He bounded ahead, occasionally glancing back to make sure I was still following.

"This is a lot easier than it used to be," I told him. "Even you would have struggled to get through here in those days."

Brodie snorted with derision at the thought that anything could slow him down, and left the path to prove it. He found his way back again after a few minutes, well sprinkled with leaves and small twigs.

"See what I mean?"

He ignored me and carried on.

I thought about that roof. The way it had looked against the sky. Surely the building wouldn't still be here, after all this time? It must have been knocked down to make way for the new village, if it hadn't fallen down on its own before then.

The path came out of the woods, and split. One fork ran straight ahead, wider than the footpath – perhaps a farm track – but also unsurfaced and muddy. The gravelled path turned left to run alongside the woods, with open fields on the right. We went left.

Thirty years ago the woods had been more extensive, stretching right down to the river on this side. I'd struggled through them for what had seemed like hours. Or was that just in my memory?

But then one of those terrifying flashes of lightning had lit up something that – thank God! (and I'd meant it) – wasn't branches. A regular pattern, printed on my brain in that moment of dazzling light. A roof.

A roof implied a house, a place of shelter, a place to find help. I'd fought my way through the woods, heading in the direction the lightning had shown me.

The treeline curved left again, and the path followed it. I came to the corner, and discovered a small hole in the fence. Small, but getting bigger as Brodie forced his way through.

"No! Brodie! Stop!" Fearful that he might be escaping into a field of sheep I raced forward and managed to grab a hind leg. He whined and growled but stopped moving, at least long enough for me to get a hand on his harness. With many complaints on both sides, I finally extricated him from the hole.

"Bad dog! Stay on the path!" I told him severely. He licked my hand in a mock apology that I didn't believe for a moment, then wandered away to sniff at a fence post, incident forgotten.

Still breathing heavily from the exertion, I straightened up and looked at the path ahead.

To our left, the woods continued, dark and ominous in my memories though it was a bright enough day now. To the right, fields – apparently sheep-free – stretched down to the river, with the main road back into town running along the far bank. Beyond that, the land rose up to the high and windy ridges that I had so often walked in the past.

In front of me, the river valley, climbing steadily in smoothly flowing folds, fields dotted with trees and copses. At the head of the valley a grey spire stood in a cluster of houses, marking an ancient faith as in so many other towns and villages across the land.

Conspicuously absent in Coren Hall Village, I thought. The façade was realistic, but had no roots.

"I think that must be Frayhampton," I told Brodie. He gave me a hopeful look, but I shook my head. "Too far to go today. But that's the direction I came from. Following the river path until it ran out and left me lost."

We carried on, until the sounds of traffic alerted me to a road ahead, and I stopped to put Brodie back on his lead. We came out of the path onto another bit of fresh tarmac.

"I wish this had been here back then! It would have made things a lot easier, I can tell you."

We turned left again, back towards the village. As we walked, I thought of the implications of that. If there had been a road here thirty years ago, I would have stumbled onto it, and followed it back, and… and many things would have been different.

"What if, Brodie? What if?"

We came to the outskirts of the village. More ginormous domiciles in landscaped ground where once was thick woodland.

I must have come along this way, I thought. Coming down

the valley, wandering away from the river. Somewhere very near here – perhaps in this very spot! – a younger version of myself had been struggling through the trees and undergrowth. Cold and wet and frightened but with no idea of the utter terror that lay ahead.

"You should have stayed in the trees, Sandy," I whispered to myself. "Better to have stayed there all night."

We reached the ersatz village green (too bad that hadn't been the Word for the Day that morning) and the car park. I put Brodie back in the boot, gave him some water and a few dog biscuits.

"You look after the car for me. There's something I need to do."

He wagged his tail and settled down for a snooze. I cracked open a window for him, locked the car, and walked on to the pub.

The walk had taken me from disbelief through denial to a dread certainty, without consciously thinking it through. It was no surprise when I came round the trees and immediately recognized the building.

I didn't understand why I should be so sure. When I was first here it had been just a looming darkness against the greater darkness. There had been no lights on, of course. I should have noticed that, but I was desperate to find shelter and safety.

The place had been cleaned up considerably. The derelict outbuildings that I had tripped and stumbled through were gone, giving way to another car park, well filled with big 4x4s and top-of-the-range saloons. The main structure had been cleaned and whitewashed: it looked bright and welcoming, matching the pub sign with its image of a jolly red-faced farmer sitting at his ease with a frothing pint.

It couldn't have been more different from the memories I had, yet I knew at once that it was the same building. The recognition came from somewhere deeper than mere sight. My guts felt it and cringed away.

I took a deep breath, crossed the car park, and went in the front door. All glass panels and brass furniture. My fingers remembered rough wood, the sharp prick of a splinter as I first hammered on the door then pushed and pulled at it. Another flicker of lightning – more distant now as the storm moved on down the valley – had both encouraged my efforts and shown me the latch. There had been a chain hanging from it, with a padlock – but the padlock hadn't been closed. The chain fell away, the latch lifted, and I was inside, finally out of the rain.

On that occasion I'd stepped into pitch darkness and had stopped just inside the doorway, unable to go further. This time I was stopped by a disdainful look from a waiter-type person.

"I'm afraid we're fully booked for lunch, madam." He glanced at the muddy patches on my jeans, a legacy of my tussle with Brodie, and was clearly relieved he didn't have to offer me a table.

"That's OK. I only wanted a drink."

"Of course," he said, with only a moment of reluctant hesitation. "The bar is open. Through the restaurant, at the rear of the building." He indicated the way.

The old· farmhouse had been completely rebuilt inside, internal walls replaced by occasional pillars to allow the entire ground floor to be opened up – right to the rafters in some places, with a mezzanine over the far end providing extra seating. All done out in rustic – whitewashed walls, dark oak beams and furniture, a real fire at one end.

And, as the waiter had indicated, it was very full, every table occupied by chattering people and steaming plates. The smell of mingled menus filled the room, wine was flowing, and a good time was being had by all.

I slipped past as inconspicuously as possible, keeping to the side of the room and avoiding the waiters, till I reached the sanctuary of the bar.

Thirty years ago I had groped my way down a dark passage, calling out as I did so, even though I was already certain that the place was empty. But I hoped that I might find a room with an un-boarded window that would let in enough light to change by. I was soaked, of course, but I had a spare pullover in my backpack, if the rain hadn't penetrated it.

There had been a side door, I remembered, but it was either locked or jammed. I carried on to the end door, and that creaked open. The room beyond had had two filthy skylights in a sloping roof that allowed in a little dim illumination. I'd stepped through, relieved to be out of the oppressive darkness of the corridor. Stood there for a moment, peering into the shadows that fringed the skylights and feeling my heartbeat slowing.

The sloping roof and skylights were now covered by a low ceiling. The room itself continued the farmhouse theme, but with comfortable leather armchairs, a central fireplace burning merrily, and wooden screens here and there to give a cosy atmosphere. In contrast to the main restaurant it was almost empty – just a couple whispering together in a corner, and an elderly gentleman reading a newspaper near the fire.

And the barman, much friendlier than the waiter.

"Afternoon, ma'am. Can I get you anything?" he asked with an actual smile.

"Just a fruit juice. I'm driving. Or do you have a ginger beer?"

"We certainly do. Take a seat, I'll bring it over."

I hitched myself up onto a barstool. "This is fine, thanks."

That time before I had stepped hesitantly forward, shivering with cold, my nostrils filled with the miasma of an abandoned house, all damp and decay. It didn't seem possible that this was the same place.

Until I turned on the barstool and saw the part of the room that had previously been concealed by a screen.

On the far wall was a window. Not *a* window, *the* window. The window from the picture, the window from my memory. No longer boarded, clean glass letting in a rush of autumn light. No single shaft illuminating a flower, no dim grey outline such as I had seen. But the shape was the same, even the line of the beam above it, though half concealed behind the new ceiling.

And if that was the window – then where I was sitting now…

"Are you all right, ma'am?" The bartender sounded genuinely concerned. "Only you've gone a little pale."

"I'm OK. Thank you. Just a bit of a… I'm fine. The drink will help."

I took the ginger beer from him, wishing it was something stronger. I dug out my purse, concentrated on counting out the money, the familiar act grounding me in the here and now. Pushing the memories back thirty years, where they belonged.

I managed a smile, and the bartender nodded, though still looking concerned. "Well, if there is anything…"

"Of course. Thanks." I took a drink and steadied myself. *It's in the past, Sandra.* I said it to myself, and was careful not to mutter the words, mindful that I was being watched. *There's nothing here now.*

Despite which, it was an effort of will to turn around again, and remember.

The faint grey light that made it through the grimy panes had dropped exhausted to the floor, making no effort to illuminate the rest of the room. My eyes were dark-adapted from groping through the corridor, but even so I couldn't make out anything other than flagstones, beams, and the faint outline of the window.

And something else. In the darkest shadows between the skylights, a suggestion of… something. Someone?

"Hello?"

No reply. Of course not. All I could make out was a smudge of darkness within the darkness, a shadow slightly more solid than the shadows around it.

And if it was a person they were impossibly tall, I realized. Eight foot, at least.

I stepped forward, wondering. Even as I came closer, I still couldn't make out any details.

Then my foot caught on an uneven flagstone. I stumbled, hands outstretched, grabbing for something to prevent me from falling. And as I touched the shadow, it moved.

DAY 4: SCINTILLA

It swung away from me, and I fell forward, right forearm smashing painfully into the floor but at least protecting my face.

I lay there for a moment, moaning with the pain from my arm, lifting myself up on my left hand to protect it but afraid to move further in case it was broken and I made it worse.

And behind me, above me, was a noise. The noise I would hear in my nightmares for years.

A slow, rhythmic creaking noise. From the rope, or the beam it was attached to. I never knew. The noise of something swinging.

In my dreams it always started as I went down the corridor. But it hadn't actually begun until I'd stumbled and fallen and started it swinging.

I had the bizarre thought that it was a punchbag. I'd felt some sort of cloth under my hands as I'd tried to hold it for support. Felt something cold and heavy underneath. I'd touched something like that at a gym once, something solid but not hard, covered in cloth. Something that swung when you pushed it.

For a moment I was sure that was what it was. That some past occupant had set up their own gym here in this back room and the punchbag had been left behind.

Very carefully, still protecting my right arm, I rolled over onto my back and looked up.

It was not a punchbag.

Pale in the dim light, a face stared down at me. The eyes bulged. The mouth gaped open, the tongue hung out.

As he swung, he moved towards me, then away, then back. He twisted slightly, looking first over my shoulder, then into my face, then down by my side. And back. Looking past me, through me, beyond me.

I learned afterwards that he had been wearing dark clothing, that he had long dark hair, that his hands had been forced into his pockets and a rope tied round his body to keep them there, so he could do nothing to help himself. And because of that, all

I could see in the faint light was his face, floating backwards and forwards eight feet above me.

All I heard was the creaking of the rope.

I knew he was dead. I don't know how I was so sure, and perhaps I should have tried to help him, tried to get him down. They asked me about it afterwards, and I felt guilty that I hadn't tried. But all the same, I was certain he was dead, and of course I was right.

So I didn't try to do anything for him. I just backed away, sliding myself across the floor, getting as far away as I could. I don't think I screamed. I would have done, but it was hard just to keep breathing; it felt as if the air had gone solid in my throat and I had to force it in and out.

I slid back across the floor until I reached the wall, then dragged myself up and pulled myself along it, looking for a way out. But there was only damp brickwork – until I reached the window and began pulling at the boards, but they were too well fixed, securely screwed in, and though I tore my nails I couldn't move them.

That was the same window I was looking at now.

The body would have been… I turned my head, looked up… The ceiling gave no indication of where the beams above were, but…

Just next to me. Thirty years ago, it would have been just next to me.

"What's wrong? Miss – ma'am?"

The barman was looking at me in shock. Fear even. Not surprisingly. I was shaking so hard that I'd spilled ginger beer over my hands. It was dripping on the carpet.

If he'd been here thirty years ago, he'd have reason to be in shock, I thought. But thirty years ago he wouldn't even have been a premonition in his dad's mind, let alone a twinkle in his eyes.

The thought sparked an inane desire to giggle. I choked it down, before it became hysteria, and forced myself to take another drink.

"I'm OK, really," I said, trying to control my voice to sound

OK. "Sorry about that. I thought I saw a… a spider, that's all."

"A spider?" The lad looked up at the ceiling, and down again. "Are you sure?"

"No, not really. Imagination. I don't like spiders." A lie. Spiders have never much bothered me. Not the native ones, anyway.

"I've got to go." I finished off what was left of my drink, and put my glass back down on the bar. "I… tell me, do you know anything about the history of this place? Before it became a restaurant?"

He looked confused by the sudden change of topic. "No – sorry, I've only worked here a month."

"Oh. Never mind. Not important. Well, I'll get off. Is there another way out?" I didn't want to go back through the restaurant with my muddy jeans and now damp cuffs.

"Yes – if you go down that corridor…" he indicated a passageway that ran off behind the bar, "… past the toilets, there's a fire escape. You're not really supposed to use it, but we do all the time. It just takes you out behind the bins, and then you're in the car park."

He looked relieved to be rid of this unstable middle-aged woman, and I couldn't blame him.

Back out in the fresh air, I took time to walk all round the car park. The main road out through the village hadn't been there before, of course. When I'd finally found my way out all those years ago – back along the corridor to the front door – the sky had lightened enough to show an overgrown cart track running off from the side of the building, running in the same direction that the footpath now did, I realized. Where the footpath turned, but a track continued – that had been where I'd gone. Running. Stumbling and slipping, sobbing and gasping for breath, but not daring to stop until I'd reached the main road again.

I went back to my car, opened the boot, and made a big fuss of Brodie, finding relief from my memories in the present-day reality of his warm fur and doggy smell. He, of course, accepted it as his natural right.

"Let's go home, eh? I've had enough of this place."

Brodie barked assent, so I got in, started up, and pulled away.

I took the new road out of the village, the one that would have saved me all that grief if it had been there the last time I visited. A short drive, a new bridge over the river, and out onto the main road back into town.

But we'd only travelled half a mile when I saw the lay-by on the opposite side, and made a sudden decision to pull across the road and park again. Fortunately, the traffic was still light enough to do that safely.

"You might as well know the rest of the story," I told Brodie. "This was where the cart track came out. That gate there."

He whined hopefully, wondering if he was going to be treated to a second walk.

"No, we're not getting out. I just wanted to see if it was still there."

I rolled the car forward a short distance, until we were alongside the gate. Beyond, the track continued, crossing the river on a bridge of grey stone that had probably served local farmers for over a hundred years.

It had looked no different thirty years ago. Not that I'd stopped to inspect it. But I could still feel the relief from when I'd found it and had realized that I wasn't trapped by the river.

"There was a lorry parked up just here. The driver had stopped for a flask of tea and a sandwich. His name was Godfrey, would you believe? Not a lorry driver's name at all! Godfrey Payne. A skinny little man, probably the far side of fifty. I don't know what he thought when I started hammering on his door and shouting. A young woman, soaking wet and near hysterical, gabbling on about a hanging body... But he was all right, was Godfrey. Put down his sandwich, screwed the top back on his flask, and said, 'Get in then; we'd better go to the police.'"

I remembered being in the cab of the lorry. It smelled of oil and sweat and strong tea. It was warm and dry and – most especially – safe.

Godfrey had been a star. He'd driven me all the way into town, right up to the Central Police Station, parked up, and accompanied me inside. He'd insisted on talking to an officer, made sure they were taking me seriously, and gave his own statement before he finally wished me good luck and went his way. I never saw him again, but ever since then, when people in church have talked about "ministering angels" I've thought of Godfrey.

I sent up a silent prayer of thanks for the Godfreys of this world, waited for a break in the traffic, then pulled back out and headed home.

*

My plan was a long soak in a hot bath: memory had set a chill in my bones. But as I turned the final corner and saw home, I also saw a van parked outside. It had a big blue logo on the side – "Fastrack Distribution". Which meant that Rob had dropped by for a visit.

He was sitting in the van, saw me coming, and waved. I waved back, pulled into the drive, and let Brodie out to do the greetings.

I've never known someone who changed as much and as quickly as Rob Seaton. When I first met him he was a big, shabby, friendly bloke, whose main interests in life were TV and sport. He was the sort of man who needed a good woman to take him on, but it would have been a big project and up to that point no one had attempted it.

He was still friendly, but dressed better and thought deeper. I put the change down to the influence of several women in his life, one of them dead. Laney Grey, the poet he'd accidentally killed, had catalysed a huge change in him through her death and her words.

Roshawn Skerrit, Laney's grandmother, had also made a big impression. But the biggest changes had been made by June Henshaw. They had officially been an item for at least six months now, but unofficially (because the police are cautious about relationships with members of the public they meet during the course of their duties) for over a year. It was June who had got him to ditch the tatty leather jacket, faded jeans, and grubby T-shirts that had constituted the major part of his wardrobe, and that had been a huge step forward.

I'd had a part to play as well. Mostly in educating Rob about the world of literature in general and poetry in particular, which had been – literally – a closed book to him previously. But he also came to me for advice in other matters.

After fussing Brodie for a suitable length of time, he turned to me. "Hi, Sandra," he said with a grin. It faded quickly as he composed himself to say something serious. "I've been away for a bit, but I heard what happened at the library. Terrible shock for you, it must have been."

Rob's sympathy came from a place of knowledge. He knew all about terrible shocks.

"It was. But we move on. To be honest, my big worry at the moment is for Emily. You remember her?"

He nodded. "Brown hair, glasses, very efficient."

"Yes… well, she's gone missing, and the police think she might have been involved. But perhaps June told you already?"

"No, June doesn't like to tell me about anything she's working on. She's very cautious about revealing information. Usually. I'm very sorry to hear about Emily."

"Thank you, Rob. Come in and have a cup of tea. But I hope you're not planning to ask me anything about poetry. I've had a difficult day, and I'm not in a literary frame of mind."

"Oh. Sorry to hear that. Only I *was* hoping to pick your brains about something. Not poetry, though. And it is a bit urgent, really…"

"Oh, OK then. Since I'm putting the kettle on anyway."

We settled ourselves in the kitchen with tea and biscuits.

"I've been wanting to ask how you were doing," Rob said as he dunked a jammy dodger. "I couldn't believe it when I heard what had happened. It must have been…"

"It was," I agreed. "But I'm OK now, thanks for asking."

He stuffed the soggy biscuit in his mouth and nodded. "Good. Glad to hear it."

"So what was it you wanted to ask about?" I wiped a few damp crumbs off the tabletop. June still had a lot of work to do.

"Well – this, actually." He produced a small box from his pocket, and flicked it open. The ring inside was surprisingly tasteful: diamond and sapphires in an elegant setting that hinted of hands clasped around the stones.

"Oh, Rob, it's lovely! But I shall have to talk to Graham first."

He looked surprised and shocked simultaneously. "No, it's for June, not you!"

"Really? You drink my tea, eat my biscuits, and break my heart?"

We laughed together, Rob with perhaps a touch of relief that I was joking.

"Seriously, it's a beautiful choice, Rob. I'm sure June will love it. Can I get in the first congratulations?"

"Ah. Yes. Well, that's what I was wanting to ask about, really."

I sighed inwardly. Not just a simple matter of approving the ring, then. "What's to ask? You've been going out for long enough to know, surely? And I've been thinking it was about time you moved things on a bit."

He looked at the ring, flicked the box with his finger. "You're right. It is time. But... thing is, Sandra, you and Graham have been together for a long time. Which is good. I admire that. That's the sort of relationship that I want. I'm just not sure..."

I broke into the pause. "Not sure about what? Not sure about June?"

He shook his head vigorously. "No, not that. It's me. I'm not sure if I've got what it takes. To be that long-term. I... I just don't want to let her down."

I sat back and cradled my cup. "I'm not sure that I'm the best person to advise you, Rob."

"You're the only person I know well enough to ask. The only

person who knows all about long-term relationships, anyway. How can you be sure of staying in love that long?"

I met his gaze. "You can't be sure. That's the thing about love. It's not a fairy-tale fantasy, it's not guaranteed. What is guaranteed is that you will let her down sometimes. And she will let you down. Just as Graham has let me down and I…"

Unexpectedly, I choked. Something had caught in my throat. I washed it down with tea.

"Someone explained it to me like this, Rob. Love isn't a hole you fall into. It's a wall you build together. Or maybe a bridge would be a better picture? Either way, it's made of bricks and cement. The bricks are the shared experiences, the things you do together. The cement is commitment. Keeping your promises to each other. You commit to each other, and you share your life, and sometimes you feel great about it but sometimes you don't, but you keep on sharing. And eventually, you find you've built something. You've built love. And that's the thing that lasts."

I watched him think about it. It reminded me of when I'd first tried to explain poetry to him.

"It's just an illustration," I added. "Perhaps it helps, perhaps not. It doesn't work for everyone."

"No, I get it. It does help. It's just that you make it sound like hard work!"

I spread my hands. "Good. I'm glad you get that. It is hard work, Rob. Not all the time, but definitely sometimes. And of course it's other things as well. There's a lot of joy, and laughter, and companionship. But it's also hard work, and you need to be clear about that from the beginning. You need to ask yourself, 'Is June worth that much hard work?' Do you want to be with her that much?"

He sat back and thought about it for a moment. When he started to open his mouth, I held up a hand.

"Don't tell me." I closed the box and pushed it back across the table towards him. "Take this home, think about it some more, and tell June. Either way. She should know."

He took the box and put it back into his pocket. "Right. OK. I'll do that." He stood and headed for the door. "Thanks, Sandra. I really appreciate being able to talk to you."

"That's OK. Any time I can help."

Then, as he was halfway through the door, a question dropped into my mind and straight out of my mouth.

"Have you ever been to Coren Hall Village?"

He stepped back in. "That new place? All incredibly expensive houses?"

"Yes. There's a pub there – used to be a farmhouse – the Farmer's Rest."

He nodded. "Had a job over there a while back. The village was still half built then. I thought I'd go in the pub for a bit of lunch, but the look the waiter gave me put me off! That and the prices."

"Yes. I think the waiter's still there. I just wondered if you knew anything about the background to the place. Like who owned it before it became a pub?"

"No idea. I only went there to drop off some equipment. Someone who'd just moved into one of the houses and wanted a whole lot of security stuff fitting, all top of the range. The leccy doing the work got us to deliver to the site. They do that sometimes if it's a big order or a rush job, and this was both. Huge house."

"Most of them are. Anyone living there must have money to spare!"

"Well, this one was owned by a 'Sir', no less. Or so the leccy said. Sir Arthur. That stuck in my mind. I don't get many knights on my round. Long days, but no knights!" He laughed at his own joke, then noticed I wasn't joining in.

"I don't suppose that was Sir Arthur Templeton?" I asked, wondering if this could possibly be as significant as it felt. "Only he's the patron of the art club that was supposed to be putting on the exhibition."

Rob snapped his fingers. "Yes, of course! Templeton! I wondered why that name seemed familiar. Bit of a coincidence, eh?"

I remembered my morning's word. "Just a scintilla."
Rob raised an eyebrow.
"Just a little thing."

DAY 5: AMBAGE

There was a lot I wanted to talk to Graham about, but he didn't get home till late and was very tired when he did. Too tired even to tell me off for not calling him as I'd promised, which worried me. His health is more fragile than he'll admit. So there wasn't much conversation had that evening.

In the morning, I left Graham sleeping in while I contemplated the day's word over my toast.

"Ambage: *noun*: a style that involves indirect ways of expressing things: circumlocution."

I didn't see much possibility for using that word: as soon as Graham was up and ready, I intended having a clear and direct conversation with him. About the past and its results. My expedition, and the conversation with Rob, had brought some things into focus.

But before Graham was even moving about upstairs, I had a call from DI Macrae.

"Good morning to you, Mrs Deeson. I wanted to let you know that we've now released the scene, and you're free to get your library back in order. Sorry for the delay."

"That's OK, Inspector. Thanks for telling me. I'll get the cleaning company in."

"Ah, yes, there will be a wee bit of that to do, I'm afraid." He paused before moving on to a new topic.

"Apart from that, there was something I wanted to talk to you about. In person rather than over the phone. Some further developments. And information that has come to light."

There was a leap of hope inside me. "Have you found Emily?"

"Ah, no. Not as yet. But I can tell you more at the station. Could you come down for about ten this morning?"

I glanced at the kitchen clock. How had it got to nine-fifteen already? "Yes, OK. Ten. Or perhaps a little later. I've got a few things to do first."

"That'll be fine, Mrs Deeson. I'm in the office all morning, in any case. Till later, then."

He hung up, and I wondered if that conversation could count as "ambage".

I got to work on the phone, contacting the cleaning company and updating Yvonne. It left me precious little time to get myself presentable and drive into town. And Graham was just awake, but still groggy. Our conversation would have to wait.

In spite of my rushing, it was nearly ten-thirty before I pulled into the visitor's car park at the Central Police Station. I was lucky to find a space – every time I'd driven past it before it had been filled with marked-up police cars. I took an extra moment to check my hair in the mirror.

A younger face stared back for a moment, the blonde hair – no grey streaks – plastered to her head with rain and fear. I hadn't worried about my appearance then, when Godfrey parked in approximately the same place and took me inside to make my report.

The old wooden doors had been replaced with steel and glass that slid smoothly aside at my approach. The counter had been remodelled as well, and the blue light that had been outside now perched incongruously above the computer screens and keyboards.

There was a short queue ahead of me: a respectable middle-aged man and a wild-looking lad with an over-abundance of rings and tattoos. The middle-aged man, it transpired, was there to fulfil his bail conditions, and the wild lad was reporting a burglary. This was a lengthy process, as it may have happened sometime last week, and may have been through the back door or an open window, and a laptop may have been stolen or possibly not. It took a quite some time for the woman on duty at the desk, a person equipped with saint-level patience, to extract all this information. I was trying not to appear to be listening, but was getting quite interested in finding out what had happened to the laptop, when Macrae appeared from the door marked "Authorized Personnel Only", caught my eye, and nodded towards the front door. I followed him out.

"I saw on the CCTV that you'd arrived," he said. "It looked like you might be there a while, so I came to you. I needed to get out of the station anyway, and there's something I'd like you to see. If you don't mind a wee trip out, that is?"

"No, that's fine. I expect you must get a bit bogged down with the office work sometimes."

"Oh, aye. You've got to expect it, of course, but I didn't join the force to stare at a computer all day!"

"Is Sergeant Henshaw coming as well?" I glanced around, but there was no sign of June.

"No, I've given her the day off. I'm afraid you'll have to manage without a chaperone!" He smiled broadly and led the way to the car park.

His vehicle was an old and somewhat battered BMW estate. "Sorry. I know detectives are supposed to have antique Jags!" he said with a smile.

"Columbo didn't," I pointed out.

"Well, it's nothing fancy, just transportation," he said, in what might have been intended as an American accent.

I smiled. "You're very good at this. Making small talk to ease the tension."

"It's an essential skill. People talk more readily when they're relaxed, and it's these little social rituals that help to do that."

He pulled out of the car park and onto the main road. At the roundabout, he took the first exit and was quickly brought to a standstill by the traffic backing up from the next roundabout. A well-known local phenomenon, but I supposed that he hadn't had time to get used to the traffic patterns yet. I'd have warned him if I'd known where he was going.

"So, this information you mentioned – it's not Emily, then?"

He gave me a sympathetic look. "Well, her car's been found. I can tell you that much. But keep it to yourself, if you would."

"Of course. But – if you've got her car, that's good, isn't it? It can help narrow the search?"

"I'm afraid not. Not in this case. It was in London. Near Heathrow, in fact." The brake lights on the car in front went off, and Macrae eased forward a few inches, but there was no further movement.

"But – she wouldn't just get on a plane, would she? Would she? Where would she be going?"

"We've no reason to believe that she did fly out. They're still checking passenger lists and the like. But Heathrow is a major transport hub. From there she could have gone anywhere in the world. If she was there at all."

"What does that mean?"

"Just because it was her car, it doesn't mean she was in it. Someone could have dumped it there."

There was some definite movement ahead, and we shuffled along for two or three car lengths before coming to a halt again.

"I'm very worried about her."

"Aye. So am I. We'll not stop looking."

Behind us, someone hit their horn several times, a totally useless gesture. Macrae glanced in his mirror and shrugged.

"You know, I'm often fascinated by how people react to things. Like that idiot back there. He can't do anything by blowing on his horn like that, but he does it anyway."

"Just venting his frustration, I suppose."

"I suppose so. But you can learn a lot about someone from how they react to things." He glanced across at me. "I'm minded of how you reacted to finding a body in your library."

"I fainted."

"Which is no more than natural, in the circumstances. But it was how you were afterwards that impressed me. When I spoke to you the following day, I thought how well you were coping with such a terrible experience."

I wasn't sure what to say to that, so I just shrugged. I had a feeling he was leading up to something. I didn't like where he might be going.

"But then I found out that it wasn't the first time you'd had such a thing happen to you, was it?"

I met his eyes. "You've been checking up on me."

He nodded. "I'm a detective. It's what I do."

"I don't see how all that's relevant. It was a long time ago. There can't be any connection…" Except, of course, through the picture, but I hadn't told him about that yet. I blundered on, hoping not to reveal that I'd been withholding information. "In fact, I'm surprised there was even anything left to find."

He laughed, gently, and moved the car forward again. "You should know that the police hate throwing anything out. Certainly not murder files. And, in any case, you'd be surprised at how much is still out there in the public domain. Just Google yourself under your maiden name."

"That was a long time before Google."

"A lot of records have been put on the internet now. Newspaper reports, for example."

"It's not something I want to revisit."

"But it seems to have revisited you."

The traffic moved on further. Staring past Macrae, I saw two young lads in a Golf with a customized paint job. *No ghosts in their past*, I thought. *Too young to have a past.*

The boy I'd found hanging hadn't had much of a past either.

They estimated his age at seventeen. Possibly younger. Not much past and no future at all.

One of the lads saw me staring and made a rude sign in my direction. I looked away.

The traffic flow improved, we finally reached the roundabout, and Macrae took us out onto the ring road, where things were at least moving steadily, if slowly.

"OK. Perhaps I should have told you. I know it seems weird, the same person finding two unidentified bodies. But there's thirty years between the two incidents! It's just a bizarre coincidence."

"I don't like coincidences. Not in a murder inquiry. Using the 'coincidence' label can be just an excuse to ignore awkward facts."

"What awkward facts are those?"

We were passing the exit into an industrial area. Macrae had to brake sharply as a van made a late decision to leave. He said something under his breath, pulled out, and accelerated past it. When he spoke again, he made one of those sudden shifts in the conversation that I'd noticed before.

"When I started looking into that past business, there were two things that particularly struck me. The first being your persistence."

He paused, inviting a comment, but I ignored him and stared out of the window at the warehouses and industrial units we were passing.

"It was impressive. You practically put your life on hold to try to identify this laddie and find out who killed him. You wrote letters, you sent out photographs, you put up posters... you must have interviewed every person living in a ten-mile radius. Even tracked down some of the ones that had moved! And you stayed with it for over a year."

Another long pause.

"Why was that, Sandra? What made you carry on when everyone else wanted to draw a line and forget about it? When the police investigation had been closed, and you were being threatened with prosecution if you persisted?"

"It wasn't just prosecution," I heard myself say. "Some people were much more... direct... in their threats."

"Because you wouldn't shut up about it?"

"Somebody must have known something!" And suddenly, it all came back, a wave of raw emotion that had been penned up for thirty years. "Somebody KNEW! He had a name, he was a person, and SOMEBODY KNEW WHO HE WAS!"

I was shouting. I felt like sobbing. It was hard to hold it back.

"He was just left there, hanging there, like a piece of meat, but somebody did that and somebody knew him and he must have had a NAME!" I swore, dredging up the worst words that I knew and spitting them out, and hammered on the dashboard as I did so. "They wouldn't talk – none of them would talk, they just let it happen – but somebody MUST HAVE KNOWN SOMETHING!"

Macrae wasn't at all disturbed by my outburst or my language. No doubt he had heard much worse. And it was probably what he wanted anyway, I realized, as I began to calm down again and sat back, feeling exhausted. That was the entire point of this trip: to crack me open and let out some more information.

My eyes were wet. I fumbled in my handbag for a tissue. Macrae leaned across, opened the glove box, and handed me a full box.

"You came prepared for this, then," I said, trying to sound light and matter-of-fact.

"Used to be a Boy Scout. Always prepared!"

We came to another exit road and he pulled off. I didn't know this route, still couldn't work out where we were going.

"You were right, you know."

We were on a B road, narrow and winding, so his concentration was on driving. But I knew that he wouldn't miss the slightest flicker of reaction from me.

"About what?"

"Somebody knew something."

"Nobody ever said anything. Not to me, not to the police."

"Aye. Which tells me that those who knew had an interest in keeping it covered up."

I nodded. "That was obvious. From early on. But it didn't make any difference. There was no evidence, nothing to point in anyone's direction."

"Well, that was the other thing that struck me. No evidence. None at all. No leads, no information. Not just dead ends, but not even any beginnings. In a case like that, I'd have expected that there'd be at least some line of inquiry to follow, however weak. But not according to the case files. Tell me, Sandra, what did you think of the police investigation at the time?"

"It was OK at first. There was a DCI Farrow in charge." He'd interviewed me back at the police station, after I'd been to hospital to be checked. A big man, blunt in his approach but he got things moving. They had dogs out in the woods and forensic teams all over the farmhouse before the end of the day, and they were back again at first light. "But then another officer took over. DCI Greer." Thin, acerbic, always behind his desk. "Different sort of person, different approach. Very by the book, and he didn't much appreciate me getting involved. He was the one who threatened me with prosecution when he closed the case and I wouldn't leave it alone."

"By the book. Aye, that's just the words that came to mind when I looked through the files. It was all done exactly by the book, all the boxes ticked – and that was all. Nothing you could point at and say, 'That wasn't done right,' but if you read between the lines, nothing was done that didn't absolutely have to be done. I've been in this job long enough to know when someone's just doing the bare minimum. And that was what Greer was at."

"That was the impression I had. But I couldn't understand why he was so negative about it."

"I don't either. But he was close to retirement, not in good health, and basically just marking time until he could finish with the police for good. My guess is that he was given the case for that precise reason – because he could be relied on to wrap it up neatly and without any fuss. The real question, of course, is who was responsible for taking the job from Farrow and putting Greer in charge. And that's something we can't know. It's not in the case files. Farrow and Greer are both dead, and even the younger officers on the case are all retired now. I haven't been able to find anyone who knew anything."

We sat in silence for a while, thinking through the implications, while the road wound its way through damp woodland. Autumn was reaching its height, all the trees ablaze in shades of orange and yellow that shone even under the overcast sky. But the leaves were falling fast, drifting across the road and being turned into mush under our wheels. Glory was a fleeting thing, I thought, and the very process that gave the leaves their brilliant colours also killed them.

"OK. Let's agree that that investigation was dodgy. But how's it connected to this one?"

"You remember I was talking about coincidences? You finding both bodies is the first. The second one is that someone is trying to close this investigation down as well."

"You're joking!" I glanced at him and saw at once that he wasn't. He sounded calm enough, but he looked furious. "No, you're not," I corrected myself. "But who's doing that?"

"Not sure. But it started after Sergeant Henshaw and I went to visit Sir Arthur Templeton. Only, we didn't. His nephew – Carr – met us at the door, refused us entry without a warrant, told us that Sir Arthur was unwell and couldn't talk to us. So we left, and the next day I'm called in to the divisional commander, who wants to know why I think Sir Arthur is of interest in the case. And of course, my reasons aren't good enough, Sir Arthur is an important and respected local citizen, good connections, blah blah, reputation of the force, blah blah, not to be bothered without reason and if I had reason I was to speak to him first."

"I didn't know that could happen. I mean, even a senior officer shouldn't be interfering in your case, should they?"

"No, they should not," he said tightly. "And I told him that. Which didn't go down well, and by the time I got back to my office my own boss is sitting on my desk, telling me to play along, not a good time to rock this particular boat, etc. So I can't go near Sir Arthur. And then my request for an art expert to look at that painting is turned down. I thought that it might give us a possible ID for the painter, but apparently the budget won't stretch that far."

"Always a good excuse for not doing something."

"That's right. And not something I was happy with. But then there was a new factor. Do you remember a cigarette end found at the scene?"

"Yes. PC – um – Newbold? He saw it."

"That's right. Well, it went off to the lab, and came back with a hit. Full DNA profile."

"Well, that's good news!" I looked at his face, and revised my statement. "Or is it?"

"The person who smoked that cigarette is a local man. Lives within half a mile of your library, in fact. Vincent Doddridge. And he's got a bit of a record. Tried his hand at a few things, has Vince – bit of burglary, bit of car crime, that sort of thing. The last thing he did was receive and sell stolen car parts, and that got him a short stretch. He's only been out a few months."

"A career criminal, then?"

"Aye. And on the face of it, well in the frame for this job. But he didn't do it." Macrae spoke with absolute confidence.

"How can you be so sure?" I asked.

"There's no history of violence. And if you saw him you'd know why. He's a wee, skinny man – shifty, for certain, you'd not want to buy a car off him, but he isn't the sort to smash a man's face in. Or to be stealing paintings either."

"So you think he had an accomplice?"

"I don't think he was ever involved at all."

"But – the cigarette end? Isn't that conclusive?"

Macrae smiled grimly. "Oh, aye, that's what everyone thinks.

Say 'DNA' and that's case closed. But then it's not that simple. A cigarette end, for example – that's a moveable object. And here's an interesting fact for you: Vince Doddridge does his drinking at the Royal Lions, which is a pub no more than five minutes' walk from the library. He was there the evening before the murder – he's said so, and witnesses confirmed it. Stayed for a few hours, had a few drinks, went outside for a smoke."

He glanced at me, to see if I'd made the connection.

"You think that the cig end came from the pub." I thought it over. "Whoever did it was in the pub that evening, and took Vince's cig end to leave in the library?"

"Well, I wouldn't go that far. It could be that they just took the cigarette from one of the bins behind the pub where all the ashtrays get emptied."

"How would they know it was Vince's, then?"

"They wouldn't. But I'm guessing that they wouldn't need to. They weren't looking to frame Vince in particular, just trying to confuse the investigation with false evidence. All they needed was a random cigarette end. And that pub has a dodgy reputation. You could pick any cig end at all from there and have an odds-on chance that it would get a DNA hit. Most of the clientele have got themselves onto the police database at one time or another."

"But in that case, why arrest Vince?"

"I didn't. Not at first. We had the hit back in twenty-four hours, and went to see Vince straight away. He didn't have much of an alibi, but it was obvious what had happened there, so I didn't pursue it. Not until yesterday, when I was ordered to arrest him and charge him with the offence."

"You were ordered... immediately after you tried to talk to Sir Arthur!"

"Exactly so."

The country lane had taken us over a ridge and down into a grey little village. It looked familiar.

"This place – it's Frayhampton!"

"Aye. Thought you'd know it."

We came out into the little square in front of the church. The bus stop where I used to get off to begin my walks was still there, though now with a shiny modern shelter. Macrae made a left turn, and now I knew where we were going.

"What made you give up searching?" he asked as we drove out of the village.

"Graham did. My husband."

He said nothing, and after a while I carried on.

"I lost my job. I was a junior reporter on a local newspaper. *The Echo*. After I found the body, I wrote several articles about it, followed the investigation, tried to get some answers. But then the editor told me to drop it. 'Old news isn't news,' he told me. And of course he was right. There was nothing more to say, even the police inquiry had been wound down. But I couldn't leave it alone. Kept pushing, kept digging, kept asking questions. Kept submitting stories, which he turned down. Eventually there was a bit of a row. I said some things I shouldn't have and really he didn't have a choice but to fire me.

"I still wouldn't leave it, though. And Graham – he was another reporter at *The Echo* – he was the only one who supported me, who stuck with me. Helped me get information, went with me to interview people. When I got too persistent and too rude with my questions, he was the one who rescued me!

"But after about a year, when there were literally no more questions to ask and no one else to talk to, he was the one who told me it was time to leave it alone. And, because he'd earned the right to say it, I listened to him. And I stopped asking questions, stopped talking to people, stopped sending letters and visiting the police station."

"And you got married."

I smiled. "Yes. Later that year. It was the only good thing that came out of it."

We were getting close to the turn for Coren Hall Village.

"When I first joined CID, up in Glasgow, I had a case that got to me the same way. A man beat his wife to death. Nasty business. We couldn't get any evidence on him though. I didn't want to leave it, but my sergeant told me that I had to learn to walk away from some jobs."

"And did you?"

He looked at me, then signalled and turned off down the new road into Coren Hall Village.

"Two weeks before I left Glasgow to come down here, I arrested that man. On a different matter, but he knew what it was really about. No, I never did walk away entirely. And neither did you, did you, Sandra?"

I said nothing as we drove into the village and past the little green. Macrae parked up on the roadside a bit further on.

"Here's another coincidence," he said, pointing to the large house opposite. It was one of the biggest in the village, and set well back behind ornate iron gates and a fence to match. And a lot of trees. If most of the leaves hadn't already fallen it would have been nearly invisible from the road. "And one that I definitely don't like at all. That house is where Sir Arthur Templeton now lives. Just a short spit from the farmhouse where you found that body hanging – which, by the way, is now a restaurant."

He was watching me as he spoke, and even though I leaned forward to peer at the house, he understood my reaction. "Ah, but you already knew that, didn't you?"

"I knew that Sir Arthur lived in the village. I didn't know where, exactly."

Macrae smiled. "Somehow, I'm not surprised. You would have been an ace reporter – or one heck of a good detective, for that matter."

I shook my head. "I'm a librarian. Why are you telling me all this?"

"I have a small favour to ask you. And it's not one I'd bother you with, except that I think this is something you'd want to do."

I said nothing at first. I sat back, stared out of the window, and watched the autumn leaves dancing away from their tree in the breeze, never to return.

Sometimes you find yourself faced with a decision that you know could change your life irrevocably. Usually, you see it coming. You take this course or that, choose this career or another one, get married or not.

This one had come out of nowhere, yet I felt it could be the most important decision of my life. I didn't know why. I didn't even know what Macrae wanted me to do. But in that moment I had the sense of standing on the brink of something. Maybe a precipice, maybe a ladder. Which way I stepped would make the difference.

I watched the leaves. It wasn't their decision to leave. It was just their time.

"What exactly do you want me to do, Inspector?"

"I asked you before: call me David."

"Why?"

"Because I can't ask this favour as Detective Inspector Macrae. This isn't official. This is a personal request, from David Macrae to Sandra Deeson."

"OK, then. David. What is it you want me to do?"

He leaned over into the back of the car, picked up a large envelope from the back seat, and pulled out the painting. The window, the dead flowers, the living one. He put it down in front of us, wedged behind the gearstick and leaning against the dashboard.

"I've had it remounted. The original mount went to the lab for chemical treatment, and that makes a terrible mess of things. They got plenty of fingerprints, but only Emily's – and the dead man's. The artist, that is; I'm very sure of that. Oh, and your own, of course."

"And?"

"And I would like to know what Sir Arthur thinks of it."

I turned the idea over in my mind. "That's all? Take the picture in and show it to him? What do you think that will achieve?"

"Perhaps nothing. But my instinct says that there's a connection here somewhere. Between Sir Arthur, the painting, what happened in the library a few days ago, and what happened in the farmhouse thirty years past. *I* can't pursue that line now. But there's nothing stopping you, as a private citizen, going to visit a famous local artist to ask his opinion about a painting you've recently acquired."

I still hadn't said yes, but I hadn't said no, either.

"The thing is, Sandra, I'm running out of leads on this. We can't find Emily, we can't identify the artist, and the only forensics we have is that dodgy cigarette end. Somewhere there's a studio where this artist worked, but we've no clues on that either, and I'm being pressured to take this inquiry down the path of least resistance, wrap it up quickly. This connection is the thing I've got at the moment, and I can't even follow up on it myself. I don't like to be asking this of you – I wouldn't if I could see any other way forward – but if we let this go, then there'll be another laddie who died without a name."

He knew how to press my buttons. Not that he had to press very hard. I'd already decided; I just didn't want to look too eager.

I picked up the painting and slid it back into the envelope. "Is the gate locked?"

"The main one is. Opens on a remote signal. But there's a side gate that they leave unlocked during the day. Access for the domestic staff – they have people in to clean and cook and look after the grounds. But they all live off-site. There's only Sir Arthur and his nephew actually resident there."

"If Carr refused you entrance, why would he let me in?" I remembered how he'd looked when confronting the PCSO. Not someone I'd care to be in an argument with.

"He might not. But as it happens, he's currently back at Central Police Station, with the art club chairman and one of my DCs, going through the CSI photographs to double-check that no other paintings are missing. A perfectly legitimate exercise, and not something that he could object to. So you should have an hour or so with Sir Arthur. And I'll be just here the whole time, mind."

"You'd better be. I'm not walking back."

"Keep your mobile handy. If I've any concerns, I'll call you."

"Right." I opened the door, got out, and reached back to get the painting. A thought struck me as I did so.

"The roundabout route you took to get here – and getting stuck in that traffic jam: I thought you just didn't know the area, but it was deliberate, wasn't it? To give Carr time to get clear?"

Macrae didn't bother to look guilty, instead giving me a wink. "And to give us time to have this wee discussion."

"You're devious and manipulative, David Macrae," I said, taking the painting and shutting the door before he had time to answer. I tucked it under my arm and crossed the road.

I should have felt apprehensive, at the least. Instead, I was eager.

I strode up the long drive and felt the way I had in that other life, when every meeting, every interview could hold the answer, could be the clue that would give me the name. I'd told Macrae that it was Graham who persuaded me to give up, but that was only part of the answer. I'd given up when I finally lost hope.

Now it was back.

The house was three storeys of pseudo-Georgian red brick. White trims round the windows and white columns flanking the door, which was all black and shiny and wouldn't have been out of place on Downing Street. There was nothing as commonplace as a doorbell, of course, just a neat brass intercom grille, placed discreetly behind one of the columns.

There was also a little hemisphere of dark glass set in the ceiling, which reminded me that Rob had been here delivering security equipment. Such as, for example, CCTV?

CCTV meant that my visit here was probably recorded, and that if someone, such as Jonathan Carr for example, looked at that recording he would know that I'd visited.

Of course, Macrae hadn't bothered to mention it.

I almost turned round and walked away, but it was too late. Leaving now might raise even more questions than staying. After all, I could still give a good reason for being here. And even without the camera, Carr would probably have found out about my visit eventually. Sir Arthur would probably tell him.'

Nevertheless, I indulged in a futile glare back down the drive to where Macrae's car was just barely visible behind the trees. And probably even less visible to CCTV, I assumed. He would have thought of that and parked accordingly.

Glare over, I pressed the intercom button.

A little red light came on, but nothing else happened.

"Hello?" I said to the intercom. "Is anyone there?"

I waited. Nothing happened. I was starting to feel cold. I hadn't dressed for door knocking.

I pressed the button again. One more try and then I'd give up, I thought.

The light turned green. "Hello?" said the intercom in an old man's voice.

"Oh! Yes. Hello – um – is that Sir Arthur? Sir Arthur Templeton?"

A pause. "Who is it?"

"Yes, hello. I'm Sandra Deeson. From the library where the exhibition was held. Was going to be held, that is. I was wondering if I could have a word with Sir Arthur Templeton?"

"The exhibition? That was all arranged by my nephew. Jonathan. I'm sorry – he's not here just now."

"Yes. I understand. But I actually wanted to talk to you. If you are Sir Arthur, that is?"

Another, longer pause. Then, a little reluctantly it seemed to me, he admitted that he was. "What is it you wanted to talk to me about?" he continued.

"I was hoping to meet you at the art club exhibition." Not totally a lie. I had had some mild interest, though I'd been more concerned with making sure everything ran smoothly. Hah! "There's a painting I have that I would like your opinion of."

"Oh. I see. Very well, just give me a few moments."

A few moments stretched into a few minutes. The chilly dampness of autumn was seeping into my bones.

Then there was a click of locks, and the door swung open.

"Sir Arthur?" I asked.

He didn't look much like a "Sir". He'd probably been tall once, but he was stooped over, which made him about my height. A few strands of grey hair, liver-spotted skin, thin face with a wary expression, thin hands clutching at the door, as if ready to slam it shut at the slightest threat. He was wearing an old blue boiler suit, stained with multicoloured paint and other less identifiable marks. A pencil and a couple of brushes were sticking out of the breast pocket.

"I'm sorry if I interrupted you working," I continued.

He glanced down at himself, as if slightly surprised to discover what he was wearing. "And I'm sorry I'm not properly dressed to receive visitors." He glanced up again and smiled. A surprisingly warm smile. "Time was that I wouldn't have dreamed of meeting a young lady in such a state! But now I'm afraid that what you see is what you get." He stepped back from the door and gestured me inside.

"Time was when 'young lady' would have been an accurate description," I answered. "Thank you for seeing me, Sir Arthur."

"It's all relative," he said ruefully. "From my point of view, every lady is a young one. There's no one left whom I could call an old lady!"

He chuckled, and I joined in with him. Slightly to my surprise, I found myself liking Arthur Templeton. He had a natural charm that made that easy.

"And please drop that 'Sir'," he continued. "It's very useful on occasion, but to be honest, I've never really felt comfortable with it. Just 'Arthur' will do."

"OK, but then I'm Sandra."

We were standing in a semicircular hall, polished tiles reflecting ornate plasterwork in keeping with the exterior. A rather grand staircase circled the room, sweeping up to the next floor from left to right. Directly ahead of us, on the wall above the staircase, was a large portrait: a young man, dark haired and incredibly handsome, half sitting and half leaning against the bonnet of a silver sports car, backdropped by some stately home that I didn't recognize.

I stared at it for a moment before recognition clicked in. "That's you!"

"Oh, good. I'm glad that there are still traces of the original underneath this worn old canvas!" He looked up at it with a smile. "A little narcissistic to keep it up there, perhaps, but it's a reminder of other times and places. And it's the only one of my early paintings that I still have."

"Really? You must have painted hundreds of portraits." I continued to stare up at the young Arthur Templeton, a man with all of life before him. With those looks and that natural charm – not to mention his talent – it was no wonder that he was such a social success.

"Almost all on commission, and the rest were sold when I went travelling." I glanced at him but he carried on without looking at me. "I painted that as a way of advertising what I could do – worked quite well, too! Put it into storage for a long while, but now I seem to be finally settled here, I thought it was time to get it out again."

"It's very impressive." I meant it. The painting wasn't just technically good, it conveyed a strong sense of the person who was both subject and artist. There was confidence, a certain amount of arrogance perhaps, in the careless way he reclined on the expensive vehicle. A challenge in the direct gaze. And something in the smile that took the edge off it; that said, "This is fun, don't take it too seriously!"

"Well, thank you." Sir Arthur inclined his head. "Would you like to come and see my studio?"

He said it with a coy little wink, but at the same time there was something in his face which I couldn't quite identify. A sort of shy hopefulness that seemed out of place for someone as rich and famous as him.

"What girl could resist that line?" I smiled. He laughed and led the way through a door and down a long corridor towards the rear of the house.

"I was sorry to have missed my visit to your library, Sandra. Terrible, terrible tragedy, of course. But apart from that, I was looking forward to seeing the place again."

"You know the library? Bromwell Street?" I'd known he was a local man, but the connection still came as a surprise.

"Oh, yes. Or at least I used to. When I was a lad I spent more time in there than I did at home! I dare say it's changed a bit since then, though."

"There's probably a lot you'd recognize," I told him, thinking of all the original Victorian architecture. "Possibly even some of the same books!"

He chuckled. "This place, on the other hand, is brand new." He waved a hand at the corridor, which was in keeping with the entrance hall – spotless and beautifully decorated along its length – but it had an empty feeling. It didn't feel like somewhere that people lived. "Paint's barely dry… I would have preferred something with a bit more character, and perhaps a bit smaller. Ridiculous, just the two of us rattling around in here. But Jonathan, my nephew, wanted something a bit more…" He flapped a hand around to indicate the "bit more".

"Plenty of room for guests, though?" I suggested.

"Guests? Oh, I suppose so." We'd come to a set of double doors at the end of the corridor. "But it does have other advantages – such as…"

He pushed the doors open.

Beyond them was a conservatory – quite a large one; probably as big as the entire ground floor of my house. Walls and a ceiling of glass filled the space with light, even though it was a dull day. But instead of housing comfortable furniture and pot plants – which is what I would have had in a conservatory – the room had become an artist's studio.

There were at least half a dozen easels scattered around the room. Some had sketches, some had photographs pinned to corkboard, some were occupied by paintings in various stages of completion. More canvases were stacked against the walls, and a large table in the middle of the room was cluttered with rags, pencils, paints, brushes, sheets of paper, mugs, plates, and a sleeping cat.

I stepped into the room and sniffed, inhaling at full strength the same odours that had clung faintly to the envelope.

"Distinctive, isn't it?" Sir Arthur stepped in behind me. "I love that smell! Though I'm so used to it that I hardly notice it now."

"I thought you'd given up painting."

He shook his head. "Never! No, I never gave up. I did put things on hold for a while. But that was always only a temporary thing." He led the way into the room and gestured at the easels. "I've given up on portraits, though. Gone back to my roots, as it were."

I took a longer look at the various photographs, sketches and paintings, and saw a common theme. They were all buildings, streets, factories and shops and warehouses. The people in them were there as part of the whole, not distinctive subjects in themselves.

"Not many people remember that I started with industrial landscapes, and that was where my real interest was." Sir Arthur peered critically at one of the paintings. "Portraits turned out to be where the money was, though, so that's what I mostly did, until I… decided to leave it all behind for a bit. But what really interests me isn't so much individuals, but the things we humans do together. Recognize that?" He tapped the canvas he had been looking at. A large one, at least five feet long and four high.

It was nearly completed, I saw, and it did look familiar: a towering edifice to industry, red brick and grey slate. "Hmm… is it the Arkwright Mill?"

"Masson Mill, in Derbyshire. One of Arkwright's mills. Built in 1783 to harness the power of the River Derwent. Still impressive now, isn't it? But can you imagine how it must have appeared to people back then? How stunning, how exciting it must have been?"

He was laughing, thrilled with his vision – and relishing the chance to share it with someone else. It wasn't hard to play along with him, the enthusiasm was contagious.

"And that's what you're trying to capture?"

"Oh, it's more than that. Look closer! Look at the people!"

I turned back to the painting and followed his instructions. It wasn't easy to make out details, for whereas the building itself was sharp and clear, with fine detail brought out in the brickwork and windows, the people entering and leaving and passing by were slightly blurry, insubstantial even. It took me a moment to realize that they were shown in the clothing of different periods. Long skirts, full skirts, short skirts, and minis; coats with tails, double-breasted coats, anoraks, and parkas; top hats, wide hats, bowler hats, and hoodies… all mingled, all busily about their ephemeral business in their different times, while behind them the great mill stood solid and unchanging through the years.

"We build these places, but then they outlast us – we create them, but then they come to define and control us. We fit our lives in and around what we have built." He shook his head. "I first saw that mill when I was a boy, and was fascinated by the thought of all that history, all those people whose lives have touched it. Or been touched by it. I've wanted to paint it ever since. I'm working from photographs now, getting too old for wandering around with an easel! But I'm realizing a dream at last. Saying something I've always wanted to say."

He touched the painting again, almost caressed it.

"That's wonderful," I said, in all sincerity.

"Thank you. Very good of you to say so. But I'm waffling on about all this, and you wanted to show me something?" He raised an eyebrow and nodded at the envelope I was carrying.

"Oh, yes."

I opened the envelope and took out the painting. The vivid colour of sunlight on the flower, its contrast to the grey death all around it, made me catch my breath all over again.

"Oh, my. That's rather powerful, isn't it? May I?" Sir Arthur took it from my hands and held it out at arm's length, examining it intently. "How did you come by this?"

"It was a gift." I hesitated, unsure of how much to tell him. "I was wondering what you could tell me about it."

"Well, it's obviously mixed media, and clearly the intention with that was to emphasize the difference between the living flower – which has the light – and the dead ones." He took it over to an easel and put it in place, covering some assorted sketches of Masson Mill. "Quite good work. A little raw, perhaps – some of it could have been more subtly executed, but the artist is clearly very talented. Do you know who did it?"

I shook my head. "It's anonymous."

"That's a pity. But also very curious. Because as it happens I also had an anonymous gift recently – and… well, see for yourself."

He went over to a stack of canvases leaned up against the wall, and pulled out a mounted picture from behind them. It was about the same size as mine. Sir Arthur took it to another easel, which he then moved until the two paintings were next to each other.

My jaw dropped.

Both mixed media. Both featuring a dramatic pool of colour in a room of black and grey. Side by side, the similarities were obvious – and stunning.

The subject matter, however, was different. Sir Arthur's painting was set in a large room, which might even have been called grand – except that strips of wallpaper hung loosely, and plaster had fallen from the ceiling to form dreary piles on the bare and dirty floorboards. Such furniture as there was appeared worn and shabby, with cushions torn and legs broken. All this meticulously executed in pencil. Not as dark as my painting – there was even a large bay window in the background with no curtains, so the room should have been well lit – but it still had the same atmosphere of gloom. Nothing outside the window could be seen; anything beyond was obscured in a heavy mist.

In the centre of the room was an easel. And on the easel a painting glowed in brilliant colour.

The painting in the painting was of the same room. The same layout, the same furniture, the same bay window. But light flooded through this window and filled the whole space. A golden-hued wallpaper, clean and intact, accentuated the sunshine, the plaster was intact, the furniture immaculate, and bright rugs lay over polished floorboards. Beyond the window could be seen trees and fields stretching off into the distance.

"Of course, it's all about the contrast, in both pictures. Not a hugely original idea, but very well executed." Sir Arthur looked from one to the other, comparing. "I would say that the contrasts in the paintings are meant to represent another contrast – something in the artist's mind, in their life perhaps?"

"Do you think they're by the same person, then?"

He shrugged. "I'd have to study them more closely. But given the coincidence of style and timing, it would seem very likely. How did you receive yours?"

"It was left for me in the library."

"Oh? Mine was left at our cleaning lady's house. She says that she found it propped up against her door one morning when she was leaving to come here. With my name on, so she brought it straight to me. No clue as to who left it."

"Was there a note or something like that?" I was thinking of the little Post-it that had accompanied mine.

"Yes. Quite interesting, actually, though it only deepened the mystery. It said, '*Hope you enjoy a trip down memory lane. Come for a visit soon!*'"

"Handwritten?"

"Yes, on one of those little yellow stick-note things. But I didn't recognize the writing, if that's what you were thinking."

"Can I see it, perhaps?"

"Sorry, I threw it away. Didn't seem that important. Though there was something curious about the message itself. 'Memory Lane' was capitalized, like a title. And the thing is, the first painting I ever sold was one I called 'Memory Lane'." He smiled, half to himself. "Not bad for a twelve-year-old boy. It was of the street where I lived – just rows of terraced houses. I didn't start from privilege! I put it into a little art competition that was running in the church hall. Didn't win any prizes, which was a disappointment, but then someone offered me five pounds for it, which I was thrilled with!" He grinned. "Five pounds was a lot of money in those days – especially for a kid."

I grinned back. "A fortune, in fact!"

We laughed together, and in one of those incredible moments of connectivity that happen so rarely between people, I knew we were sharing the same thought. That five pounds was nothing compared to what his portraits had sold for. But no amount of money could have matched the thrill of that first experience. Because it wasn't about the money at all: it was knowing that you had done something which had value.

But I needed to get back on track. "When did you get the painting, if you don't mind me asking?"

"Not at all… Let me see, it was just before the exhibition was supposed to happen. About six or seven days ago, I think? I'm afraid I don't keep track of time as well as I might, holed up here on my own!"

I stood next to him, looking at the paintings. "They're saying something, aren't they? There's a message in each one, something about the exhibition." I took out my mobile. "Can I get a picture of your painting?"

"Of course."

I went to the camera app and started taking photos. Different angles, to get different light: long shots and close-ups. "Do you recognize the place at all, Sir Arthur?"

"Please. Just plain 'Arthur' is quite sufficient for informal occasions! Actually, I have thought that there's something familiar about it, but I'm not sure what. Somewhere I visited a long time ago, perhaps?"

Thirty years ago? I wondered, but didn't say it. I hesitated over telling him what I knew about my painting. Would it help things along or not? It depended on whether he knew about the farmhouse – and what had happened there.

As I was putting my phone away, it buzzed. A text – from Macrae.

"Carr has left the station, in a hurry, presumed on his way back. Finish up and leave."

Something inside me turned icy cold. I glanced at my watch. How long would Carr take to get here? Not long, in that Porsche, especially if he ignored the speed limits. Of course, he might get stuck in the traffic as we had – but more than likely he knew his way around and would avoid the worst bottlenecks. And I didn't know how long ago he'd left the station. I might have ten minutes. Or perhaps only five.

"Urgent message?" asked Sir Arthur.

I nodded. "Someone's waiting for me. I'll have to go."

"Oh, that's a pity. This is a fascinating little puzzle we have here. As you say, there is a message here. Or two messages, perhaps. Of course, art always has a message if it's of any value at all. If you know how to look at it, that is. Often it says as much about the artist as the subject, but sometimes you have to know something about that artist to understand where he or she is coming from. I don't suppose you have any clue at all as to who painted these?"

I shook my head. "No. There isn't even a signature – at least, not on mine, and I don't see one on yours either. Of course, you didn't sign your paintings either."

He chuckled. "I did have that reputation." He peered at my painting again.

Another buzz on my phone, which I still held in my hand. Another text from Macrae.

"Get out NOW!!!"

"I'm sorry, er, Arthur, but I really have to go…"

Sir Arthur wasn't looking at me. He was still staring at my painting, but his face was pale, and the expression on his face was of utter shock.

"Sir Arthur?"

He ignored me, turned his attention to the other picture. He put his hand to his head in a gesture which would have seemed theatrical if he'd shown the slightest awareness of my presence, but for the moment I was forgotten. He said something, but not to me. Low and under his breath.

It was a bad time to be going, but with Jonathan Carr about to come up the drive at any moment, it was a worse time to be staying.

"I'm really sorry to rush out like this, but I do have to go. I'll see myself out." I snatched the painting off the easel, picked up the envelope, and headed for the door.

"And thank you!" I called out from the corridor.

He made no reply. He was still staring at the picture, and wiping his eyes with his hand.

I broke into a run down the corridor, wondering what I'd do if the front door was locked, but whatever other security mechanisms it might have had, it was held only by a Yale, and I was outside in a moment, and starting down the drive. Still running.

My phone buzzed yet again, and at the same time I heard a high-powered engine approaching at speed.

No time to answer the phone. I could guess what it said, anyway.

I veered off the drive, running flat out across the lawn, heading for the trees.

The engine noise was very loud, then there was a screech of

brakes just outside the gates, and I knew I wasn't going to make the trees.

But there was a bush in the middle of the lawn. Not a big one. Maybe big enough.

I dived behind it just as the Porsche came up the drive, accelerating then braking into a skid-stop just outside the door.

I scrambled to keep myself behind the bush, and peeped round the edge just in time to see Carr opening the front door and disappearing inside. I could hear him though, shouting for his uncle.

How long would that conversation last, I wondered?

"Where is she?"

"Just left!"

It might be that quick and then he'd be out again and after me.

I was already running again when I thought that. Sprinting flat out for the gate at a speed I hadn't attained since my last school sports day. Perhaps not even then.

Out on the road again, and Macrae had his car turned round and parked opposite the drive so that I could dive straight into the open door, phone still clutched in one hand and painting in the other.

He was already accelerating down the road as I managed to get myself properly into the seat and fumbled for the belt.

"Well, that was exciting," he said calmly.

"What… happened?" I asked between pants. "I thought… we had… more time?"

"So did I. But according to my DC, Carr had some sort of message on his phone. He just looked at it and left in a hurry."

"A message? Sir Arthur didn't make any calls."

"Not while you were there, perhaps. But he could have called before he let you in. Or it might have been an automatic notification from the intercom. And perhaps he had a link to his CCTV as well."

I lay back in the seat and shut my eyes. "Whatever. Too close."

"Yes. Sorry. But it's good to get the adrenaline flowing now and then! Let's you know you're alive, right?"

I opened one eye and looked at him. "Next time I want to know if I'm alive, I'll go and see my doctor!"

He took the direct route back into town, and drove fast, so that by the time I had all my breath back and my nerves in order he was pulling into the police car park.

"So, did we get anything useful from that wee exercise?" he asked as we came to a stop.

"That 'wee exercise' was a lot more exercise than I've had in a long time, and not at all welcome either," I told him. "But yes, we may have something from that."

I related the full story to him. He was a good listener, keeping focused on what I was saying without any interruptions.

Finally, when I'd finished, he put in a question. "So have you any idea what he saw in the picture that caused such a reaction?"

I shook my head. "We were talking about artists' signatures. I thought he must have seen something like that, but I've checked and checked that painting, and I'll swear on a Bible that there's no signature there. I don't think there was one on the other painting either. I'll take a closer look at the images I recorded, though."

"Aye, do that. And if you could Bluetooth those pictures to me now?"

We got out our phones and made the transfer.

"I suppose this counts as another of those coincidences you don't like? I mean, myself and Sir Arthur both getting these pictures and at about the same time."

"This goes way beyond coincidence." Macrae was staring out of the windscreen, frowning and drumming his fingers on the dashboard. "I'm wondering if he recognized the location of your picture."

"Possibly. I didn't have time to dig into that, and I hadn't actually told him where it was. But if he did know the place – and what happened there – then that would explain his reaction."

"Back when you were chasing this yourself, Sandra, did you ever make a link to Coren Hall?"

"In my mind I did. Well, it was an obvious jump to make. Unidentified teenager found dead within a mile or two of a school and home for orphans? Of course I considered a link. But – as you probably know – the police investigation discounted that. All the Coren Hall pupils were safe and accounted for. No one from the school had ever been near the farmhouse. Didn't even know it existed." I sighed, remembering past frustrations. "Of course, I tried to check that out for myself. I was allowed one interview with a member of staff, who called himself Mr Hargrove. Deputy head. By telephone. All he did was confirm what the police had said. No further information. No other questions allowed. No contact with pupils allowed. No visits allowed. I went out there, couldn't get past the gate. Short of breaking and entering, I couldn't go any further."

"How often did you think of doing that?"

I gave him a sharp look; he gave me a poker face, but with a twinkle in his eye.

"About as often as you would have, I suppose! But Graham talked me out of actually doing it. So in the end I just had to accept the police account."

"As a police officer, I must advise against any criminal activity on your part, Mrs Deeson, however good the motive, and commend your husband on his good advice. But as David to Sandra, you might be interested to know that the farmhouse was originally part of the Coren Hall estate. So was most of the land around there – including all that is now Coren Hall Village."

"That's interesting. And who actually owns it? The Hall, the farmhouse, the land?"

"Ah, now that's a very good question. But not an easy one to answer. There's a note in the file from the original investigation about joint ownership, but no details. And so far, all I've been able to discover is that there's a company called 'Coren Hall Estates' that holds the paperwork for it all. But the names behind that are elusive. The real names, that is."

"You'll let me know what you find?"

"As much as I can." He caught the look I gave him, and sighed. "You understand that DI Macrae has to operate within the constraints of his job, and that David Macrae has to respect that?"

"A bit late to be playing that card, isn't it? Well, I appreciate you have to be careful, but keep me in the loop, OK? You owe me that much."

He nodded. "I do indeed. And I want you in the loop anyway. Unless I'm very wrong about all this, you've been part of this story from the beginning, and my gut tells me that you need to be in it to the end."

"Thanks. I think." I shook my head. "I am part of it. I wish I wasn't. I wish I'd left it alone thirty years ago. I wish I could leave it now. But I can't. I can't stop caring about who these people were, about why they died. I know I care too much. But I can't help it."

I opened the door and began to climb out, but was stopped by his hand on my arm. "Sandra – I don't think you can care too much."

I looked back at him. "You don't know what it cost me," I said, and got out.

My plans for a frank and open discussion with Graham needed some serious revision after the morning's adventure. I wasn't sure how to tell him that I'd gone right back to where I was before we were married. And besides, I had left Yvonne coping with things at the library, which wasn't very fair on her. So I decided to let the problem stew in my subconscious for a while and went back to my day job, stopping on the way to pick up some takeaway lunch as a peace offering.

There was a large white van parked outside when I arrived, with Yvonne sitting in her car a few spaces behind it. I parked in the nearest gap, waved, and went over to join her.

"So how was the dishy DI, and what do I tell Graham if he asks? And I hope that pizza's for me. I'm starving."

"It's for sharing," I told her. "And there's something chocolaty for dessert, providing you say nothing to Graham."

"Deal." We sat and munched on a deep pan spicy meat feast while watching anonymous figures in all-enveloping white suits going in and out, carrying various unidentified items.

"They've got more equipment than the CSIs had," I commented after a while. "And better suits."

Yvonne nodded. "When they started going into the van and coming out dressed like that, I asked where their spaceship was and if this was an invasion. But they didn't seem very amused. Probably heard it before."

"Probably, and it wasn't very good the first time. Did they say when they'll be finished?"

"Hopefully by about five tonight, they think. I was going to leave them to it and come back, but they've got some company policy about having a member of staff on hand."

"Oh, yes. I think there was something about that in the small print. Sorry, I'd have gone for a different company if that had registered."

"Not to worry. I'm treating it as a quiet day at work and catching up on some reading. We should be OK to go back in tomorrow morning and get the place opened up again."

"Are those paintings still there?"

"No. The chairman – what's his name, Ferrers-Manton? Anyway, he turned up with some of the other members this morning so it's a good thing I was stuck here. They've arranged an alternative venue for their exhibition. Guild Hall, I think he said. So they took everything down there. I say they, but he didn't do much. Stood around for a while telling everyone else what to do. Talked a bit about the investigation, sort of trying to imply that he was helping out the police, but also asking questions about what was happening – just like Carr did – so I don't think he really knew much. Then he announced he had an important meeting at Central Police Station and would have to leave them to it. I don't think anyone cheered, but there was relief all round when he left." She gave me an appraising look. "This meeting at Central

Police Station – that wasn't anything to do with you, was it?"

"No, not really." I wasn't going to tell Yvonne about the morning – certainly not before I'd talked to Graham. And perhaps not then – she knew my past history almost as well as he did and would be even quicker to set me right about digging up the past. "Macrae just wanted to bring me up to date with a few things, that's all."

"I see. And that mud on your face: was that part of the dating – sorry, updating! – process?"

"What mud?"

I pulled down the sun visor and looked in the mirror. There was indeed a big dirty streak along my cheek. And, when I looked, another one on the sleeve of my coat – in about the same position as the sore spot that I was starting to become aware of. All legacies of my dive behind the bush, I realized. I hadn't even noticed before – though it did explain the strange looks I'd got in the pizza shop.

"Oh, that mud," I answered myself. "It's nothing. I fell over."

Yvonne raised an eyebrow. "And when you weren't falling over DI Macrae, did he tell you anything useful? Like have they heard anything about Emily?"

I winced. "Sorry. I should have told you first." Except that with everything else that had happened, that had dropped out of my mind. "They've found her car, but they don't think it helps much. It was near Heathrow, Macrae said, but he thinks it might have been dumped there as a distraction. Oh, and he also said I should keep that to myself – so please keep it to yourself, Yvonne."

She sighed and tossed the empty pizza box into the back of her car. "Bring on the chocolate and my lips are sealed."

"You'll find it hard to eat then."

"I'll find a way, don't worry."

She proceeded to do so. I helped. While we did that, I considered what to do with the rest of the day.

"Yvonne, why don't you get off home for a bit? I'll stay here and babysit."

She considered it. "I don't suppose you can get into too much trouble just sitting in the car."

"Trouble? Why would I get into trouble?"

"Says she with mud all over her face!" She fumbled around in the door pocket and produced a packet of wet wipes. "Here, that'll help with the mud and the chocolate stains." She fussed over me until I was presentable, then sat back with a serious look on her face. "Tell me honestly, Sandy – how are you? Because with all you've been through in the last few days, I don't think you should be here at all. If you didn't want to stay at home, you should be jetting off to somewhere sunny."

"Sweet of you to worry, but I'm doing fine."

"Are you sure? Because the last time something like this happened, it was pretty devastating, wasn't it? And that's the sort of experience no one should have even once in their life, let alone twice."

There were far too many people who knew about my past. I'd told Yvonne the story years ago – or some of it – and of course, she wouldn't forget something like that. I certainly wasn't going to tell her about the connections with recent events.

"It's not the same at all. Maybe it looks similar, but I'm a different person, the circumstances are different..."

"OK. If you insist. But if you take over here this afternoon, you leave things to me tomorrow. In fact, you should take a few days off. I've got it covered."

I knew that look, and there was no arguing with it. Besides, I could probably make use of the time.

"Oh, all right then. And thanks."

"You're welcome. Now get out of my car. If I get going I can still catch the afternoon soaps!"

She drove off, waving, while I was making myself known to the cleaning people and letting them know that the shift had changed. The person in charge, a dour little man who looked as though he'd spent too much of his life cleaning up after other people's evil, had bad news for me. Bad enough that he pulled down his mask to convey it.

"Sorry to say, but it's going to be longer than we thought. That superglue's a b... a bit more difficult to shift than we'd hoped."

"So what time?"

He scratched at his chin. "Six-ish, I hope. Or perhaps seven?"

"Right. Well, whatever it takes." I couldn't do anything about it, anyway.

I phoned Graham, and explained where I was and what I was doing, making no mention of this morning's adventures, of course.

"Do you want me to come and sit with you?" he asked.

I considered this and was tempted. His solid presence and the warmth of his company would have been very welcome.

But, on the other hand, it would have been very difficult to sit next to him for hours and not talk about everything that was happening. Of course I was going to tell him. But in my own time.

And besides, he was recovering from a heart operation. Had to keep remembering that.

"Thanks, but there's no point. It'd just be pretty boring for you. I'll call you later, when I'm finished up. How about we go out to eat tonight? Down to The Plough, perhaps?"

"Sounds good. Call it a date, then. But you will let me know if you need anything, won't you?"

"Of course I will. Bye now."

As soon as I'd broken the connection, I regretted it. Without Graham, without Yvonne, without even David Macrae, I felt far too much on my own, and far too vulnerable. The memory of Jonathan Carr storming up the drive returned to me, and with it the thought, *"What if he'd seen me? What if I'd been thirty seconds later coming out of that door?"*

Of course, Macrae had still been there. Carr couldn't have actually done anything. And in any case, it was beside the point. He hadn't seen me.

But of course he had seen me. On the CCTV.

I looked around nervously.

"Pull yourself together, girl!" I said sharply. "If he does turn up, you've got a perfectly valid reason for being there, and Sir Arthur will back you up. And he's not going to do anything, because that would just give David an excuse to go after him."

Sound logic, I thought. I hoped.

Comforted slightly by my reasoning, I thought over what had happened that morning, trying to be objective about it. What was the link between the two paintings, and what had made such an impact on Sir Arthur?

They were linked by style, and by the timing of the delivery. Both just before the exhibition, though I hadn't seen it until afterwards.

I remembered the note that had been in with mine, and getting out my phone, I scrolled through the images until I could see it again.

"Dear Sandy, This is a personal gift for you. You'll understand why when you've seen the exhibition paintings. We plan to donate prints from them to the library, once things have quietened down a bit! But we thought that this would be appropriate for you to have. Emily."

Something had been planned for the exhibition. Something that was going to cause a big sensation – because it would need to "quieten down a bit". Something that probably involved the dead man and the missing paintings.

And something connected with Sir Arthur, as well.

I looked at the images I'd recorded that morning, searching for clues in Sir Arthur's painting. Something in his past, perhaps, given that note referring to "memory lane". Or was it, for some reason, referring to Sir Arthur's own picture, his own "Memory Lane"?

I wondered where that was. Was there an actual street called Memory Lane?

I tried an online search, but the internet connection was too slow. I'd do better if I could get in the library and connect to the

Wi-Fi – or even use the PC there – but there was no sign of the cleaning crew finishing yet.

So, I put that aside for the time being. What else had I learned?

The connection between Coren Hall and the farmhouse was interesting. I hadn't known that at the time, though it probably wouldn't have made much difference if I had.

I leaned back, closed my eyes, and thought about the one and only time I'd actually visited the place. Or attempted to.

My attempts to arrange a proper visit over the phone having failed, I decided to go out there and make a nuisance of myself until they let me in and talked to me properly. I'd borrowed Graham's car – he had a rusty little Mini in those days – and driven myself out. No satnav in those days, of course, but with an old-fashioned map and a bit of luck I'd eventually come across a narrow lane flanked by crumbling stone pillars and a barely legible sign announcing "Coren Hall". It also had a much newer and more readable sign just above it: "NO UNAUTHORIZED ENTRY. WARNING – GUARD DOGS. TRESPASSERS WILL BE PROSECUTED".

Friendly sort of place.

I'd driven up the lane until it widened out into a patch of weed-grown gravel in front of large iron gates with elaborate stone posts and a gatehouse inside on the right. They would have formed a grand entrance in their day, but the stonework was chipped and overgrown with moss, the gates were rusty, and the gatehouse looked semi-derelict, with most of the visible windows boarded up.

There was, however, a shiny new chain holding the gate shut, with an impressively large padlock securing it.

Beyond the gate, a drive ran off up a hill and disappeared behind some trees. Roofs and short turrets loomed above them, presumably the Hall itself. There was no one around, and no obvious means of attracting any attention.

I got out and tried the gate. It was as well secured as it had appeared. I shouted, hoping someone might be in the gatehouse. No result. I found a stone and banged on the gates. It didn't make as much noise as I'd hoped, so I got in the car and started blowing the horn.

And I kept on doing it. I was going to keep it up until either someone took some notice or the horn broke.

After fifteen or twenty minutes of this, I finally got a result. Two figures were coming down the driveway towards me. I gave the horn a rest, got out, and waited for them.

They weren't alone, I noticed. They had dogs with them. Quite large dogs, it appeared. Not a breed I recognized, but the way they were straining at their leashes wasn't encouraging.

Both men were dressed in countryside chic – green waxed jackets, dark trousers and wellies, flat caps. The older one, heavily built and ruddy faced, had a shotgun hanging over his left arm and a dog pulling on the other one. His companion was shorter, younger, and thinner, but with a distinct family resemblance. No gun, but two dogs. It looked like the squire and his son out for a day's shooting rather than school staff coming to answer the gate.

And they didn't look welcoming, either. The "squire" looked angry, his son looked mean, and the dogs looked vicious. I stepped back a bit from the gate.

"Hello!" I called as they came closer. "I'm Sandra Reynolds, from *The Echo*." Not strictly true, as I'd been fired the week before, but they didn't know that. "I'd just like to ask –"

The older man interrupted me. Not with any response to what I was saying. He just talked over me.

"If you're not on your way in thirty seconds, I'll open the gate and set the dogs on you."

I was slow to react. I'd never come across such concentrated hostility before. The man's face and tone and whole manner said that he hated the sight of me – even though we'd never met before. The voice was familiar – it was probably the same person I'd spoken to on the phone – but I couldn't grasp the sheer venom he was directing at me.

DAY 5: AMBAGE

I think I must have gaped at him, before starting to protest. "But – I only want…"

As soon as I started talking he handed his dog's lead to the younger man, and stepped towards the gate, pulling out a bunch of keys as he did so.

The dogs had been largely silent up to now, though they were looking at me with a fixed intensity that didn't promise friendly relations. As the keys came out they began to snarl, and pull forward so strongly that the younger man had trouble holding them back.

From the look on his face, though, he didn't intend to do so for long. For a moment, I caught his eye, and the eagerness I saw there chilled me. It was even worse than the older man's anger. He didn't want me to go. He wanted to set the dogs on me.

There was a click as the key turned in the padlock, a rattle as the chain was unwrapped, and an increase in volume from the dogs. I turned and ran to the car, leaped in, and slammed the door. I'd left the keys in the ignition, which was fortunate, because my hands were shaking so hard I could hardly even turn them – I would have struggled to get them in. Fortunately, the engine started first time. I pulled the Mini round in the sharpest, fastest turn I could manage, and headed down the lane at full speed.

A glance in the mirror showed me that the gate was open, and the dogs were charging through. I tried to push the accelerator into the floor, and shot past the stone pillars at the end of the lane, barely managing the turn into the road beyond. If there'd been any traffic along there, it would have been fatal.

I finally managed to get control of myself enough to pull into a lay-by, and I sat there for a long time, shivering and crying. I told myself that they'd been bluffing, that they wouldn't actually have let the dogs do me any harm. And really, I should go back and confront them.

But then I remembered the dogs charging down the lane behind me. And I remembered the expressions on the faces of the two men. Hatred and anger on one, a sick eagerness on the other.

After all; there was a warning sign. Not their fault if some young reporter ignored it and got herself torn apart. Very tragic, of course, and the dogs would have to be put down. And perhaps there would have to be an investigation. But they looked as if they were ready to take that risk – and it would have been far too late to help me.

I could have gone to the police and reported it. But DCI Greer had already made it clear that I should not be getting myself involved. I wasn't likely to get a sympathetic hearing. In fact, I might even have been charged with trespassing!

I'd thought about it for a long time. Then I'd driven home.

Looking back, I realized that that had been the beginning of the end for me. That was when I'd realized that I was beaten. I'd kept on trying for a while, but inside I'd given up.

I'd never gone back to Coren Hall, or anywhere near it.

Coren Hall – the farmhouse. And Sir Arthur. All somehow linked. And the library. The unknown artist, so terribly murdered, and the hanging body. Both unknown. And the paintings. The missing paintings, the painting I had. The flowers in the farmhouse. The painting Sir Arthur had – a picture in a room. A painting of a painting… Memory Lane…

All the different elements were whirling around in my brain. *Too much information, too many facts, too many coincidences*, David Macrae would have said…

There was a tap on the side window and I jerked upright, suddenly realizing that I'd fallen asleep. It was dark, and the cleaning crew boss was tapping on my window impatiently.

"OK. Just a minute." I tried to roll down the window, but electric windows don't work without power and my keys were still somewhere in a pocket. I opened the door a crack instead.

"We're all finished. Just need you to come and sign off on it."

"Right. Yes. Of course. What's the time?"

"Er – about half past seven."

"What? You said six!" I pushed the door fully open, making

him move back, and got out. I was cold and stiff and my bruised arm was really painful now.

"I said six or seven." He frowned at me as if it was my fault. "Can't be precise about these things, and this was a tricky one. But it's all done now." He held out a clipboard. "Sign here, please."

I wasn't feeling very accommodating. A long day, bad memories and a sore arm didn't help my mood. "I'll take a look first."

"No need for that," he protested. But I was on my way to the door.

The lights were still on in the library. I walked round, checking everywhere for signs of powder or superglue residue, but they'd done their job well. A faint whiff of chemicals hung round the place, but I supposed that that would disperse eventually.

I managed to squeeze some graciousness out, and smiled as I signed his clipboard. "Looks good. Thank you."

He grunted something that I chose to assume was "You're welcome", ripped off a copy of the job sheet, and thrust it at me before scuttling out.

My mobile rang. Graham calling. "Are you still at the library? Only it's gone eight o'clock – I thought you'd be home by now."

Gone eight? I glanced at the clock behind the reception desk, but it had been one of the things smashed by the intruder. "Sorry. I didn't realize how late it was. The cleaning crew have only just finished." If I'd realized just how generous the boss had been when estimating his crew's work rate, I would have been a lot less gracious towards him.

"OK, then. Do you still want to eat out?" It was a good thing that Graham was a lot more gracious – and patient! – than I was.

I considered it. I did, but... "To be honest, I mostly want a long, hot bath just now. Sorry, but I don't think I've got a night out in me."

"That's OK. How about I order a takeaway instead, then start the bath running?"

"You are the perfect husband."

"This is true. Chinese or Indian? Or pizza?"

I'd already had pizza. "Chinese, I think. Nothing too elaborate. Lemon chicken, boiled rice, and… oh, I don't know. Surprise me."

He laughed. I always loved his laughter, soft and warm and rich. "I'll do my best. You get yourself home!"

He hung up. I went to the door, then paused, and looked around again.

The sliding doors to the Laney Grey Wing were still open. I'd become used to them closing on their own, but they weren't doing it. Yvonne must have put in the code to keep them locked open, which would have made sense with the cleaning crew going in and out all the time.

I went over to the keypad to rectify that, and noticed something that made me even more annoyed with the cleaners. On the far door there was still evidence of the CSIs' work: a little black arrow was still stuck there, pointing down.

"Sloppy, sloppy, sloppy!" I muttered, and went to pull it off. I wondered why it was there anyway. What had the CSIs been marking in that position?

It was about four feet up from the floor. Just below it, as indicated by the arrow, there was a small V-shaped indentation in the wood.

It was, I thought, the sort of mark you might get from the head of a flat screwdriver if, for example, someone had forced a screwdriver in between the closed doors and tried to lever them apart.

I remembered June saying something about marks on the doors. She'd been expecting to see marks on both sides, but could only see them on one.

I turned to look at the other door. The marks she had seen were still there. Slightly rounded indentations in the edge of the wood frame. Marks that you might get from the shaft of a screwdriver if you were forcing it that way… in which case the head would leave a mark on the other side of the door…

The two marks were at the same height.

June had only been able to see one set of tool marks because the door had been closed and the others had been hidden. But of course the CSIs had found them and marked them.

I peeled the sticker off, or half of it. The rest had to be scraped off with my thumb.

It wasn't a very big mark. Which was fortunate from the point of view of the damage done, but surely that implied a small screwdriver?

The doors were massively over-secure. When closed, they automatically locked together at four points, plus putting steel pins into the floor and ceiling. No way they could have been forced open by a little screwdriver.

Of course, if you didn't know that, you might expect that a bit of leverage would be sufficient. Who bolts up a library door like Fort Knox, eh?

I shook my head. I didn't understand what had happened here, and I was too tired to work it out. Probably Macrae had it figured out already, but if so it wasn't something he'd shared with me.

I finished locking up and went home. Sleeping in the car hadn't refreshed me; I was still dozy and found myself rubbernecking at the traffic lights. I wound the window down, trying to revive myself with fresh air, but got a heavy dose of diesel fumes from the big artic in front of me.

Home was a slice of heaven. Warm lights in the gloom, Graham opening the door as I approached, Brodie wagging his tail and sniffing for a fuss.

"The bath is ready, milady," Graham announced. "And the evening meal will be served in the banqueting hall at your convenience."

"Thank you, you're a ministering angel."

"Want help undressing?"

"Don't push your luck, mister."

An hour or so later, I was clean, warm, full of lemon chicken and rice, snuggled up against my cuddly hubby. It seemed a pity to break the mood, but I needed to talk to him.

"Graham… I have to tell you something."

"OK, but if we're sharing news, then me first! Sam's been in touch again."

I sat upright. "Is he OK?"

"Yes, he's fine – just wanted to let us know he was moving on from Thailand."

"Where to? Did he say?"

"Not really… he sorted of hinted that he was leaving Asia, but more than that…" A shrug. "Somewhere different, I suppose. Somewhere new."

"There isn't anywhere new. He's been everywhere!"

"It's a big world, Sandy. And our lad wants to see it all."

There was a long pause while we thought of our globetrotting son.

"It's my fault," I said.

I hadn't meant to say it. It wasn't what I'd planned to say at all. But I said it.

Graham looked puzzled. "What is?"

"Sam. It's my fault that he dropped out and… went away and… he never comes home…"

Tears were flowing now.

And Graham… Graham held me close. "No it's not, Sandy. It's just who Sam is."

"But – I drove him away… always wanting him to be safe, to know where he was; always wanting to make sure he was protected… Don't you remember that big row we had? When he was off to university and I was marking his stuff, all his clothes and everything – name and address and UV pen marks and… like he was on his first day at infants' – and he was so furious with me and stomped out and didn't speak to me again – just went off to uni. Then he hadn't been there six months and he dropped out and took off… It was me, Graham! I did that!"

"No, no. Listen, Sandy…"

But I was beyond listening. I was too tired and too hurting to listen, and the past had come back too often to hide from it any more.

"I blamed him and I blamed you and I blamed God – and Sam won't talk to me and I don't talk about him to you and I can't talk to God about anything because I know it was really my fault and I've always known it and I… I just couldn't bear to think of something happening to him and no one knowing who he was."

I couldn't see properly. Graham was right next to me, but his face was blurred. I rubbed desperately at my eyes.

"I still can't," I added in a whisper.

"Oh, Sandy… You've been carrying this all these years? I thought you understood. I thought I told you. Why didn't you hear me?"

"Hear what?"

He grabbed my hands and held them. "It wasn't because of you that Sam dropped out and went travelling. He just decided that he needed to do it. University doesn't suit everyone. Sam just couldn't cope with academic life. He felt trapped, stifled. He had to get out and just go."

"But we had such an argument."

"Yes, and that didn't help. But he would have gone anyway. To be honest, I think I – we – made a mistake encouraging him to go to uni in the first place. He was under pressure from us and from his teachers, because he's bright enough, for sure – but it was never in his heart. He was always going to be a wanderer."

I looked at him. "If that's so, why doesn't he ever talk to me?"

Graham shrugged. "I don't know for sure – but what I think is, he feels guilty too. He knows how much it hurts you, what he's doing, how fearful you are. And that's hard to live with. Easier to keep you at a distance, perhaps?"

"I would never have held that against him."

"No more than he would have held that argument against

you. But guilt does that. Keeps people apart. Both of you blaming yourselves."

"I wish I'd known."

"I have tried to talk about it. But – until this business brought it all out – you just wouldn't talk about it."

Which reminded me of something else. "Ah, yes. About that – there's some other things I need to talk about."

"Oh yes?" he said, with a wariness born from past experience. "Well…"

We were interrupted. Brodie, who had been dozing in his basket nearby, suddenly leaped up, barking furiously, and ran out into the hall.

"What the heck's got into that dog?" Graham got up and followed him, and as he reached the hall door there was a whooshing noise, and fire licked round the top of the door and into his face.

He fell back with a shout, beating wildly at his hair. Brodie dashed past him, whining.

My mind froze. I saw what was happening, but couldn't understand it. Where had that flame come from? A gas explosion? But the boiler was in the kitchen, not the hall. Had Brodie set something off? How could he have done that?

Yet somehow, even while my mind spun in circles, my body was moving. I had hold of Graham, pulling him back from the hall, while in my other hand I had snatched up Brodie's water bowl and flung it over Graham's hair. I dragged him into the kitchen, had the tap running, and was throwing more water over him and the dog before seeing the fire blanket on the wall, pulling it out of the container, and rushing out towards the hallway.

A blast of intense heat struck me in the face. I raised the fire blanket as a barrier ahead of me, wrapping it round my fingers, and tried to peer at the front door.

It was all orange flame and black smoke. The entire hallway seemed full of it.

"Out, Sandy! We've got to get out! Now!"

Graham grabbed me from behind, pulling me away and back through the kitchen, out into the garden, the fresh air feeling raw and sharp on my lungs but the coolness an incredible blessing.

There were people around, neighbours. Mrs Steel from next door, wrapped in a huge flowery dressing gown, taking charge. "Get them into my house!" she ordered. "Quickly now!"

And the young couple who had just moved in across from us, her on her mobile, him half supporting Graham, and I remembered Graham's heart and grabbed at him, but Mrs Steel and another woman were all around me, hustling me away, and Brodie was whining, but somewhere near, thank God – not still inside.

One of the other men from nearby, I had forgotten his name, had an extinguisher and was blasting it through the letterbox, but the orange glow from inside the glass panels seemed unaffected, and I wondered if we would lose the house. "Oh God, please, not the house," I sobbed, then saw Graham sinking to the ground still half supported by the neighbour, and I prayed, "Not Graham! The house we can lose, but I can't lose Graham!"

In the distance there were sirens. We were inside Mrs Steel's house, so I couldn't see any lights, but the sirens were getting louder. I wondered if it was an ambulance or a fire engine. I hoped it was both.

DAY 6: SINISTROUS

Sometime in the small hours, an A & E doctor looked me over. I had some minor burns on my face and hands, sore eyes and a raw throat from the smoke, but apart from that I was fine. Painkillers, treatment for skin and throat, and an overnight stay for observation.

Graham, I learned, was in a worse state, with more severe burns on his head. They had him in an isolation ward – severe burns carry a high risk of infection – and under sedation. After I begged long enough, they let me see him through a window. That might have been a mistake. His head was bandaged, there was a drip in his arm, and he was so terribly still.

They persuaded me, eventually, that he was fine under the circumstances, and that there was no more I could do. Finally I gave in and let them put me to bed in a nearby ward.

I didn't really expect to sleep. My face hurt too much, my head was too busy. But the painkillers took the edge off, and my whirling thoughts faded into darkness.

I woke up to warm sunlight and bustling nurses. My face and hands and throat all hurt, but my head was a lot clearer, and my first thought was of Graham.

"I'll ring his ward," promised the first nurse I managed to grab hold of – literally – clutching at her arm as she paused by my bed. Amazingly, she responded with a smile before detaching herself and carrying on.

Even more amazingly, she came back to me in thirty minutes or so. "He had a good night, and he's awake and comfortable. He'll be seen by a burns specialist later today – that's Mr Cromarty, he's very good – and they'll have someone from Cardiology check him out as well, in view of his history."

"I need to see him. Can I, please?"

"I'm sure that will happen later, but it would be better if you stayed here for now, until the doctor's seen you. I think that they'll probably discharge you anyway, but best to be sure, right?"

"Yes. Thank you."

She smiled again and moved on to the next demand, and I did my best to relax.

It was a frustrating time. I had too much to think about, and not enough information. It was hard not to keep coming back to that terrifying wall of flame that had filled the hallway.

I didn't even have my mobile phone with me, to make contact with someone and find out what was going on. Had the house survived? Where was Brodie?

And, of course, who had done it?

I had my suspicions on that. But no facts. So I lay in increasing frustration, forcing myself not to keep bothering the nurses and other staff with endless questions that they couldn't possibly be expected to answer.

I did consider discharging myself and going to look for some answers in person. But there were practical difficulties in that – such as the fact that the only clothes of my own I had were the dressing gown and nightdress that I had put on after my bath, both of which had been singed and smoke-stained. I was left wearing hospital pyjamas, and I was not going out and about dressed like that. I'd be in the psychiatric ward tonight if I tried it.

So I was left to fret and worry through a hospital breakfast that I had a surprisingly good appetite for and then on through the morning while I waited for the doctor. But it was David Macrae who came to my rescue, at least as far as my need for information went.

"Visitor for you," said a nurse, and he was standing by the bed with a grim expression.

"Sandra – I can't begin to say how sorry I am."

"Why? Did you do it?"

"You know what I mean. I put you in harm's way, getting you to go to see Templeton. I just didn't expect a reaction like this."

That answered one of my questions – or confirmed my suspicions. "Carr?"

He shrugged, and pulled up a chair. "There was a silver Porsche seen making off from the area, at speed."

I managed a smile, though it hurt my face. "You've got him then!"

He shook his head slowly. "Well, it's not that easy. We haven't got the number plate, and there's no description of the driver. So no actual evidence that it was him. Of course, we'll be talking to him about it – silver Porsches aren't exactly commonplace round here – but they're not unique to him, either. Unless forensics comes up with something, we won't have enough to charge him. And I have to tread lightly, in view of our little adventure yesterday. That could come back to bite."

I controlled a desire to swear. "David – we could have been killed! You can't just let him get away with it!"

"As I said, I'm sorry. I shouldn't have put you in this position."

I sat back and stared into the distance. Well, across the ward, anyway. The woman opposite me hadn't forgotten her mobile when she came in, and she was talking on it now. She had been since before breakfast. I wasn't sure if it was the same conversation or just another in an endless series.

"How are you doing, anyway?" he asked after a moment.

"I'm OK. Well, not OK, but not too bad. Just a little scorched.

Graham's worse – he got a fireball in the face – but what I'm hearing is that he'll be all right. What actually happened, anyway? All I can remember is that the dog was barking, and next thing the hallway's in flames."

"It seems like a standard letterbox arson. I just talked to the Fire Investigator – that's like the Fire Service's CSI – and he's quite confident of that. Some sort of accelerant was poured in, then a bit of rag or paper pushed in behind it, and lit from the outside. The pattern of marks it leaves is quite distinctive."

"And how much damage is there?" I asked, trying to be calm. I loved that house. We'd been there nearly twenty years. The thought of it being gutted was a worse pain than my face.

"Not too much. The fire was mostly confined to the doormat, which soaked up the accelerant, and the UPVC door itself. I'm afraid you'll need to replace it, and perhaps some of the floorboards and wall coverings, but the rest is just smoke damage. A terrible mess, for sure, but nothing major."

"Really? I mean – it's a relief to hear that, but I saw the flames coming into the living room – right into Graham's face, in fact. I thought it must have spread further."

"That was just the initial fireball. See, when the accelerant ignited you got a big ball of flame that went up, travelled along the ceiling, then down and round the top of the door. Fortunately it didn't contact anything volatile, so wasn't sustained. Of course, that would have been different if your neighbours hadn't been so quick. Someone saw the flames and dialled 999 almost as soon as it happened, and those lads were on the ball!"

"And Brodie? Our dog?"

"I understand that one of your neighbours has him safe. A bit of singed fur, that's all, though I dare say you'll want a vet to take a look at him."

"Yes, I'll certainly do that."

The woman across from me finally finished her conversation. But only long enough to press a speed-dial button and start another.

I wondered what make it was. I'd have to get one – the battery life must be phenomenal.

"Of course, the real question is why would anyone do this?" I mused. "Though if it was Carr, I suppose that answers itself. He was trying to shut me up."

"Or just warn you off," Macrae suggested. "If he'd intended to kill you, he'd have been better off waiting till later, when you were all off to your beds. And the fact that he used his own car suggests that it was a message. I think he wanted you to know who did it – but he was careful to make sure we couldn't prove it."

"Trying to scare me off," I said bleakly. I thought of Coren Hall, and the dogs. "And will he do anything else, do you think?"

"I doubt it. He's sent his message – and you can be very sure I'll let him know that we'll be watching him." He stood up. "I'm sorry, but I have to be on my way. I've a lot happening this morning, as you'll no doubt understand. But there's a constable outside who'll get a statement off you if that's OK? And once again, I apologize."

"No. Don't." I met his gaze. "I agreed to go and see Sir Arthur because I wanted answers as much as you did. I could have said no. But I didn't, and that's my responsibility."

Macrae had a wary look to him. "Sandra, I'd not want you taking on a load of guilt about this."

"Guilt?" I suddenly thought of the conversation I'd been having with Graham just before the fire. "No. I'm done with feeling guilty about the wrong things. This was down to Carr."

He smiled. "Well, that's yet to be proved. But that's the way to think. I'll keep you informed."

Things moved a bit faster then. The constable took my statement, and then the doctor came round and agreed that I could be discharged, though I was to see my GP within the week. I made a phone call from the nurses' station – fortunately, Yvonne's number was one of the few I had actually memorized.

"I've been phoning all day!" she remonstrated. "Ever since I heard! I was just about to come to the hospital anyway, now we've got the library sorted."

"I didn't have my mobile with me," I explained. "Thanks for dealing with the library. I need a favour though: I'm stuck here with nothing but hospital jim-jams to cover my embarrassment. Could you pop over with some clothes and give me a lift home?"

"No problem. I'll be about twenty minutes."

"No, don't rush. I've got to go and see Graham. Give me an hour."

Then I went along to Graham's ward, where I was pleased to see him now awake and sitting up in bed. He gave me a wave through the glass door.

"You can go in," confirmed the nurse on duty. "Actually, your timing's perfect. He's just back from Cardiology, and there're no issues in that regard."

"Thanks. That's great!" I said from my heart.

"And there's more," she continued. "The burns specialist has had a look, and things aren't as bad as we'd feared. He probably won't need skin grafts, and the damage to his nose and throat is minimal. He'll be in here for a while, but it's all looking positive."

I grabbed her hand and squeezed, momentarily choked with relief. Of course, I'd known he was going to be OK. But I had been more worried than I'd realized.

She smiled, a burst of brightness on a tired face that made me realize why she was in the job: for those moments when she could give good news like that. "Go on in. But don't let him talk too much; he needs to rest. Especially his throat." She gave me a meaningful look. "And so do you, actually."

I nodded and went in. Leaned over the bed and gave him a very gentle hug.

"Hi, you," I said.

"Hi, yourself," he croaked back. The damage to his throat might have been minimal, but he sounded awful. "I think next time we should go out for dinner. Don't you?"

I laughed, and he started to, but then broke into coughing. I handed him a glass of water and helped him take a few sips, after which he leaned back into his pillows.

"I'll talk, you just nod or shake, OK?"

He nodded.

"Right. Well, DI Macrae has just been to see me. It was arson – someone poured something through our letterbox and set it alight. There's some damage, but mostly to the door and the mat. And to you, of course. Nothing that can't be fixed. Brodie's OK, and so am I, thanks."

"That would have been my first question," he whispered. "Because you don't look it." He started coughing again, and I gave him some more water.

"What did I tell you? Stop talking!" He opened his mouth and I raised a hand. "Shush!"

He subsided with a petulant look on his face and a twinkle in his eye.

"Better. Now, I've been discharged, Yvonne's giving me a lift home, so I'll be back later with some things for you. I'm afraid you're going to be in here a bit longer. Which is fine, because it means I can get the house sorted out without you getting in the way."

He mimed horror, followed by indignation. I smiled and continued.

"You will be wondering who might have done this and why." He nodded vigorously. "Well, Macrae told me that there was a Porsche seen nearby which might belong to Jonathan Carr."

Graham tried to raise an eyebrow. Hard to see, under the bandages, but I correctly interpreted the twitch of an eye followed by the wince of pain.

"Yes, that's right. Secretary of the art club. And as for why…" I took a deep breath. "There was something I was going to tell you about. Before we were interrupted."

I gave him a thumbnail sketch of recent events. My visit to

the farmhouse, and then to Sir Arthur's place with Macrae. I told him of my growing certainty that there was a link between the two murders, and that Carr was somehow connected with them.

"The attack on our house was a warning. It was telling me to keep my nose out. So that's why it's happened. That's why you are here now."

Graham had listened carefully. Now he squeezed my arm and shook his head. "Not your fault. His."

I squeezed back. "Actually, that's what I thought. You were right, what you said about guilt. I've had a bit of time to think about that, but I knew you were right as soon as I heard it. I held on to that guilt for too long. I'm not planning to add any more."

He smiled. "Good. What... now?" He breathed the words.

"Oh, I'll get the house sorted, find someone to come and fix the door, then get back with your stuff and see about getting you better."

He shook his head.

"No?"

Graham looked at me steadily then shook his head. He indicated the water, and I helped him to have a long drink.

"Do you know why I fell in love with you?" he said. There was a nasty rasp in his voice, but I could tell he wasn't going to shut up this time.

"You said you had a thing for blondes?"

He grinned and nodded. "That as well. But I fell in love with a girl who wouldn't give up. You cared about that unknown boy. You did everything you possibly could to get justice for him. To get his name."

He paused, but then carried on. "When you had to give up, it left something incomplete in you. Now you've got a chance to sort it. Go and do what you have to do, Sandy. Be the girl I love."

"You mean that? Of course you do. But..."

He leaned forward, staring intently at me. "Thirty years of unfinished business, Sandy. Thirty years I've prayed for a resolution for you. Just be careful."

He leaned back, coughing again. I helped him to some more water, but then he waved me away and leaned back into the pillows, eyes closed.

"Go on," he muttered. "Leave me to the nurses. Especially the blonde one."

A nurse came in as he was speaking. Not blonde, but quite pretty. "I'm sorry, but I think you should let him rest for a bit now," she said. She was trying her best to sound firm, but was a bit too young and unsure of herself, so it came out a little hesitant.

"It's OK. I'm going now," I assured her. Leaning over, I gave Graham a kiss on the cheek. "See you later, love. Be gentle with the nurses."

Yvonne arrived shortly afterwards bringing with her – apart from the traditional bunch of grapes – a tracksuit, some T-shirts, socks, underwear, and a pair of trainers. All brand new. "Did a bit of shopping on the way over. Don't make a fuss, it's all cheap stuff."

Pink and lime green – with electric blue trainers – wouldn't have been my choice of colours, but it was a big improvement over hospital pyjamas. We left the grapes with Graham – now sleeping again – and headed for home.

There was a CSI van parked outside. I recognized Alison Kepple sitting in the driver's seat, writing.

"Hi!" I knocked on the window and she glanced up at me. "Did you get anything?"

She wound her window down, shaking her head as she did so. "Just photographs. There isn't usually much forensic evidence to recover from scenes like this. The offender didn't have to touch anything except the outside of the letterbox, which is a poor surface for prints anyway, and if he or she was wearing gloves..." She shrugged. "I'm glad you got out safely. And your dog as well, I understand from the neighbours. That's really good. I had an arson once where the dog was trapped inside and..."

"Yes, OK, thanks, but I don't need to know that." It wasn't just the job, I decided – she really was insensitive. "Is it all right for me to go in and get things cleaned up?"

She gave me a puzzled look, as if unsure why I had interrupted her. "Yes, of course, I'm all finished."

Yvonne insisted on coming in. She was uncharacteristically silent as we entered through the kitchen door and were met by a stomach-churning smell of smoke and ashes.

There were black stains on the ceiling of the living room above the door, preparing us for what was to come. In the hallway, the entire ceiling was soot-stained, and the marks continued up the stairs. Ugly lumps of melted plastic hung down where the light fittings and smoke alarms had been, looking like diseased stalactites, while the door itself was black and distorted.

"Looks like you'll need a new one," Yvonne said eventually. "Frame as well."

"No, really? I thought I could just wipe it over with a damp cloth."

She forgave my sarcasm with a hug. "Don't worry, we can fix this. But you'd better come and sleep at ours tonight. You can't stay here with this mess."

"Thanks. I do appreciate that. But I've got other plans."

She gave me a suspicious look. "Like what?"

"Oh, I'm going to treat myself. I'm going to a hotel tonight. Coren Hall Hotel."

*

They'd moved the entrance to Coren Hall. The new route in was from the village, on the opposite side of the Hall from where I had been chased off on my visit. And it was a lot nicer too, in my opinion. No more rusty gates, crumbling stonework, and overgrown drives. Now there was a proper noticeboard which said "Welcome" and promised all sorts of comforts and luxuries. Over and above the meals and beds which you'd expect from a hotel, there was a spa including a sauna, a massage parlour and beauty parlour, a golf course, tennis courts, gymnasium, and (coming soon) a swimming pool.

None of this was a surprise; I'd checked the website first. I'd also checked the prices and had nearly given up on the idea. They were almost as frightening as the dogs I'd met previously. But I'd already made up my mind – I was going back to Coren Hall and this time I wasn't going to be put off.

I drove through the entrance – flanked by very new looking granite pillars – and up a long, sweeping, and well-tarmacked drive. It continued to sweep, curving round to the west and back again to show the Hall from several angles. Perched on top of the hill, the square Georgian building looked suitably impressive. Especially as the lowering sun tinged the grey walls with ruddy gold.

It had taken most of the day to get there. Contacting our insurance company and arranging for the door to be replaced had taken several hours by itself. Checking on Brodie, arranging for him to stay with Mrs Steel overnight, thanking neighbours, and assuring everyone that I was fine and Graham was going to be – that took up another considerable chunk of the day. Sorting through some clothing for him and for me took a while – nearly everything seemed to smell of smoke. Fortunately, my best jacket and skirt ensemble had been inside a suit bag, which seemed to have protected it. I was relieved to get out of the tracksuit and trainers, which were starting to hurt my eyes.

I'd also fitted in a little research and contacted Coren Hall to book my room. It was late afternoon by the time I'd finished everything, tossed Graham's things into one bag and my own into another, and headed for my car. Then headed back into the house for the painkillers I'd left behind, and for my laptop, in case I wanted to do some more research. Finally, to the hospital again, to see Graham and drop off the various items that I'd collected for him, before getting out of town.

Now I was here, I wondered again why. I had to admit it was partly because I was being stubborn and bloody-minded and someone had tried to scare me off again. But this time, I wasn't having it. So I was picking up the trail where I had left it the last time.

DAY 6: SINISTROUS

I told myself that there was a certain logic in that. But my reasons went beyond logic. There was a conviction that somehow this was the next step. That there was a connection between events that ran through Coren Hall.

And I did need somewhere to stay for the night.

The drive finally brought me to a wide gravelled space, where I parked my Fiesta alongside a clutch of shiny luxury saloons and sleek, expensive sports cars, took my bag, and went up to the grand double doors. They opened smoothly at my approach, ushering me into the entrance hall: two storeys of marble columns and wood panelling, with reception desk to match.

The woman behind the desk was so perfectly turned out that I thought she might have been installed along with the desk. However, she proved to be human, at least enough to look momentarily shocked at the sight of my face. She was quick to hide her reaction behind her professional mask but I wasn't surprised by it. I'd felt the same way, looking in a mirror. The dressings were off, and I'd found a hat to cover my forehead, but my cheeks still looked like raw skin.

Good thing I'd changed out of the pink and lime green tracksuit, I thought. That really would have been too much. I hoped my best Sunday wear was acceptable.

"Sandra Deeson," I announced. "I phoned earlier." My voice, I thought, had a very husky tone to it. Small reward for the raging sore throat.

"Certainly, ma'am. Just one moment, please." The mannequin raised a perfectly poised arm and pressed buttons on her keyboard. "Ah, yes. Mrs Deeson. Room 34." She passed over the key – actually a strip of plastic with the number on the outside and no doubt a small computer's worth of electronics on the inside.

"Thank you. And can I get something to eat? I haven't managed any lunch today."

There had been endless cups of tea or coffee as I did the rounds of the neighbours, along with various selections of cake and/or biscuits, but I'd had nothing substantial since the hospital breakfast. I wasn't sure how much I could actually swallow, given the way my throat felt, but my stomach insisted that I should try.

"I'm afraid dinner isn't available until after seven." She sounded desperately sorry, in a very practised and professional way. "But they are still serving afternoon tea in the small dining room. I can have your bags… bag sent up for you if you want to go straight there?"

"That would be fine." I hoisted my battered black sports bag onto the polished wood of the reception desk, feeling as if I'd committed an act of desecration. "Which way, please?"

In a beautifully choreographed movement, she pointed across the room. "Through the doorway, and straight along the corridor to the end. I do hope you enjoy your stay with us, Mrs Deeson."

I nodded and followed directions, repenting of my catty thoughts as I did so. She was probably a very nice person if you got to know her outside her job, and certainly wasn't responsible for my poor temper. But then again, considering the sort of day I'd had, and how I felt, a bad temper was only reasonable, and at least I was only thinking things, not saying them.

The corridor was a long one. Long and high, with polished wood panels, parquet flooring, large paintings (mostly reproductions of Constable or Turner, or knock-offs done in their style), and some uncomfortable-looking chairs here and there. I tried to imagine it as a school, with kids going to and from lessons. It wouldn't have looked so grand then, with the floors scuffed and the panels scratched.

I'd never been able to get a clear idea of how many pupils the school had had, or even of what sort of school it was. One version I'd heard was that it was a charitable institution for orphaned children, many of them from other countries. Another, that it was a special private school for the offspring of rich families who had – as we would now say – "special needs". Or, less diplomatically, a place where family embarrassments could be hidden away. Whatever the real truth was had been kept hidden: Coren Hall School had been a shrouded place. Churchill's phrase – "a riddle wrapped in a mystery inside an enigma" – fitted it perfectly.

Doors and corridors opened off the main passageway at regular intervals, most of them with discreet little brass plaques to assist guests: "Drawing Room" – "Games Room" – "Sauna and Massage Parlour" – "Orangery". I peered hopefully down passages and around doors, not knowing what I was looking for but irrationally certain that there was something to be found.

Irrational or not, I was right.

The doors at the end of the corridor were open. As I came close enough to see through, I felt the hairs on the back of my head rising. They really did. And the air seemed to get thicker and harder to breathe, while the walls and side passages faded out of my vision so that I barely noticed the plaque announcing that this was the "Small Dining Room". All my attention was focused on the space that opened up in front of me. A room I had never been in before, but which I recognized instantly.

I stood in the doorway and tuned out the extraneous noise. The tables and chairs, the small group of people chatting over tea and cakes over by the windows, the man on his own to my left, sipping daintily at a cup. The waiter coming towards me, his smile of welcome turning slightly bemused as I just stood there and ignored him.

With those elements mentally deleted, it became clear. The proportions were the same, the tall bay window at the far end was the same.

I had seen this room before. In the painting Sir Arthur had shown me.

A discreet cough from the waiter brought me back to the present. "Will madam be taking afternoon tea?" he enquired.

"Er – yes, madam will," I confirmed. He showed me to a table, provided a menu, and after a few minutes of perusal, I ordered something that would be gentle on my throat and not too harsh on my bank account.

The chattering group finished their tea and left. The solitary man was reading something on his mobile, while the waiter – having served me with commendable speed and efficiency – busied himself with clearing away the tea things. I was left to consider the room over a three-tier stack of crust-less sandwiches, cream cakes, and a pot of tea. Far too much for one person, but I was hungry and ready to make an effort.

I had hoped to find something, expected it even. But actually doing so was still a surprise. I fumbled for my phone to check the pictures I had taken.

The phone was wrong. The buttons weren't where they should be. I stared at it blankly for a moment before realizing that I had Graham's phone.

I remembered the rush with which I'd packed a bag for him. I'd actually put it in the car before realizing that I'd got his charger, but not the phone. I'd gone back inside, found it, and put it in my handbag. Then, at the hospital, I'd forgotten to take it out again.

So that meant I'd have to make another trip to the hospital! Well, I was going back to see him tomorrow anyway. It could wait until then. He probably wouldn't be needing it overnight.

I slipped it into a pocket, where I was less likely to forget it. Then I fumbled some more, found my own mobile, and scrolled through the photos.

Yes, it was definitely the same room. In much better condition now than shown in the painting, but the same.

I thought through the implications. The unknown artist had been here – here at Coren Hall! Probably when it was a school. And he had been at the farmhouse. He'd known both places: the link between them was established beyond all doubt. It was not so much a revelation as a confirmation. I'd always suspected it.

And it also made a link between Coren Hall School and Sir Arthur, I realized. He may not have recognized the depiction in the painting, but it had been a long time ago – and he had admitted that it was familiar. Moreover, the artist clearly thought that Sir

Arthur should know it. The note had talked about a trip down memory lane, hadn't it?

Well, actually (I corrected myself), it had said specifically "Memory Lane". Which Sir Arthur had thought might be a reference to his first painting – something so far in the past and so obscure that very few people would know about it. Apart from Sir Arthur himself, of course.

And, perhaps, anyone he had told about it?

My head was spinning with the abundance of new thoughts and new possibilities. This could be crucial information, I realized, and David Macrae should know about it as soon as possible.

I finished off a cream bun – the fresh cream did seem to be good for my throat – and called him.

It went to voicemail. I considered calling June, she should probably be back at work by now – but then again, perhaps not. I smiled, remembering Rob and the ring. It might be that June had taken a little more time off to deal with personal matters. In any case, there was no need to bother either of them, it wasn't that urgent.

Instead I sent Macrae a text. *"Re. painting sent to Sir A. Location is a room in Coren Hall! Interesting implications, call me when you can."*

And returned to enjoying my afternoon tea.

I was just using the last of the pot to wash down my next dose of painkillers, when my phone rang. Not David, June.

"Hi, June – have you got any news to tell me, then?"

"What? Yes. Yes I've got news."

She sounded grim. Not like someone about to announce their engagement. Had something gone disastrously wrong? But she was still speaking.

"The DI got your text. Where are you now?"

"At the hotel. Coren Hall Hotel, that is. Why? Where's David?"

"Who? Oh, Jimmy. He's in a meeting. Listen, Sandra, you've got to get out of there!"

"Get out? Why? I've only just got here and I need to look around a bit more…"

"No! Don't look around, don't do anything! I'm sending a police car for you. Be ready!"

"A police car?" I had a vision of being bundled down the steps into a marked-up vehicle, with blue lights flashing and guests watching. "No! No need for that. I've got my own car. I'll leave immediately. But – what's going on, June?"

There was a brief pause. I could hear background noises – an office it sounded like. A very busy office. Frantically busy, even.

"OK. Sandra, we found out today that the hotel, the village, the farmhouse – the entire estate in fact – is owned by Sir Arthur. Was owned by him, that is. Though Jonathan Carr seems to have been in charge and responsible for all the work done in recent years."

"Oh, I see. But surely that doesn't mean I'm in danger, does it? I'm sure not from Sir Arthur, anyway, and even Carr wouldn't do anything in a public place – would he?"

Another long pause. One which to my mind had ominous tones.

"Right. What I'm going to tell you – keep to yourself. Absolutely to yourself, you understand, Sandra? The press doesn't know yet; we want to keep them out of it as long as possible. There's going to be a media circus when it hits."

"When what hits? What are you talking about, June?"

"Sir Arthur is dead."

I felt myself gaping.

"What? How? I mean – was he ill? Or an accident?"

"No. None of that. Sandra, he was murdered. Shot. Sometime last night, or early this morning."

"Shot – but who? Why?"

"Obviously we're working on that. But our immediate concern is that Jonathan Carr has disappeared. No trace of him anywhere. And in view of recent events, we're very concerned for your safety. We've got a police officer at the hospital for your husband, but you're in a very exposed position just now – that's why you have to leave there immediately!"

"OK. Right – I understand. I'm leaving. Ah – where to? The police station?"

"Yes. Oh, on second thoughts, perhaps better not. It's a madhouse here at the moment; you'd end up sitting in an interview room all night."

"Well, I can't go home. There's friends I could go to – but if Carr knows about them, I can't put them at risk like that." I thought of Yvonne, who would certainly take me in no matter what. But Sir Arthur had been shot! And perhaps by his own nephew. I couldn't expose her to that danger. "Haven't you got some sort of safe house?"

"We're the police, not MI5!" she retorted. "OK. I understand what you're saying. You need somewhere that has no connection with your work or normal life at all."

"Yes."

"Right then. Go to 24 Northumberland Avenue. Near Eastgate. Have you got a satnav?"

I confirmed that I had, and she added a postcode. "Go there and wait outside. Text me and I'll come and meet you."

"I'll do that. But whose house is it?"

"Mine. Not a problem. I've got a history of taking in strays. Ask Rob. Got to go now."

She broke the connection.

Mechanically, my mind numb, I put away the phone, picked up my handbag, and left the room. Back along the corridor to reception.

The same girl was still at the desk. "Ah, Mrs Deeson – I've had your bag put in your room."

"Thank you. Can you get it back again, please?"

She looked puzzled. "I'm sorry, is there a problem?"

I nodded. "I'm afraid so. I've had to change my plans. I won't be staying."

"Oh. Well, I'm afraid a cancellation at this stage…"

"Yes, right, whatever. I'm sorry, but I must hurry. Please can I have the bill? And my bag?"

She seemed to take it personally, but got over her upset and produced a bill which made afternoon tea the most expensive meal I'd ever had. My bag was returned, and I was back outside, in my car, and driving off again.

It was dark. I concentrated on the road, and the satnav, especially as I got into an unfamiliar part of town. Especially as I was trying not to think about Sir Arthur. About that charming, enthusiastic, brilliant man. About his latest painting, his vision of past and future drawn together, which would never now be finished.

My eyes were blurring. I had to pull over and wipe them before I could continue.

Could Carr really have shot his uncle? I knew he was unpleasant, a bit of a bully. And I could even believe he'd committed the murder in the library. But his own uncle?

And the answer was, yes, of course he could have. Why not? History is full of family members killing each other.

I reached the address, a well-kept semi, and sent the text. June sent back that she was on her way, and sure enough, pulled up behind me ten minutes later.

She gave me a long look as I got out of the car. "I hate to say this, Sandra, but frankly, you look like. . ."

"Yes, I know!" I was getting good at interrupting people. "It's been a rough week." I glanced down at her hands, and sure enough, something glittered that I hadn't seen before. Not on her finger, anyway. "Interesting week for you, though."

June looked at the ring with an expression I couldn't quite decipher. Like she was thrilled by it, but wondering why she was. "Yes, certainly that. Can you believe Rob's timing? Right in the middle of a murder investigation!"

"If you want sensitivity, you'll have to look further I'm afraid."

She grinned. "If I wanted sensitivity, I wouldn't bother with men at all. Come on, let's get you settled down inside. I'm afraid I'm going to have to leave you on your own for a while and get back to the station. The news has got out, the media are all over it, and we desperately need to get some traction on this. So far, there's no sign of Carr and nothing useful from forensics."

She unlocked the door, let me in, and gave me a quick tour. "Help yourself to whatever's in the kitchen. The bed in the spare room's made up, just make yourself at home, OK? I can't say when I'll be back, probably late."

She left with a final admonition to keep the door locked. I dumped myself down in the living room. It wasn't as luxurious as Coren Hall, but it was comfortable. I glanced round. Clearly, June liked things neat, without being obsessive about it. However, there were indications that someone with a more relaxed attitude to life had been here: the jacket tossed onto a chair looked like Rob's. They'd have to find their own point of balance, as all serious relationships must.

The TV control had slipped down a side cushion, which I guessed was another indication of Rob's presence. I worked out how to switch it on, and found a news channel.

Sir Arthur's death was the third item, right behind an international crisis and a political scandal. Not much actually in the item: some old footage of him in his heyday, a map showing Coren Hall Village, and the bare bones of the story: "Police confirmed that Sir Arthur had died from gunshot wounds at his home..." etc.

But then, "Our Arts Editor looks back on his life and work."

I sat up and paid close attention, as the picture switched to the inside of an art gallery, with the reporter standing in front of what was clearly one of Sir Arthur's portraits. I even recognized it – a member of the Royal Family, but not in the full regalia. Instead, she was wearing mud-stained country clothing, sitting on a low stone wall, and apparently drinking something from a thermos. She was gazing out of the picture with a look of amused irony. I could almost hear her saying, "What? Surprised to see me looking like a normal person?"

"Sir Arthur Templeton was perhaps the most famous portraitist of his generation," began the reporter. "Known internationally for his paintings of the rich, the famous, and the great: known too for his ability to look past that wealth and fame and greatness and show something deeper and perhaps more real in his subjects."

The picture faded to a montage of other Templeton portraits, with particular points highlighted by the commentary, before coming to a grainy black-and-white photo of a scruffy schoolboy accompanied by a pretty but tired-looking young woman.

"But Arthur Templeton was not a native of the high-flying and glamorous world that he came to both inhabit and depict with such skill. He was born Arthur Waterhouse, in very humble circumstances which soon became outright poverty when his father, a farm labourer, died. His mother moved into town to find work, and it was there that she met James Templeton, a widower and the owner of the factory where she was employed. Both she and Arthur took on the Templeton name, a family including an older brother and sister, and a much more comfortable life with better prospects."

The reporter went on to talk about Arthur's early signs of talent, his attendance at art school, and the contacts he made there which led to his first commissions and the beginning of his rise to fame. But – apart from noting that there was no mention of "Memory Lane" – I tuned out of that part. My mind was full of these new revelations about Sir Arthur's past.

"Older brother and sister." Presumably that meant that Carr was the son of Sir Arthur's half-sister or half-brother. Did that make him a half-nephew?

The reporter had moved on to interview one of Sir Arthur's contemporaries, an artist whom I'd never heard of. He seemed to be aware that no one had heard of him, and was bitter about it. A poor choice for an interviewee, I thought. Probably the first person they could find at short notice who had known Arthur well enough to talk about him: but while saying all the right things, he still managed to give the impression that Arthur's success was more due to social skills than to artistic talent.

"Catty little man," I said, resentfully.

"Of course," the reporter was saying, "one of the things Sir Arthur was known for was that he never signed his work. Why was that, do you think?"

The interviewee, a flamboyantly dressed figure with a ridiculous goatee beard over a double chin, waved a hand dismissively. "Oh, that's what he liked people to think. It was part of his mystique, as it were. But the truth is he did sign everything. Even his rough sketches, would you believe! Though the dear man did love to talk about how recognizable his work was, he never quite had the courage of his convictions, and he always put his initials in there somewhere. For instance, look here..."

He pointed to a part of the royal portrait behind them, and the camera zoomed in on the indicated section. "Can you make that out? Do you see just there in the detail of the stone wall? That mark on the surface makes an 'A' and the shadow next to it, where the blocks join, that's the 'T'. Arthur Templeton!"

The camera pulled back to show the unknown artist looking insufferably pleased with himself. "There's probably not more than half a dozen people in the world know about that!" he proclaimed. "I'm one of the very few people Sir Arthur told, and he swore me to secrecy! But I don't suppose that matters now, does it?"

The reporter wrapped up and handed back to the studio, where things moved on to sport. I switched it off.

Hidden signatures.

I remembered Sir Arthur looking so intently at one part of my painting – and his sudden shock at something he saw there. Could that have been a signature – one concealed in the same way?

Not Sir Arthur's own, of course. But someone who knew him – perhaps had been taught by him? Someone who had learned about his signatures and had used the same idea?

If it was a signature or initial that Sir Arthur had recognized, that might explain the shock.

I scrolled through the pictures on my mobile until I found the ones of my painting. The original was – I hoped – safely back at home: I'd put it near my laptop, in the office. Well clear of the fire-damaged area. I was tempted to jump in my car and go for it, but dismissed the idea. I wasn't up for any more driving, and June would not be pleased if I left the safety of her house on a whim.

So I did what I could on my phone, zooming in until the quality of the picture began to deteriorate, then slowly scanning across the surface, looking for something like a signature or an initial.

It was slow going. The resolution of the image simply wasn't good enough for such close examination. There were various blurs and marks in the shadows that could have been letters – but nothing that I was sure of.

I sat back, my eyes aching. And my head, and my throat again. The painkillers were wearing off.

Where exactly had Sir Arthur been looking? I struggled to remember. In truth, I hadn't really noticed. I'd been more concerned about getting out before Carr arrived.

But it seemed to me that perhaps he'd been looking more at the centre of the painting. In the lit area around the flower.

I went back to searching.

And just there – in the angle between leaf and stalk – was that a "V"? And if so, then next to it, the fine pattern on the leaf surface made a "T".

T – V.

I blinked, and rubbed my eyes and looked again. The T shape was surely anomalous. The veins on a leaf didn't run that way. Or did they? It was a long time since I'd looked at a leaf.

The V was just the natural shape. But the way it was shaded made it stand out. I looked at that part again. The shading continued down the other side of the stalk. So it could be an "N".

Or it could be my eyes, or my imagination, or just noise on a low-resolution image blown up too far.

All the same, I found myself wondering who "TN" could have been.

And had it been on the other painting? Sir Arthur had been looking at it when I'd left. What had he muttered?

It might have been a name. It might have been anything.

I found the pictures of the room in Coren Hall and went over them in the same detailed way.

That – there, in the shadows cast by the easel – wasn't that a "TN"?

It could be. I wasn't sure. My headache was getting worse.

I sat back and closed my eyes. Tomorrow I'd try to get home to take a closer look at the original. And perhaps Macrae could get the painting from Sir Arthur's house and look at that one, though I supposed it would be part of the crime scene.

Still thinking about tomorrow, I dozed off, and didn't wake up until June came back in.

"Hello! You can use the bed, you know!" She grinned as I peered at her through blurry eyes, trying to remember where I was.

"Oh. June? Um – what time is it?"

"Half past eleven. I've just got off. Things are pretty much at a standstill for now, so Jimmy's sent us all home so as to be bright-eyed and bushy-tailed for tomorrow. Which we hope will be a big day!"

"Why?" My brain was slowly coming together. "What's happening tomorrow?"

"I've no idea. We always hope for a big day, though. Sometimes we're right. I'm going to have a hot chocolate and get to bed. Do you want one?"

"Yes. Please. Definitely. My mouth tastes like something died in there. And I'm overdue a painkiller or two."

"Coming up, then!"

June clattered around in the kitchen for a while before returning with two steaming mugs. I took mine gratefully, wrapped my fingers round the hot china, sniffed the rich aroma, and finally took a slow sip. Hot, thick, sweet. "Heaven in a mug," I said. "Thanks."

"You're welcome. Can't beat a cup of chocolate to unwind with."

We sat together for a while in companionable silence. "How's the investigation going?" I asked eventually.

June shook her head. "No sign of Carr, no sign of Emily, no leads, no clues. Rather not talk about it if you don't mind. I need to try to switch off from work for a while."

"Of course. So – tell me what else has been happening in your life, then." I looked pointedly at her finger.

"Oh, this!" June looked at it herself, examining it curiously as if it was the first time she'd seen it. "Rob gave it me – was it just yesterday? Yes. Yesterday."

"You seem surprised."

"Well, I was. I mean, I know we've been heading this way for months. But somehow, it was still a bit of a shock. Perhaps I didn't think he'd ever get round to it. He's a bit – what shall I say? – relaxed about life? Not much sense of urgency?"

"Any, er…?" I broke off, trying to find a more tactful way to put my question, but June had already realized what I was thinking.

"Second thoughts?"

"Sorry. Not my business."

"No, it's OK. We do seem so different sometimes. Chalk and cheese. Like I said, he's so laid-back… and I can be a bit – the opposite, I suppose."

"So what convinced you, then?"

She was silent for a few moments, thinking. "You know how we met? After Laney Grey died? Of course you do, you were involved as well."

"Yes, I remember. As I recall, you saved his life."

"And he saved mine! But… there was this moment, when I thought he was about to die, when I just felt that if he did, I would die with him. Or that something irreplaceable would have gone out of my life." She threw up her hands in frustration. "I'm not sure how to say it. The words just don't do it."

"It's OK, June. I understand what you mean."

She gave a shy little laugh, and glanced at me in a way I'd never seen before. And I realized that what I was seeing was a depth of her that rarely surfaced. A vulnerability and uncertainty that lived inside the confident, professional young woman.

"The thing is, I barely knew Rob then. We'd only met a few days before. But he was already the most important person in the world to me. And I don't get it, Sandra. I just don't get it."

"Don't try to get it, June. Understanding is overrated. Some things go deeper than we can think. Love is one of them."

"So what're you saying? Follow your heart?" She grinned, making a joke of it, cloaking herself again.

I grinned back. "Well, don't switch your brain off entirely! You're going to need that as well. Just don't overthink it."

"Thanks. I'll remember that." She took a long swallow from the cooling chocolate. "Any other advice?" And before I could answer, she stopped me with a raised hand. "Nothing trite and obvious, please, Sandra. I know all about needing to talk and needing to listen and all that stuff. Tell me something real. Something from yourself."

"OK." I drank some more chocolate, thinking. "OK. Something I've only learned very recently. Watch out for guilt. It gets in the way. And it doesn't matter if it's real guilt or false guilt. Once you accept that narrative, once you start living in it, the guilt shuts down communications and colours relationships and…" I shrugged. "Yes. It gets in the way."

She looked at me and frowned. "So what are you saying? That you've had to forgive Graham something – or that he's had to forgive you?"

"Both of those. But the real problem is forgiving myself."

She finished off her drink and stared into the bottom of the cup for a moment. "Yes. I think I know what you mean." Glancing up, she caught my eye. "Thanks, Sandra. Well…" She stood up and stretched, working some kinks out of her shoulders. "I need to get some sleep. Briefing's at eight sharp tomorrow morning, and Jimmy wants to come round here to go over a few things before then."

"This secondment to CID seems to be working out well for you."

"Yes. Jimmy's indicated that he'd like me to make it permanent. But I'm not sure. I was pretty comfortable in uniform. And I've got a lot more on my mind at the moment!" She waved her ring finger at me. "Too much happening all at once! Goodnight, Sandra."

After June had gone, I took the mugs through to the kitchen and rinsed them out before heading upstairs myself. My head was still buzzing, but I was too tired to process the thoughts.

June's spare room smelled gently of lavender. I put my mobile on charge before I got into bed, and noticed that there was a stack of messages waiting to be answered. I scanned through quickly, but there was nothing from the hospital. The rest could wait.

I hadn't even checked my Word for the Day. I took a quick glance. "Sinistrous", meaning "giving the impression that something bad will happen; ominous".

"Too late," I muttered to myself. "It's already happened."

I slipped between crisp, fresh sheets and into deep, soft sleep.

DAY 7: QUONDAM

I woke up to the sound of June clattering around in the bathroom. I'm sure she wasn't doing it deliberately, but when you live alone you can make as much noise as you like, and it's hard to break that habit. Especially if you're half asleep yourself.

I could have gone back to sleep, but I wanted to be up in time to phone the hospital early on. So I forced myself out of the warm bed and, lacking my dressing gown, put the tracksuit back on. I'd packed it, reluctantly, as it was one of the few things I had that didn't smell smoky. But at least the colours helped to wake me up.

While June finished in the bathroom, I revisited my messages and started deleting the ones I didn't need to answer. The Word for the Day, I noticed, was "Dunderhead".

"Great start," I muttered. "Insulted by my own phone."

It was a boring word, anyway. Everyone knew what a dunderhead was. I'd have to find something better than that.

June finished, I made use of the facilities, and then followed the smell of coffee downstairs, to find June and David Macrae poring over a map on the table. They glanced up as I came in; I was sure that he blinked as he took in my outfit.

"Good morning, Sandra," he said. "You're looking... bright today."

"Coffee's in the kitchen," June told me. "Decaf or the poisonous stuff, which I've had to start keeping in for Rob. Until I can get him off it. I've had some toast, but there's cereal in the cupboard."

I just nodded, speech being beyond me until I was caffeinated, and headed for the kitchen and the real stuff. "Thanks, Rob," I said to myself as I sipped on it and returned to the living room.

"What's happening, then?" I asked as I entered. "Anything you can tell me?"

Macrae shrugged, and indicated the map. "We've got some possible sightings of the Porsche, but nothing confirmed as yet. We were hoping to see some sort of pattern developing, which might tell us where he's away to, but if there is one, I'm not seeing it."

"Neither can I," I admitted, glancing over his shoulder. "I'm finding it hard to believe. That Sir Arthur's dead – and that his own nephew could have killed him! Though I suppose that sort of thing happens all the time?"

"Most murders are committed by people who knew their victim," June confirmed. "Friends and family. But the motives are usually clear-cut. Jealousy, frustration, abusive relationships, that sort of thing. It's not so obvious in this case."

"I'm thinking that I may have provided the trigger that set him off," Macrae said grimly. "It was a big mistake to send you in to see Sir Arthur. What he saw in your painting – and perhaps in his as well – may have led him into a confrontation with Carr. And now you've confirmed the link between the paintings and Coren Hall – thanks for that, by the way – and therefore with the farmhouse as well, it makes it more likely in my mind that this is all tied in with what happened thirty years ago."

"Where was Carr back then?" I wondered aloud.

"Australia." Macrae fished in his briefcase, brought out a cardboard file, and opened it up on top of the map. "This is the result of all the research we've done so far. Our man Sir Arthur had a sad start to life. His father died when he was young: 1942. He was just five years old."

"There was a feature on the news about him last night," I remembered. "Wasn't his father a farm labourer?"

"They were quick off the mark," June commented. "But they got that bit right. Only John Waterhouse didn't stay on the farm. When the war started he joined up. The army sent him out to Egypt, and he was killed at El Alamein. Which was bad enough for his wife and kid, but their home was a farm cottage. After he died, they had to move out. So she came here, looking for work, and got a job at Templeton Engineering. Seems she caught the boss's eye. James Templeton was a widower, with two children – Nigel and Mary. They got married in 1948, when Arthur was eleven. At that time Nigel would have been fifteen, Mary fourteen."

"Good move for Arthur and his mum," I said.

"Aye, it was," Macrae agreed. "It seems like Templeton Engineering had done well out of the war, and young Arthur got his first taste of the good things in life. Big house, better food and clothes, good schooling – he was on his way."

"James was quite a bit older than his wife, though," June continued. "He died in 1955, with no further children. The business wasn't doing too well by then, once all the war contracts had finished, so it was sold off, and the family went their various ways. Nigel went into education, and was teaching at a fairly prestigious private school. Mary married an Aussie and moved over there with him. She became Mary Carr, and they had one son – Jonathan."

"Ah, so he really is Sir Arthur's nephew. I had wondered about that."

"Yes, it's genuine," Macrae confirmed. "But there's more. Nigel Templeton also married, but it didn't work out well. The marriage broke down within a couple of years, with one son, Geraint, who seems to have been passed backwards and forwards between the two of them for a while, before his mother disappeared off the scene entirely. Nigel wasn't doing well in other areas either. He lost his job at the private school – we don't know why – and was in some difficulties. Fortunately for them, Arthur's painting really began to take off about then, and that may have given Nigel an opportunity."

He sorted through the file and pulled out a black-and-white photograph. "This was taken in the sixties. You'll recognize Sir Arthur, unveiling one o' his paintings at some big society event. But do you see the man standing next to him? That's Nigel Templeton."

I peered at the heavily built figure. "I think I know him! I saw him once – at Coren Hall! He chased me off, threatened to set the dogs on me!"

"Coren Hall, you say?" Macrae caught June's eye. "Well, now that's interesting. You know that the Hall and the entire estate was owned by Sir Arthur?"

"Yes, June told me."

"Right. Well, his name was hidden behind a wall of paperwork, but some of our bright lads and lasses managed to dig through and get the story. The way it happened, we think, was that sometime in the late sixties, while Sir Arthur – just Arthur then, of course – was still a rising star, he came into ownership. It may have been in payment of a debt for one of his portraits; we don't know. But if that was the case, he got a bad deal, because the Hall was in a poor state. Hadn't been lived in for some years, it seems.

"But then a school opened up in the old building. It was set up as a charity for orphans, but though all the paperwork is complete, there isn't much real information to find. Arthur Templeton's on the Board of Trustees, and there's a headmaster named –"

"Nigel Templeton?" I suggested, but Macrae shook his head. "There's not a sniff of Nigel anywhere in the paperwork. The head is named as a Marcus Sowerby, who apparently was once a teacher in the state system, but none of the other names seem to have any history at all."

"I spoke to someone called Hargrove? Called himself deputy head?"

"Aye, I remember you mentioning it. The name does appear in the paperwork somewhere, but no other details."

"What about the son? Geraint, did you say his name was? There were two people there when I was chased off – Nigel, I presume, and a younger man who looked a bit like him."

"I haven't seen him mentioned. Have you, June?"

She shook her head. "No. As far as we can make out, the only definitely real person associated with Coren Hall School is Sir Arthur. And there's no other information anywhere. No staff lists, no pupil lists – nothing. If they ever existed, they were removed long ago. Or doctored into uselessness. We suspected that Nigel might have been involved in the school, and probably Geraint as well, but you've just given us the first confirmation of that."

I remembered my discovery of last night. "Have the initials T-N come up anywhere? Only I think I may have found a signature on those paintings." I explained my thinking, and showed the relevant section of the painting on my phone. "I'll have a closer look on my painting as soon as I can. Any chance of getting a look at Sir Arthur's?"

"Probably not," said June. "Because we've not been able to find it yet. There seems to have been an attempt to make it look like a burglary – windows smashed, stuff thrown about – but nothing appears to be missing. Except for that painting."

"Well, that's interesting in itself," I mused. "You know, I got the impression that Sir Arthur had been keeping it hidden. Hidden from his nephew, perhaps? It may be that Jonathan didn't know about it until my visit."

"Aye, that's possible. Something else to be thinking about." Macrae looked into his cup, found it empty, and put it aside. "Well then, we know there was some sort of school running there: there were a few mentions of it in the newspapers, in regards to Sir Arthur's involvement in charitable work. According to some articles, he regularly went there to teach painting to the pupils. He's quoted as saying that there was some real talent to be found amongst them. What we think was happening is that Nigel was the person running it, but he was keeping a very low profile, which suggests that something was going on there which he didn't want to be connected with."

"And Sir Arthur? How much did he know?"

"Well, that's the question I would have liked to ask him. But from the fact that he was the only person publicly and legally associated with it, I'd guess not much. He had too much to lose if he was linked to something criminal or even just unsavoury. I'm thinking that they used him as a figurehead, but kept him away from whatever it was that they were really doing there."

A mobile rang. Macrae fished in his pocket, took out his phone, and looked at the screen. "DCI," he said to June. "Sorry, Sandra. I have to take this. June'll tell you the rest."

He left the room, and June took over the pile of paper.

"So that brings us up to 1985," she said, and pulled out an A4 sheet. It was, I saw, a computer printout of the original news story. "*Body Found Hanging in Abandoned Farmhouse*" the headline screamed at me. I hid a slight shudder.

"I know about 1985," I assured her.

"Yes, but it's interesting to look at this again in the light of our new information. See this for example…"

Another newspaper article. "*Sir Arthur Templeton Cancels!*" ran the headline. I quickly scanned the text.

"*Britain's best-known portraitist, Sir Arthur Templeton, has unexpectedly cancelled the exhibition he was due to hold in London. The event was intended to showcase some of his most famous works from the past two decades, as well as a number of new pieces. However, it will not now be taking place. Sir Arthur has given no reason for this, and cannot be contacted for a statement. It is believed that he may be travelling abroad.*"

Those were the facts; the rest of the article was just padding in the form of speculation and quotes from people who didn't know anything.

"Of course! I hadn't made the connection before – but that wasn't long after I found the body!"

"There was no reason to make a connection if you didn't know that Sir Arthur owned all that land – which was information well hidden. And that was the last anyone saw of him for nearly thirty years." June produced a further printout, this time from a website.

"The Northdene Art Club is proud to announce that Sir Arthur Templeton, one of the greatest artists of the past century, has agreed to become the new Patron of the Art Club. Sir Arthur has recently returned to this country after many years of travelling abroad, and has expressed a desire to become involved in local art and with local artists. We will therefore be changing our name to the Templeton Art Club, and we are delighted to be honoured in this way. We also welcome his nephew, Mr Jonathan Carr, who has agreed to take on the role of Club Secretary."

There was a bit more, mostly about Sir Arthur's past triumphs. It had been posted by the club chairman, Claude Ferrers-Manton, about two years previously.

"Yes, I remember this. There was a bit of a stir in the media about Sir Arthur coming back, but he didn't do anything publicly, so they soon lost interest."

"Right. Though apparently there's been talk of him putting on an exhibition soon. He may have been intending to announce it at the library." June closed the file and sat back. "What we think may have happened is that Sir Arthur, in his travels, finally washed up in Australia and dropped in to see his family. Now his brother-in-law, Carr Senior, started out as a builder, and did quite well for himself. Had his own firm, was involved in some fair-sized projects. Jonathan is following in the family business, and when they found out that Sir Arthur still owned a chunk of real estate over here, what could be more natural than to suggest to the old man that Jonathan should come over and make a bit of money out of it? Apparently he entered the country about three years ago, and got things moving, investing some funds to get the Hall and the farmhouse renovated, and started building the village. When things were well under way, Sir Arthur followed on and settled in."

"And now…" I felt tears pricking at my eyes, and stopped, choked. "Sorry. It's just sinking in. I only just met him, and he was such a charming, friendly… such a vivid person…"

June leaned across and held my hand. "I know. Believe me, I know."

"Sorry. With all you see, you must get hardened to it."

"Yes. That's the danger."

Macrae came back in. "We've got to go, June. Briefing in thirty minutes, and the DCI wants us to go in with him to bring the Command Team up to speed. So we're away! I'll catch you later, Sandra. Come in my car, June; there's a couple of things to go over before we get there." He was gathering up his map and papers as he spoke, and was out of the door.

June stood up to follow him. "There's a spare key in the cupboard next to the front door. Come and go as you need to, but stay safe. I think Carr is long gone, but keep your eyes open and call me or Jimmy if you see anything dodgy, OK?"

Then she was gone as well, leaving me alone in the house, with not even Brodie to give comfort.

No use moping. I'd see Brodie later – after I'd been to see Graham. Which reminded me to give him a call. Or at least, give his ward a call.

Unfortunately, he wasn't available. "With the doctor just now," the nurse said. "I'm afraid he had an uncomfortable night. He had difficulty breathing and his air passages seem to be inflamed. Nothing to worry about, but we're trying to get him more comfortable. They'll be taking him down for more scans as soon as the doctor's finished with him, and we'll know more then."

He gently but firmly discouraged me from rushing straight over there. "You won't be able to go in with him anyway. And we're trying to keep him from talking as much as possible. Why don't you call back about midday?"

With my plans for the morning ruined, I rummaged through June's cupboards for some breakfast, and found porridge. Good comfort food, especially as it was looking like a cold, damp, and generally grey day. No matter, the porridge warmed me through and the tracksuit provided more than enough colour.

I went back to working my way through the messages on my phone, which included three from Yvonne, deleting the spam, and sending back general reassurances to the others. That took up an hour or so. I washed up, sat back, and twiddled my thumbs.

I'd meant to ask June or David if they'd made any progress on finding the dead artist's studio, but things had been too rushed. At the moment, their priority was obviously finding Jonathan Carr – if they could ask him some questions, it might solve a lot of problems.

Still, it would be useful to find that studio: the place where my painting and Sir Arthur's had probably both come from. And perhaps there would be copies or prints of the missing exhibition paintings. If there was a reason for taking them apart from their monetary value, then a visit to the studio might reveal that. Finding the place might not be a priority, but it could only help the investigation.

Of course, several days of intensive police searching hadn't found it, so how would I?

I did have a few clues. My pictures of the paintings for a start – but I had gone over them till my head ached. And there was the note to me – also well studied. A pity Sir Arthur hadn't kept his note to compare with it. What had it said?

I struggled to remember the exact words. Something like *"Enjoy your trip down memory lane."* Only it was "Memory Lane" in capitals, referring to Sir Arthur's first painting. First painting to be sold, that is. And there had been an invitation to *"Come and visit"*.

But visit where?

Whoever had sent that note – and I was thinking that it must have been Emily, probably on behalf of the artist – wanted Sir Arthur to come and see them. But only Sir Arthur. The invitation was deliberately obscure. A clue that only he would understand. Something in the reference to Memory Lane.

Of course, it couldn't be as obvious as an actual "Memory Lane", could it?

I pulled out my laptop, found June's router and Wi-Fi key, and got onto the internet. A quick search confirmed that although there were plenty of songs, bands, companies, and websites called "Memory Lane", there was no actual street of that name. Not in the UK, anyway.

So what street had Sir Arthur actually painted, then? "The street where I lived," he'd said.

His first home would have been the farm labourer's cottage. He would only have been a few years old when he and his mother left there, but perhaps he'd gone back for a visit. Where had it been, though?

Back to the internet.

There was a lot about Sir Arthur online. Most of the more recent posts were, of course, concerned with his death. Others were critical evaluations of his work. But at least one had a lot of details about his life, including reams of salacious gossip from his glory days. A skim read of all his supposed exploits left me wondering how he'd ever found time to paint – but of course, it was just gossip.

Some real facts were included. Such as that he had been born in March 1937 in the village of Sharnham Cross.

But Sharnham Cross was gone. It had been obliterated by new housing back in the sixties. All that was left of the old village was the church and the pub – both listed buildings. No farms, no labourer's cottages, no trace of Sir Arthur's past.

What about when he and his mother moved into the town?

No details on that. One researcher said that they had "lived in the poorest and meanest area", but that didn't narrow it down much.

There was a lot more information about the latter part of Arthur's youth, after he'd become a Templeton. Even a picture of the large detached house they had moved into. "The Limes." Not very original, but accurate enough, from the picture attached. It seemed that the house still stood, and was still surrounded by lime trees. But it didn't fit in with Sir Arthur's description of "Memory Lane" as "rows of terraced houses".

Dead end. I went and got a cup of coffee.

Arthur's mother had found work at Templeton Engineering. Ordinary people didn't do long commutes in those days, so she probably lived nearby. A bus ride, perhaps – or even within walking distance? Where had Templeton had his premises, I wondered?

Back to the laptop, and more research, this time on local history sites. The name Templeton came up in a few places, mostly to do with Sir Arthur himself. But Templeton Engineering appeared on a list of businesses that had operated in the old Delford Mills buildings.

There was a lot of local history connected with Delford Mills.

Back in the early Victorian era, Sir Martin Delford had poured all his money into constructing a vast industrial complex. And, since he also needed workers for his mills, he built streets and streets and streets of slums. Back-to-back houses, they were called. Whole families crammed into a few rooms, whole blocks with a shared toilet.

Keen to recoup his money, Sir Martin skimped as much as possible on the building work, paid as little as possible in wages, and made as much as possible in profits. And the strategy worked – he became very rich indeed, while his workers suffered in conditions that were appalling even by the standards of Victorian England.

He also became seriously obese, suffered badly from gout, and – with ironic justice – died from his overindulgence at the age of forty-five, while many of his employees were struggling to feed their families on his miserable wages.

Delford Mills, however, continued, with some gradual improvements in wages and conditions. In the 1920s a major programme of slum clearance and rebuilding began, replacing the worst of the buildings with more modern terraced housing – including such luxuries as a toilet for each house!

The original business, however, didn't survive the Depression, and various parts of the old factory were sold or rented out to new enterprises. Such as Templeton Engineering.

I found a map of the Delford Mills area from the late forties. Templeton Engineering was right on the northern edge of the site. Very close to some of the worst of the old slum areas. Some streets still had the back-to-back housing – the money had run out before those areas could be rebuilt. They'd had to settle for "renovations".

I felt my excitement building. This fitted perfectly with what I'd already found out.

There was something else as well. Those streets were within a mile of Bromwell Street Library. And what had Sir Arthur said about it?

"I spent more time there than I did at home!"

Well, you would, wouldn't you, if you were a clever lad living in the worst slum in the town? And there had once been a school at the end of Bromwell Street. Probably the closest to that part of Delford Mills.

In my imagination I saw a small boy in ragged clothing walking the mile to school every day and along to the library afterwards. Sitting and reading. I wondered when he'd discovered the art section, and how many hours he might have spent reading about Constable and Turner, Monet and Renoir, Van Gogh and Rembrandt and Vermeer and all the others, looking at the illustrations, catching the vision, dreaming the dream of becoming a painter.

I couldn't help but feel a certain pride in my library, in all libraries, and their impact on the world.

But, back to business. I was confident that I'd narrowed "Memory Lane" down to a small area on the north side of Delford Mills. But that was still a dozen or more streets, hundreds of homes, thousands of people.

DAY 7: QUONDAM

The map helpfully listed all the street names round the Mills, many of them hotlinked to further information. Someone had spent a long time lovingly researching the history of the place. Probably a resident or ex-resident. And the history was certainly colourful, if a little sad. The names of the streets spoke of that.

Murder Row, for example. Where, back in 1849, five people had been stabbed to death in their sleep and their meagre possessions stolen – in three different houses, on three different nights. The murderer was eventually tracked down, proving to be a lodger who had been sleeping in the attic of one of the houses. He had found a way through the roof spaces into the other dwellings, where he had committed his crimes to pay the rent and to supply himself with ale. For which he was quickly hanged.

That was one to put the chills up you, I thought.

What about Soldier Street? The first residents had included several ex-soldiers, it seemed, and the name had followed naturally – no matter what official name it had first been given. There had even been a pub on the corner of the street called The Barracks.

Manatee Lane was originally Sea Cow Lane. Someone had somehow acquired a skeleton that he claimed to be that of a sea cow, and allegedly charged a farthing a time for people to come and view it. During the rebuilding of the 1920s, a zealous official had declared that the correct name for a sea cow was a manatee. Of course, the skeleton was long gone by then.

And Quondam Road?

I knew that word. It had been the Word for the Day a month or so previously. Meaning "former" or "that once was".

It had, it seemed, originally been "King Street". But, again during the 1920s, it had been decided to rename it as there was already a King Street in the town. However, no decision had been made as to what the new name should be. Someone in the planning department – probably the same erudite person who had renamed Sea Cow Lane – had therefore written on the plans "Quondam King Road".

But somewhere along the line the "King" bit had dropped out, and it became simply "Quondam Road" – "Former Road". Of course, not many of the inhabitants would have known about that, or probably cared.

But a bright lad who spent most of his free time in the library might have found out.

"Not bad, for a twelve-year-old boy," Sir Arthur had said. I'd thought he'd meant his painting. But perhaps he'd meant the name. A pun. Memory Lane for Quondam Road. Not bad at all for a twelve-year-old.

"That's it," I said quietly. "That's your Memory Lane, Arthur."

And the person who had given him that picture had known that as well. They had known about Coren Hall, they had known about the farmhouse, and they had known about Memory Lane. And, what's more, they'd wanted him to go there.

Surely, I thought, it would be too much of a coincidence if the artist's studio was on the same street where Arthur had once lived? Unless it was no coincidence at all, but something deliberately planned; if the location had been chosen precisely because of its link with Sir Arthur Templeton.

Somehow, it was part of it all. Part of the murders and the mysteries that spanned the past thirty years. If you could draw a line between them – not a geographical line, but a line between events that connected the body in the farmhouse, the body in the library, Coren Hall, and Sir Arthur – it would somehow intersect with Quondam Road.

In my mind, it was a theory. But deep down, I was certain. Just as I was certain that I was going there.

After all, it wasn't that far. June's house was down in the southern part of town, the hospital was out to the east – but it was still a couple of hours before I could visit Graham. In the meantime, I could nip home, see how Brodie was – maybe go via the library, check on how things were going there – which would put me close enough to Delford Mills for a quick visit to Quondam Road.

Or better yet, I could go straight there. Ten minutes to change back into my Sunday best, fifteen minutes at the most to drive over – I might have found the studio in half an hour!

I should probably tell June or David first, but they were really busy. And there would be no harm in just taking a look.

Dunderhead.

*

Over the course of the twentieth century, Delford Mills followed a course of steady decline. The vast complex had played host to a succession of small businesses and increasingly seedy enterprises, while the poorly maintained buildings decayed around them. Various schemes were proposed to revitalize the area, none with any success.

By the turn of the century, the Mills were a national scandal, a huge blot on the town landscape. Most of the buildings – and a lot of the surrounding housing – had been condemned, but that didn't stop them being inhabited by the poorest and most desperate. Meanwhile, local and national government had argued endlessly about who should pay to do something about it.

The tipping point had come in 2010, when a rave party in one of the old factory buildings got wildly out of hand. A fire had started, half the building had collapsed, and a dozen teenagers died. The headlines were huge, heads rolled, and a consortium of government, council, and business finally found the money to do something about the place. Bulldozers went in, Delford Mills was razed to the ground, the surrounding streets were cleared out and marked for demolition, and a wonderful scale model of the shiny new Delford Mills Reclamation Project was unveiled.

But the Curse of Delford Mills (as the papers called it) struck again. Three months after work had started, it came to a sudden halt, because all the money for it had disappeared – along with several senior members of the project. And that was as far as it got. The rubble-strewn wasteland remained just that, while the addicts and dropouts and those who had fallen through the social security net – or escaped it, from other points of view – drifted back into the area and took up residence in the abandoned houses.

Crime and drugs and deprivation. The Mills' long decline seemed to be almost complete – it was hard to see how much further it could fall.

Just the previous year, Rob Seaton had nearly been murdered there, after a terrifying chase through the ruins. That had prompted a further attempt by the council to seal off the whole area, with fencing put up all round it – at considerable cost and with minimal effectiveness. It didn't keep out anyone who really wanted to get in, but it did mean that I had to drive all the way round the perimeter to get to Quondam Road.

It was an unfamiliar part of town for me, and the satnav, not being up to date with the latest road closures, wasn't much help. Navigating by guesswork, I got onto Market Street, followed it past the Plaza, and then took a left turn. Which brought me eventually to a blocked-off street, so I knew I was close. I backtracked, took another road, and eventually came out onto Queensway.

Queensway was the main route south out of the centre, a wide, fast dual carriageway. It was also the border between Delford Mills and the better parts of town. On my left, I was passing row after row of terraced housing, all brick and asphalt. On the right, separated by four lanes of traffic and a gulf of history, were neat semis surrounded by grass and privet hedges and the occasional tree.

A service road diverged from Queensway to skim the edge of the Mills area, giving me chance to slow down and look at the street names without a furious flashing of lights and blowing of horns from impatient drivers behind me.

"Manatee Lane!" I said aloud. "I'm close!"

And two roads further on, there it was. Quondam Road.

I turned into it, and stopped. This was it. Arthur's boyhood home, and the subject of his first commercially successful painting.

A stiff breeze had sprung up, shredding the clouds and

allowing a little bright sunshine through to show Quondam Road at its best. The two-storey rows of red brick had a mellow glow in that light, though it also showed up flaking paintwork and grimy glass. Perhaps it had been in better condition in his day. Or perhaps he was already seeing it with an artist's eye, looking beyond the obvious and superficial to the human life and social history that had brought the buildings into existence and given them their meaning.

A hundred yards or so down the street, the terraced houses came to an end. A cross alley marked the limit of the 1920s rebuilding. Beyond that towered the three-storey Victorian back-to-backs, bricks blackened with over a century of soot and grime. Even the brightest of sunlight could do nothing for them.

That would have been in Arthur's first painting as well. He would have been fascinated by the juxtaposition of building styles, the contrasting years they represented.

There were a few things that wouldn't have been in his painting though. The row of vehicles down the left of the street – it was too narrow for parking on both sides – wouldn't have been there in his day. I doubted if many working-class people would have owned cars back then. Even now, they were hardly symbols of affluence: mostly rusty, dented, and looking as if they'd been rescued from a scrapyard.

And another thing that Arthur wouldn't have painted was the ten-foot-high chain-link fence that divided the street, cutting off the Victorian slum from the slightly more modern housing.

I drove further down Quondam. It was narrow, the parked cars taking up most of one side and barely leaving room for me to get past. It looked as though I would have to reverse out of it.

Eventually I was able to squeeze into a space between a grey Mondeo with red doors and a rust-streaked Transit with no doors at all. I got out and approached the barrier.

"Are you from the council?"

It wasn't so much a question as a challenge, and it came from a woman leaning in an open doorway across the road. She looked a bit older than me, a bit bigger, and a lot rougher.

"No, I'm not," I assured her. My smart Sunday-best clothes were out of place here. I would have been better off wearing the tracksuit.

"You're police, then."

She said it as a statement and accompanied it with a glare. I took it that she didn't like the police much.

Coincidentally, she was wearing a tracksuit – purple and yellow – underneath her pink dressing gown. She took out a lighter and a packet of cigarettes without diverting her glare.

"No, I'm not police either." I crossed the road towards her, hoping to put the conversation on a better footing than shouting accusations across the street.

She snorted. "Why else would you be down here, then? You're police, council – or social services?"

I shook my head. "I'm a librarian."

That surprised her. So much that her cigarette nearly dropped out of her mouth. "A ruddy librarian? What the hell would a librarian be doing round here?"

"I'm doing a bit of private research. About a famous artist who used to live round here. Do you know anything about that?"

"Research, eh?" She lit up, and took a long drag, settling herself into a more comfortable position against the doorpost. "Does that pay well, doing that sort of thing?"

"Pay well? No, it's not something I'm doing for money."

Her eyes narrowed and her expression hardened. I got the impression that I'd given the wrong answer. "Waste of time then, if there's no money in it."

Finally, I got it. "Well, of course I'm willing to pay for any information you might have."

She nodded, and relaxed a little. "How much?"

I opened my handbag, took out my purse, and delved inside. I wasn't carrying a lot of cash. I pulled out a tenner.

Her expression changed into a beaming smile. "Well, I might know a bit about an artist, now I think about it. And where he lived – him and that girlfriend of his."

"Girlfriend?" My jaw dropped. Arthur had had a girlfriend?

"Oh, so you didn't know about her, then? I can tell you all about that." She reached out her free hand expectantly while taking another lungful of smoke.

She didn't mean Arthur. She would have to be in her eighties at least to remember him living here, and she didn't look that old. She was talking about another artist.

I handed over the tenner. "I'd love to hear about them."

She nodded, slipping the note into her pocket. "Well, the artist bloke – can't tell you his name, never heard it, people round here just called him 'The Artist' – he's been living round here for as long as I can remember. Was holed up in the Mills before they knocked them down, then when they cleared the old houses" – she nodded her head at the barrier – "he found his way in there, with all the dropouts and druggies. Skinny little bloke, looked like he hadn't had a decent meal in his life. Never any trouble, though. Used to come round now and then selling his paintings and drawings. They was pretty good, too. Nearly everyone round here has had something off him at one time or another. I've got a few myself. For a couple of quid, he'd draw your picture, and it was a treat to watch him. A few minutes with paper and pencil and he'd have you dead on, good as a photograph. But he didn't talk much. I don't think I ever heard him say more than two words at a time."

She paused for another smoke and gave a significant glance at my handbag. I gave a similar glance at her pocket where the tenner now resided. She frowned, but carried on.

"Well, a couple of years or so ago – more than that perhaps, I can't really say – this girl started to hang around with him. I say girl – girl to you and me perhaps, eh?" She gave me a wink that I didn't much appreciate. "In her twenties, anyway. Skinny little piece; pleasant enough I suppose but not much to her. Didn't make the best of herself – brown hair in a bun usually, big glasses, wore clothes like she just needed a place to hang 'em."

Which sounded like Emily. Just like Emily. I forced myself not to get excited, pulled out my purse again but didn't open it.

"Yes, go on."

She looked at the purse, looked at me, and considered. "So, after she comes on the scene, the Artist stops coming round with his pictures. Reckon she must be feeding him and all. Perhaps selling his pictures somewhere, and maybe getting some more money as well, because he starts looking better dressed. Used to be practically in rags. She used to park her little car here on the street – that was before they blocked off the bottom end, where the old buildings are – and brought him all sorts a stuff. Lot of arty stuff, you know."

"Canvases?"

"Yeh. Maybe."

"And where was he living? On this street?"

She shrugged, met my gaze. "Not sure if I remember, exactly."

I opened my purse, took out the last note I had. A fiver. "Are you sure?"

She looked disappointed. "Might be."

I shrugged, and put the fiver away again. "OK. Thanks anyway. I'll ask around, perhaps someone else can remember."

"It's number 17," she said quickly. "Two doors past the barrier on this side."

I took the fiver out again. "And how do I get past the barrier?"

"This corner." She pointed with her cigarette. "You'll see."

She held out her free hand and I put the fiver in it.

"No point in you going there, though. They ain't in. Ain't seen 'em round here in days. Reckon they've moved out."

She gave me a triumphant grin, having put one over on me, as she thought.

I smiled. "Thank you. That's very useful information."

She blew smoke at me and slammed the door in my face.

I walked on to the end of the street, my excitement rising. Surely, this had to be it! The Artist – and Emily – hiding out in the abandoned housing at the end of Quondam Street.

The fence had been a serious attempt to seal off the area. The base had been concreted in at several points, and the ends were screwed to the walls. But, on closer examination, the tubular steel legs at this end had been cut through just above the base, and the screws were loose in their fittings. With a firm tug, the entire section swung open. With a slight sense of guilt – and a bit of a thrill – I stepped through into the forbidden territory.

It was a depressing sight. The sunshine shone more brightly than ever, but it only served to show crumbling bricks and cracked asphalt, with weeds forcing their way through all across the road and pavement. At some point in the past, the council had attempted to seal off each house, but in accordance with the traditions of Delford Mills, they'd sought to do it as cheaply as possible. Wooden boards had been nailed across the doorways and ground-floor windows – I knew that, because a few splintered remnants were still there. The original doors were long gone, probably used for firewood, I guessed. So was most of the glass which had been in the windows, leaving gaping holes into the dark interiors.

There was one exception. Two doors down from the barrier. No numbers showing, but – counting from number 11, the last house on the other side of the barrier – it had to be number 17. Here, the ground-floor windows were covered with sheet metal, and in the upper storeys the glass was grimy but intact. The door itself was galvanized steel, bright in the sunshine. It was held shut with a massive padlock – not something that was going to be forced off with a screwdriver.

I went up to it and gave the door an experimental tug. It barely moved.

Well, there was no going any further. I wasn't skilled in breaking and entering. And in any case, whatever was in there was all going to be "evidence".

I dug into my handbag, pulled out my mobile, and started scrolling through the speed-dial page, looking for David Macrae's number.

"Don't bother with that, Mrs Deeson. You won't be making any phone calls."

I glanced up, surprised. The street had been deserted a moment ago.

A short, rotund man. Red face under a black hat. He also wore a strange expression, a sort of calm fury. As if it was something he was used to keeping suppressed, but was now leaking out.

Seeing him out of his normal context, it took a moment before I could remember his name.

"Mr… Ferrers-Manton! But – what are you doing here?"

"The same as you, of course!" He smiled. It looked more like a snarl. "Looking for an artist. Or rather, their 'atelier'. Their studio, that is."

"Yes, I know. But I still don't understand how you found this place at the same time I did," I said, puzzling it out as I spoke. "Unless… you weren't following me, were you?"

He shook his head. "Nothing so primitive, I assure you. Nobody follows anyone nowadays! Not when these things are so easy to obtain."

He fished in the pockets of his trademark coat, and produced a small black box. "The word these days is 'track'. I've been tracking you for a few days. Stuck this on your car while you were sleeping in it, outside the library! I'm afraid I'd quite run out of ideas, and I couldn't let the police find it first – but I had some hopes for you, with your skill in following clues! Not to mention your stubborn persistence. And it seems that I was right."

He tipped back his hat a little to gaze up at the building. "I must admit, I never would have thought of looking here. On Arthur's old street, of all places! Of course, it can't be just a coincidence. I wonder if we'll ever know the story behind that, eh?"

I shook my head in confusion. Too much sudden strangeness.

My brain was racing to catch up. "No. I mean – why? Why were you following me? Tracking me. Why –"

"Too many questions!" he interrupted me, and now the anger was much clearer. "Always too many questions with you, Deeson! Just open the door. We're not having this discussion out in the open."

"But it's locked…" I began, but he'd put the tracker away and pulled out a key instead. He tossed it at me, and I caught it automatically.

A big key. The sort that might fit a big padlock.

I looked at him. "Go on," he said. "Try it."

My phone was still in my other hand. "I need to phone someone first," I said.

"No you don't. In fact, it would be better if you gave that to me." He held out a hand.

"What? No!" I shook my head. "Look, Mr Ferrers-Manton, I really don't understand what's going on here, but investigating this place is a matter for the police and I'm phoning them now."

"I don't think so!" he snapped. He reached inside his coat and produced a gun. A large black automatic pistol. It looked huge in his pudgy little hand, but he held it very steadily, and it was pointing at me. "Now, throw your mobile to me."

"You've got a gun," I said. Not the brightest observation ever, but I was in shock.

He rolled his eyes. "Yes, Mrs Deeson, I have a gun, and I will use it if you don't do as I tell you! Now give me your phone and open that door!"

I looked at the gun. It's true what they say: the muzzle looks huge when it's pointed at you. But I clung to my phone. It was my only chance of getting help.

"Someone will hear a shot," I told him.

"Someone might, but round here I doubt if anyone will do anything. And you'll be dead anyway! Last chance – give it me or I'll put a bullet between your eyes now!"

I tossed the phone at him. He made no attempt to catch it, just let it land on the ground then stamped down on it. Glass fragments scattered.

"That's better. Now, the door if you please?"

I stepped over to the door, finding it hard to take my eyes off his pistol. The key fitted smoothly into the lock, which opened with a well-oiled click. I took the padlock off, and turned around.

"Drop it on the floor."

I did as I was told. "The only people who would have had keys to that lock were Emily and the Artist," I said. "So you must have…"

I couldn't finish the sentence.

"Yes, I did," he confirmed. "I'll tell you all about it if you like. When we're inside." He nodded at the door again.

I lifted the handle and pulled. Like the lock, everything was well oiled. *Emily*, I thought. *She was always so efficient.*

Inside was very dark.

"Go on," said Ferrers-Manton.

I stepped forward. The sunshine through the doorway illuminated bare floorboards, worn by the human traffic of nearly two hundred years. I suddenly wondered if that was the last sunlight I would ever see, and began to tremble.

There was a strong smell of damp. Damp and rot and decay. With faint overtones of petrol and old food and – turpentine?

"Light switch. On the wall to your left." Ferrers-Manton's voice came from close behind.

I reached out and pressed the switch, not expecting anything, the mains electricity had been cut off here years ago, but several low-energy bulbs glowed into life, and I looked around as the shadows faded out.

When the money for rebuilding had run out, the council had settled for refurbishing. Originally, the little ground-floor room – barely ten feet square in Delford's houses – would have been a kitchen and scullery. Above it was another room the same size, and another above that with a low ceiling. Plus an attic space which often got pressed into service. The council had expanded things a little by knocking out intervening walls, making two houses into one, with three larger rooms. Then, later on, doorways had been made through into the house behind, so that four of the original houses had become one, with finally a decent amount of room for a family, and luxuries like gas, electricity, and water supplied.

Of course, by that time the ancient buildings were dilapidated and crumbling. It cost so much to shore them up that it would have been cheaper to demolish and rebuild after all.

This enlarged room was mostly empty, though. To judge by the black mould creeping up the walls, this was where the smell of damp and rot originated.

"Charming." Ferrers-Manton pushed me further into the room with the pistol, then shut the door behind us. "Do keep walking, Mrs Deeson. We want to see the rest, don't we?"

A doorway – no door – led into a back room. Also empty, though one end was curtained off. A strong chemical smell overlaying something less pleasant emanated from that direction. Toilet facilities, I surmised.

Another doorway, this time with a door, took us to a set of stairs. As we went up, the damp odour was left behind and the other smells became stronger.

We emerged into grimy daylight, the windows dirty but intact. The back room was in use as a storage space. Over on one side, unused canvases and paper were stacked and ready. On the other side, paints and oils and brushes and other art supplies were organized into neat piles. Under the boarded-up window on my left were several rows of car batteries, which explained where the electricity came from. There was even a portable generator with them, ready to charge them up. Hence the petrol smell.

"My, this is a nice set-up," said Ferrers-Manton. He went over to the generator and sniffed. "I wonder if this is leaking?"

He crouched down next to it, keeping the gun pointing at me

while he twisted the cap on the petrol tank. "Well, look at that. Not fitted properly! That's a fire hazard."

"Well, shouldn't you put it back on, then?" I asked.

He looked up at me, his face shadowed under the brim of his hat, but his eyes gleaming. "Oh, I don't think so. I think the more petrol vapour round here the better. I think that after I've left, there might be a bit of a fire. What do you think, Mrs Deeson? This place would make quite a bonfire, wouldn't it?"

I glanced round, remembering the fireball that had burst into our living room, and shuddered involuntarily. In this place it would be much, much worse.

"Oh, does that bring back bad memories?" Ferrers-Manton chuckled. "Sorry about that." He didn't sound sorry at all.

At the front of the house were the living quarters. A camp bed with a sleeping bag. A motley collection of chairs with a rickety table. A portable TV in one corner, and a gas camping cooker in another. Shelves with food cans and packets. There was even a sofa. I wondered how they'd got it up there. Presumably it must come apart.

There were paintings on the walls. Prints of some famous artists, including a lot of portraits. Templeton portraits.

Ferrers-Manton sneered at them. "Very cosy." He stared up at one of the Templetons. "Oh, yes. That's the famous portrait of Duke... whatever."

The hat brim obscured his vision as he looked around the walls, and he swept it off impatiently, tossed it onto a chair. Its absence revealed a shiny bald head with a fringe of long greying hair.

"This arty-farty persona I've been using has worked very well. People expect an artist to be a bit eccentric. But it's starting to irritate me now. Perhaps it's time for a change."

He seemed to be intent on the pictures. I glanced at the doorway and the stairs beyond, wondering if I could make a run for it. But when I looked back he was watching me. Amused.

"Don't even consider it, Mrs Deeson. Come on. There's nothing of any value or interest here. Up we go!"

There was no door this time, just an open staircase. At the top we found that the entire floor had been made into one room. Pillars had been fitted in place of load-bearing walls, and the bricks had been whitewashed. Even the windows had been cleaned. Light flooded in from both sides.

"Ah! This is what we were looking for." Ferrers-Manton came up the stairs behind me and looked around. "Impressive, isn't it? They must have got someone in to do this – amazing what a bit of money can do, even in the Mills. And my, wasn't he prolific?"

The room was full of paintings. They hung or leaned against every wall, they were mounted on easels and propped up on tables – a riot of colour and shape compressed into dozens of canvases in different sizes.

I stepped out into the room, still very conscious of the gun pointing at me, still unable to understand what was going on, but momentarily distracted by what we'd found.

My mind began to make sense of what I was seeing, sorting it into order. There were about half a dozen distinct sections of different paintings round the room, all following different themes. An easel formed the centrepiece of each section, usually with a work in progress mounted on it, while paintings and sketches of that work or something related were collected around it.

To my left, as I stepped off the un-railed staircase, were flowers. Charcoal and pencil, acrylics and watercolours, and oils and mixtures. Most of them were shown as withered and dead, but a few – including the almost-completed one on the easel – were bursting with light and colour.

Next to them was a collection of studies of a room. A room I knew all too well – the room in the farmhouse. Nearly all these were charcoal, or painted in dark shades.

There was another room depicted in the next station – which I also recognized, both from the painting sent to Sir Arthur and from my own visit to Coren Hall: the room where I had enjoyed a cream tea. That same room, in all its contrasting incarnations of dull decay or colourful restoration.

"Why, I do believe that it's Sir Arthur's classroom!" Ferrers-Manton peered over my shoulder, nudging me with the gun barrel as he did so. "The place where I first learned to daub paint! I would hardly have recognized it."

The place where the Artist had discovered his talent, I realized, and another part of the story slid into place.

At the end of the room, beneath and alongside the windows, were stacked completed paintings of various other subjects – buildings, landscapes, portraits – none of which I recognized. A stepladder stood by itself in the corner. Then, as I moved around the room, another workstation. This time, the subject was faces. Young faces, mostly, boys and girls. Sometimes full face, sometimes seen from the side. Sometimes alone, sometimes in groups, or in a row. All looking upwards, with expressions of shock or horror or utter terror.

"Ah. Now we're getting to the good bit!" Ferrers-Manton had been following me round, looking where I looked. He sounded almost jovial.

The next set was a hanging man. *The* hanging man. The one I had found all those years ago.

Not so much a man as a youth. I could see that better in the paintings than I had in real life. There was more light, the detail was sharper, clearer. And horrific.

He was depicted from several angles, but one predominated – looking up from below and in front. Not very different from the view I'd had after I'd fallen, turned over, and looked back.

In my head, I heard again the creaking of the rope. I turned away from the pictures, rubbing at my eyes.

"No, no, you should take a proper look! They're really good – such an excellent likeness. You might almost say lifelike!" He laughed. "Except that's not totally accurate, is it?"

I shook my head, not looking. "I don't need to see them. I was there."

"Yes, you were, weren't you? Interfering cow!" The humour had entirely gone from his voice. "Well, you can look anyway!"

He grabbed my hair, pushed the pistol against my head, and forced me to turn back towards the hanging man.

"How long did you spend trying to find out who he was? Eh? Well, this is your happy day, because now you can get your answer at last! Just ask me!"

"But..."

"Ask me!" He ground the muzzle painfully into the side of my head.

"Who? Who was he?" I gasped out.

"That's better..." He took the gun away, let go of my hair, and stepped back. "Malcolm Eridni, that was his name. Or Eradnu, something weird like that. Pretty Malcolm. Except he didn't look so pretty hanging up there, did he?"

"How do you know that?" I couldn't grasp the link between Claude Ferrers-Manton and the farmhouse. I knew it should be obvious, but my mind was still whirling with fear and shock.

"Still haven't worked it out? Really, Mrs Deeson, I thought you'd be quicker on the uptake. But, to be fair, no one else did either. Not even Terry. Not until it was too late. All that money I spent on plastic surgery turned out to be a good investment, eh?"

"Terry? Who's Terry?"

He sighed. "Do try to keep up, Mrs Deeson. Terry. The Artist. We're in his studio, for goodness' sake! Terrance Naylor."

"T – N. His initials on the paintings!" I said to myself.

"He initialled his paintings? I hadn't noticed. Well, I didn't spend time studying them. Once I realized what they were – and to be honest, I hadn't recognized Terry until I saw the paintings – my first concern was to get rid of them. And him, of course."

"So you killed him."

"Oh, yes." A savage look came across his face. Savage –

and gleeful. "With the library's fire extinguisher. I hadn't gone prepared. I just wanted to see who this hotshot painter was that Carr was pushing me out of the way for. I asked when I could see him and his work, and Emily said, 'Tomorrow, at the exhibition.' She intimated that she was helping him bring the paintings over that night. So I came back after you closed up, hung around, and when they arrived, I followed them in. Emily had gone up to the office, so I caught little Terry on his own, setting up his paintings. Imagine my surprise when I saw what they were!"

He indicated the next group of paintings.

Here, the artist – Terry – had started putting the various elements together. The room in the farmhouse. The frightened kids sitting on the floor in a circle, staring up at the hanging man.

At Malcolm.

There were several different versions, different angles, different mediums. All of them, however, had one extra element in them.

Just outside the circle there was another figure. Bigger, older than the rest. A young man, heavily built with powerful features, and an expression of... pleasure.

"His exhibition pieces were a selection from some of these groups."

He waved his arm around the room. "One of the kids' faces, one of Malcolm, one of all of us together. I thought he might have some more pictures stashed away, and it seems I was right – though I hadn't realized how many versions he'd done of each one! Good thing we managed to track them down, eh?"

"There was space for four pictures in the exhibition," I said.

"Oh, yes. Terry included a self-portrait." Ferrers-Manton indicated one of the children in the circle. "That's him there. Quite a good likeness, actually. But of course, you wouldn't know. I made quite a mess of his face."

I shuddered, remembering. He smiled. And although the features were different, I recognized the expression.

"That was you at the farmhouse! You. You hung that person. Malcolm. You..."

"Ah! Now, at last, you're starting to get it."

There was another memory trying to come forward. Another time I had seen that expression.

"And he was – you were – at the gate that day. At Coren Hall. With the dogs – and the older man..."

He raised an eyebrow. "Oh, you remember that? You got off lightly. I didn't want to give you any warnings, just set the dogs on you. But Father wouldn't let me. He was angry enough to do it, but he was scared as well. After all the trouble you'd already caused, he thought it would stir things up too much if you disappeared. That was always his problem. Never wanted to go the full distance, did old Nigel. Left that sort of thing to me. Should have left it to me then."

"Nigel. Nigel Templeton? So you must be – Geraint?"

He took a little bow. "Yes! Good. You got there in the end. Well done. You're only the second person to figure it out. Third, if Terry realized before I hit him with the fire extinguisher. And Sir Arthur only recognized me after he'd been given a clue from that painting he was sent. Terry's painting, of course."

"Why? Why kill anyone in the first place?"

"Oh, heavens, not more questions!" He shook his head. "You've got all the names – that's what you've been searching for all this time. Really, there's no satisfying some people." He glanced at his watch. "OK, then. We have a little time. Why don't you sit down and make yourself comfortable?"

In the middle of the room, behind one of the pillars, was a table not covered in brushes and paints, but with a laptop, some A4 paperwork, and a digital camera arranged neatly on top. There was a printer on a shelf underneath, and a chair behind it.

I sat down. Ferrers-Manton, aka Geraint Templeton, moved behind me. It was even worse, somehow, having him out of sight than it had been when he was in front of me and pointing the gun at my face. I turned in the chair and watched as he went over to the windows at the far end and began opening them.

"Let's have a bit of fresh air in here," he said. "A bit of extra oxygen to feed the accidental fire that's going to happen!"

I wondered if I could make it to the stairs and get down before he noticed, but even as I thought it, I realized that he still had the pistol aimed in my direction. He smiled brightly, as if he'd read my thoughts, and walked over to stand behind me, peering over my shoulder at the A4 sheets.

"I do believe that Emily was planning to make a speech at the exhibition. Why don't you read it out to us? It would be interesting to find out what she knew."

I hesitated. "Emily's dead, isn't she?"

"Well, of course she is! If she was alive I would have got her to bring me here, and we'd never be having this conversation! Silly girl tried to run away when she saw what I'd done to Terry. I threw the fire extinguisher at her. Clumsy thing to throw, but it caught her on the leg and she went down. Hit her head on a bookshelf. I took her back to my place, hoped she'd come round, but she died after a day or two without recovering consciousness."

I was crying. "She was still alive? You could have taken her to a hospital. She might have survived!"

"Don't be ridiculous! Of course I wasn't going to let her live." He tapped me on the head with the pistol. "Read!"

I took a deep breath, wiped my eyes, and began.

"*Good afternoon. My name is Emily Coombe, and I am here today on behalf of the artist who painted these remarkable works, Terrance Naylor. Terry has opted not to come in person today, and I think that when I have told his story, you will understand his reasons.*

"*I first encountered his work some five years ago, shortly after I had moved here and started work at the library. At that time I was living in rented accommodation on the edge of the Delford Mills area of town, and going into a local shop one day, I noticed some drawings for sale.*"

Emily's talk had been intended to go with a media presentation.

DAY 7: QUONDAM

At several points there were references to "Slide number..." and thumbnail pictures. In this case, it was a pencil sketch of a shop front.

"*They were very rough pencil drawings, on cheap paper, but had been done with remarkable skill. I have been a lover of art and an amateur artist myself for many years, and as soon as I saw these I realized that they were the product of an amazing talent.*

"*However, the shopkeeper was unable to tell me who the artist was. He talked vaguely of some 'down and out' who lived in the abandoned housing round the demolished Mill buildings, and who occasionally came round selling his drawings. They were, he conceded, 'not bad', and he usually gave the man a few quid for them.*

"*I bought all he had, and began a search for this mysterious artist.*

"*It took me all of a year to track him down, and as long again to gain his confidence. Eventually, with gifts of food and clothing and – most importantly! – art supplies, I was able to find out where he lived.*

"*At that time he was occupying part of an old back-to-back house on Quondam Street, and living in the most appalling conditions of squalor imaginable. I did my best to get him to move to somewhere better, but he absolutely refused. He was tied to Quondam Street for reasons I only discovered much later. So I was forced to adopt a different plan. I set about cleaning out and renovating one of the better of the abandoned houses.*

"*Eventually, I was able to introduce Terry to much better living conditions, and a proper studio for his work.*

"*In all this time, he rarely spoke more than a few words to me. It was very clear that he had, at some time in his past, suffered some terribly traumatic experience that had rendered him all but unable to communicate and indeed terrified of most human contact. Clearly, he needed proper professional help, but he utterly refused to meet with anyone else but me. I could only continue to try to build our friendship, hoping to get to the point where I might be able to introduce him to someone else.*

"*In the meantime, there was his painting.*

"With the access I provided to proper materials, his art flourished, and he soon showed that he had a natural mastery of all mediums. With only occasional help from me, he was soon working in oils, acrylics, and watercolours, as well as his original pencil or charcoal sketches.

"I wanted to start showing these to a wider audience, but Terry was absolutely insistent that no one should know his name or where he lived. He trusted me and, to some extent, some of the local people – but he was terrified that someone, and he would not or could not say who, might find him.

"So I selected the best of his work, and offered it to the market through some dealers I knew of in London. Like me, they quickly recognized the quality of his work, and it began to sell.

"But some paintings Terry refused to let me put on sale. There were certain themes that he returned to obsessively, painting the same or similar scenes over and over again, and these he absolutely refused to show to anyone else.

"Most often, there was a room, an ugly place in some old building. I thought at first that this was somewhere in the Mills, but Terry indicated otherwise. The only description he would give was 'Farmhouse'.

"Sometimes he depicted himself or other people in this place. It became clear to me that this was somehow tied in with his traumatic past. I encouraged him to explore this in his painting, because I felt that bringing these things out into the open might be the best or only way to deal with them.

"And so it proved. Though it was sometimes incredibly painful for him to revisit these memories, every time he went there it became a little easier, he was able to show a little more, and sometimes even say a bit about it. In time, Terry was able to produce the paintings you see here today, and I was able to put together the terrible story behind them.

"Terry was an orphan, and he knows nothing of his parents or even where he was born. His earliest memories are of being in some sort of institution, or institutions – he can't even be sure how many places there might have been. But sometime in his early teens (he thinks) he was sent to Coren Hall.

"I think it likely that Terry already had problems with communicating before that happened, and Coren Hall was supposedly a special school and orphanage that would help young people like him. But it soon became clear that it was something else, something that was – and I do not think this is an exaggeration – evil.

"To put it bluntly, Coren Hall was a high-class paedophile brothel."

I had to stop at that point.

"Oh, come on now!" Geraint sounded impatient. "All that time you were investigating, surely you must have had some idea what was going on?"

"I – I suppose it occurred to me. Only, I didn't want to think that that was possible."

He chuckled. "Not many people did want to think about it then. Apart from the ones who thought about it all the time, of course! That worked to our advantage. Carry on."

"I will not tell you here everything I learned from Terry. I have written a full report separately and that will be going to the proper authorities. And I suspect that most of what went on there he still cannot talk about. Perhaps he does not even remember. But there is no doubt that he and others there were systematically abused over a period of years.

"There was one bright spot in the darkness that covered Coren Hall. That was the occasional visit of someone whom Terry would only refer to as 'The Sir'.

"Terry wanted to make it absolutely clear that this person had never abused or taken part in any abuse of himself or any of the other inmates of Coren Hall. It is possible that he did not even know about the true nature of the institution. He came every now and then to teach a class in art, and whilst he was there, none of the other 'guests' came to visit. It was some time before I came to understand that this person was none other than Sir Arthur Templeton.

"From what Terry has told me, I believe that Sir Arthur genuinely thought that he was donating his time to a charitable foundation."

Geraint sniggered. "That's true. Gullible old fool was always congratulating Nigel on how he had such a wonderful heart for the kids! You should have seen his face when we finally told him the truth!" He shook his head. "Those art classes were a pain in the neck, though. We had to keep the customers away while he was there. I had to join in the classes as well. Just to keep an eye on what was happening, make sure none of the brats talked out of turn."

"And it was in these art classes that Terry discovered and developed his artistic talent. Sir Arthur recognized it early on, and gave him extra tuition."

"That's when things really started getting difficult. Uncle Arthur was wanting to pop round every week to check on his star pupil. Of course, he didn't have much time for me, even though I was his nephew!"

"For Terry, these classes opened up a whole new world. One that gave him an avenue of communication that he had never had before. He has acknowledged that, and the debt he owes to Sir Arthur, with a special painting."

The thumbnail was, of course, of the Coren Hall painting that Sir Arthur had received.

"But something even more terrible was about to happen at Coren Hall.

"Discipline had always been harsh. Direct physical punishment was rarely used, but the 'pupils' were forced into submission with threats and deprivation of food and, above all, fear. As part of this cruel treatment, offenders were taken to an abandoned farmhouse near the Hall and locked in. Sometimes they were left there for days on end, without food or water."

"Days on end? That didn't happen much. Overnight was usually enough. The little bastards –" Geraint sniggered, "– that's literal truth in most cases, I'm not swearing – were absolutely terrified of the farmhouse. Psychology, you see. Didn't want to do anything to damage the merchandise physically, our customers liked undamaged goods, even the ones who wanted to play rough. But get them frightened of something, and you don't need anything as crude as a beating."

My eyes were stinging. I turned to glare at him, ignoring the pistol. "You – you… monster! You treated these children like… like…"

He shrugged. "Like merchandise. As I said. They were no good for anything else."

I continued to look at him, but no longer glaring. I just stared, totally unable to understand a mind like his. Other people were no more than commodities to him – I realized that, but I couldn't grasp it.

"I can't imagine what it must be like to be you," I said. Softly. Almost to myself.

He smiled. "Well, it's pretty good, actually. But please read on. We're getting to the fun part."

I turned back to the sheets of paper, rubbing my eyes.

"This part of Terry's story was the hardest of all for him to put into words, though it was the major theme of his paintings. What I came to understand was that one of the older boys managed to escape. I don't know how it was managed – according to Terry, the grounds were patrolled by ferocious dogs, trained to attack anyone trying to get in or out."

"Well, you know that bit's true!" Geraint said. "We made sure all the kids saw the dogs rip something up – a rabbit or once it was a sheep – and that kept them from wandering around at night! But Malcolm, he was a bit smarter than the rest. Hid himself in the boot of a customer's car. Got himself locked in, though, and when he was discovered, they brought him straight back."

"The escape ended in failure, and resulted in a terrible punishment. The day after the escape attempt, the entire school was marched down to the farmhouse. You can see from the paintings exhibited here how they were forced to sit in a circle, and made to watch whilst the escapee was murdered by being hung from the rafters.

"And you can also see the person responsible. Standing behind them, making sure they didn't look away.

"This was the traumatic event which, above all, scarred Terry's life. A memory so terrible that he could never escape it; a fear so profound that it remained with him forever."

"Did the job, then!" Geraint said with satisfaction.

"However, it also marked a change in things at Coren Hall. Over the next days and weeks, the 'customers' stopped coming. There were rumours that the police had visited, though they didn't speak to anyone except the staff."

"That was your fault!" Geraint's tone of jovial self-congratulation changed abruptly to a petulant anger. Without warning, he hit me on the side of the head with the pistol barrel. Hard enough to almost knock me out of the chair. I managed to stay upright, even though I was dizzy with the sudden pain. "You ruined everything, snooping about, poking your nose in! What were you doing in the farmhouse anyway?"

I put my hand to my ear, and it came away bloody. "I was lost. In the woods – with the storm. I was just looking for shelter."

"So you thought you could just wander in anywhere you wanted?" He raised the gun and I flinched.

"I knocked. I shouted. There was no one there. And the door wasn't locked."

"Ahh. So that's it! Baz forgot to lock up after us!"

"Who was Baz?"

"Barry Hargrove. Big lad, ex-con. We used him for a bit of muscle round the place. Happy to do anything to anyone for a bit of dosh. None too bright, though." He shook his head. "He was giving me a hand with that little job, in case any of them kicked off. Last one out, he was supposed to put the lock on. We were going to go back later and get the body, but then the storm broke and we decided to put it off till the next day. Except that the next day the place was swarming with police! I never did understand how you'd got in there."

I thought back over that day, and shuddered. While I was on the bus, going out to start my walk, Geraint was marching children down from Coren Hall to witness a murder. About the time I got off in Frayhampton, he was stringing one of them up.

Malcolm. He had a name now. When I was making my decision

to go down the valley instead of along the ridge, Malcolm was choking to death.

"Of course, we had to put a hold on things whilst all that was happening," Geraint continued. "Couldn't have the customers running into the Old Bill, could we? But Dad had a word in a few ears, made sure that things were wrapped up quickly and neatly." He glanced at his watch again, and frowned. "Let's finish Miss Coombe's story, shall we?"

I flipped over the page and continued reading.

"Several months went past. There were still no 'customers'. Terry couldn't say much about this period: it is probably that he was still in a state of shock after what he had seen. But I was able to piece together what had happened to change things at Coren Hall: and it is largely due to the work of a remarkable woman whom I am proud to know personally – Mrs..."

I stopped abruptly. And felt the gun muzzle poke against the back of my head.

"Don't be shy! Too late for that now. Read it!" Geraint hissed the words into my ear.

"Mrs Sandra Deeson."

I paused again, the gun ground harder into my skull, and I felt a shudder go through me. Geraint felt it as well, and it seemed to amuse him. He chuckled, his mood switching abruptly from anger to good humour, and he pulled the gun away.

"Quite the hero, aren't you? Do let me know what Miss Coombe had to say about you."

"Mrs Deeson was the person who discovered the body and who alerted the police. But she did not leave things there. She continued to investigate, even after the police investigation had been completed with suspicious speed and without anything being learned. Determined to discover the identity of the body, she refused to let the matter be brushed under the carpet. Even when her persistence cost her her job, she carried on.

"I believe it was as the direct result of this that Coren Hall was suddenly closed, nearly a year after the murder. Terry recalls that suddenly

the children were told to pack their belongings – such as they had – and were sent away. He never saw Coren Hall again.

"When I told Terry about Mrs Deeson and the part she had played, *he began producing a new series of pictures. He had often used the image of dead or dying flowers to represent his time at Coren Hall. Now he began to show sunlight breaking in to bring those flowers back to life. In this way, he felt, Mrs Deeson's actions had brought him hope and had delivered him from the terror and darkness of the Hall."*

"Oh, well done Mrs Deeson!" Geraint sounded angry again. Aware now of how rapidly his moods could change, I braced myself for another blow to the head, but instead he began clapping – or as well as he could with the gun still in his hand. "I expect you feel very proud of yourself, don't you!"

I turned and looked at him, thinking about how I felt as I did so.

"Yes. Yes I do, actually. For the last thirty years I've been telling myself that I wrecked my career with a pointless obsession, and now I've found out that it wasn't pointless at all. I stopped you. I put an end to the evil thing you were doing at Coren Hall, and I gave Terry and those other kids a chance at freedom. And that's something I can feel very proud of."

He frowned, and his hand holding the gun seemed to shake. I closed my eyes. How stupid was it to wind up an emotionally unstable murderer with a gun pointed at you?

But he didn't hit me, and he didn't fire.

"That's something else I didn't understand." He sounded genuinely curious. "Why did you do all that? Why go to all that trouble? At first I thought you were after some big news award or something, but even after you lost your job you carried on. It made no sense. There was nothing in it for you at all!"

"I cared. That's all. I cared about somebody being murdered and just left hanging there like a piece of meat in a butcher's shop."

He raised his hands in exasperation. "Yes, I get that. I get that you cared! But why? He was nothing to you! You didn't even know him!"

"And that is exactly why I cared. Because no one should die like that, and no one should be left without a name to say over their grave and to be remembered by. No one should be uncared for."

We looked at each other, a few feet apart in distance; light years in understanding.

"The world doesn't care, Sandra." He said it quietly, earnestly. Trying to convince me. Or himself. "I realized that a long time ago. Nobody really cares, everyone is out to get something, and caring is part of the scam, part of the trick, but it's not real. The only person who cares about you is you. Everything else is illusion."

"And that's how you've lived all these years?" I asked.

"It's the truth!" he snapped. "You just care too much!"

"Someone told me recently that you can't care too much. I wasn't sure then. But now I believe it. Now I have proof. My caring made a difference. It helped."

"Your caring just got in the way!" He clenched his teeth, got control of himself. "And if it had been left to me, you would have been got out of the way! But dear old Dad didn't have the stomach for it. Didn't want any more bodies. And when things started going wrong, when the customers stayed away because of the publicity, and some people began hinting that they might not be able to keep on protecting us if you continued to stir things up, and when you wouldn't damn well stop, even came right up to the Hall... Old Nigel decided to chuck in the towel. Paid off the staff, got rid of the kids..."

He saw the look of horror on my face and chuckled. Good humour restored again. "No, not like that. Not that it wasn't an option, in my opinion, but the Old Man wouldn't have it. Too many bodies. He was terrified of another one turning up. So we just fed them back into the system. I was pretty sure that they wouldn't talk. Wouldn't be believed if they did. Made sure they got spread round the country, different places so they couldn't get together. Then we left. Took the money and went off abroad."

"What about Sir Arthur? Why did he leave?"

"Oh, he came round wanting to know what was going on and why we were closing up – and what was happening to his star pupil, little Terry. So we told him. Well, I told him. The whole story. And made it clear how implicated he was. His was the name on all the official documents, he was the source of all the contacts we'd made. If we went down, he went down as well. I suggested that perhaps he should take a holiday, as it were. And sure enough, he ran just as fast as Nigel. Hard to believe that there was no blood relationship, they were so alike in that way."

He nodded at the papers. "Finish it off. I want to know what happened to Terry."

"Terry spent the remaining years of his childhood in various homes and institutions. The terrible things he had experienced had rendered him almost mute and I think it likely that he was considered and treated as 'subnormal'. If so, any treatment he received was ineffectual.

"At some point, he left the system, either pushed out or escaped. I could never get a clear understanding. He made his way back here, and eventually became one of the hidden community of people living in the ruins and abandoned housing round Delford Mills. He was particularly drawn to Quondam Street: because that was where Sir Arthur had lived as a boy. There Terry felt close to the one man who had recognized his talent, who had shown him kindness and given him an identity. And as I have said, that was where I found him.

"These paintings, then, reveal a terrible and tragic story. One which still, some thirty years after the events took place, casts a shadow over Terry and any other victims of Coren Hall who still survive. One which cries out for a justice which has been so long delayed but which I hope may now be, in some measure, achieved.

"But it is also a story of a remarkable talent, something which could not be crushed, a voice that could not be silenced, and which is now revealed for you all to see. Thank you."

I laid the last sheet of paper down. The brief silence was broken by Geraint, applauding vigorously.

"Oh, marvellous! Well done, Miss Coombe! Magnificent! What

a speech!" He winked at me. "Well, it would have been if she'd ever got to give it, eh? But in any case, it turns out that she was wrong. Little Terry's voice was silenced, and no one will ever know his sad, sad story." He shook his head in mock grief.

"But why did you have to kill him? And Emily? What difference would it have made after all this time? You said yourself, even Terry didn't recognize you."

"He didn't then, but who's to say he wouldn't have, given time? I wasn't going to take that risk, now, was I? And in any case, I didn't want the whole Coren Hall thing coming out. A great deal of my current income derives from keeping it all hush-hush."

"Blackmail, you mean?"

"Well, I prefer to think of it as accepting a small gratuity for keeping a discreet lid on things! Of course, many of our original customers have died, but most of them had family. Families who may or may not have known what Grandad or Uncle or whoever used to do for recreation, but they'll certainly pay a bit to make sure no one else finds out!"

He took another look at his watch, and I finally realized why he was doing that. And why he was happy to keep me talking.

"You're expecting someone, aren't you?" I asked, and felt my stomach clench as he smiled back at me.

"Oh, how very smart you are, Mrs Deeson! Yes, I've arranged for some, ah, acquaintances of mine to drop by and take you off my hands. They should be here any time now – so if you have any more questions, now is the time to ask."

My first question would have been, "What will they do with me?" But I could guess the answer to that, and I didn't want it confirmed. So instead I asked, "What happened that night at the library?"

He nodded. "Yes, I might as well tell you that story since I can't tell anyone else, after all! Let me see – I already told you what happened with Terry and Miss Coombe, didn't I? Well, that left me with something of a dilemma. One dead man, one unconscious woman, and four paintings that I had to get rid of. I needed to think fast!

"The paintings were the first thing. I took those out to my car, and as I did, I worked out a plan to make the whole thing look like a burglary gone wrong. Send the police off on the wrong track. So I went round to a place I knew of nearby – terribly seedy little pub, all sorts of villainous types hang out there! – and collected a cigarette end from the bins. My idea was to leave it inside then take the body, leaving the police with a fine puzzle! But to my annoyance, when I got back I found that the doors to the exhibition had shut and locked themselves. I had a go at prising them open, but the only tool I had was a dinky little screwdriver from the car, and it was clear that that wasn't going to do the trick.

"So I had to think again."

He was looking ridiculously pleased with himself. Boasting about how clever he was. I thought of Terry's body as I'd found it. I thought of Malcolm. I thought of Emily. And the fear began to fade. Replaced by fury.

"You left the cigarette end by the exhibition doors. You took Emily; put her in your car, I suppose. You opened the windows in the toilet and smashed the alarm box. You made a bit of a mess in the library, then you phoned the police."

He looked surprised, then nodded. "Of course, I was forgetting that you'd been there. So sorry for disturbing your sleep! You're not quite right, though. I had to get someone to get rid of Miss Coombe's car before I could call the police. Fortunately, I have a few contacts who will do that sort of work for a price. The same people that we're waiting for now, as it happens! After that it was mostly a matter of watching and waiting. Trying to find this place" – he waved his gun around to indicate the studio – "and keeping an eye on the police, to make sure they didn't find it first. Had to call in a few favours, remind a few people of things that I knew about, put a bit of pressure on to make sure the investigation went the way I wanted it to. Just like old times!"

There was something hard in my jacket pocket pushing uncomfortably into my ribs. I moved a little to ease it and he raised his gun in warning.

"Please do sit still, Mrs Deeson. I would prefer not to shoot you. The preferred plan is for you to be in a fatal car accident, and a bullet would spoil that. But of course I will if I must. So the quieter you sit, the longer you'll live."

I should have been terrified, but I was too angry. "You've no conscience, have you?" I said as scathingly as I could manage.

"None at all," he agreed. "Such a weakness, I've always thought."

"Was it you who firebombed our house?"

He looked shocked. "Goodness, no! No, that was my cousin, Jonathan. He was very protective of Sir Arthur – well, he had a bit of an investment there – and perhaps the old man told him the full story about Coren Hall. In any case, he wanted to scare you off. Very clumsy business. I told him so, when I went to see my uncle."

"You could have gone to see him any time. Why then?"

"Well, that's true. I'd been settled back here for a while – ever since old Nigel finally kicked the bucket – when Uncle Arthur and Cousin Jonathan turned up and began renovating the old Hall. I did think of introducing myself but why stir things up? I preferred to watch and see how their project worked out. It was amusing when Jonathan made contact with me – well, with the chairman of the art club. I thought I'd been recognized, but it turned out that he wanted a way to get Arthur back in touch with the art world. The artist persona was a very useful cover, but I certainly never saw it working out in quite that way!"

"Why did you decide to kill him? Your own uncle?"

"I hadn't intended to. I was hoping that Arthur might have a clue about where Terry's studio was. But he'd worked it all out and knew who I was, and things got a little ugly. He was going to call the police, and Jonathan was getting aggressive, so I had to shoot him. Then, of course, I had to shoot Arthur. I don't think he had any idea where Terry was anyway. He was still getting used to the idea that his star pupil was still alive."

A big smile lit up his face. "But then things came together so well! With Arthur dead, I only had to get Jonathan to disappear and he takes the blame for everything! And it wasn't even hard to arrange. I made a call, and away he went along with his car, never to be seen again. And the police will join the dots, as they do, and announce that Jonathan killed his uncle and the artist in the library and Miss Coombe. Then he tried to kill you before leaving the country."

"The police will find him, though. They're looking all over for him and his car. When his body turns up with the same bullets in that killed Sir Arthur, they'll know that someone else is involved!"

"Good luck to them! Jonathan and his Porsche are at the bottom of Sheerside Quarry. Which is flooded to a depth of five hundred feet or more! They won't even look there. No, Jonathan's disappearance will remain a mystery, and I'll finally be able to get on with my life."

The hard object in my pocket was Graham's phone, I realized. Where I'd put it, so I'd remember to give it back to him.

"So you think," I said, without knowing what I'd say next. I didn't have a plan. I hadn't worked anything out. But words formed in my mouth without even seeming to go through my brain. "But the police will be here any minute now, and they've already heard everything. Everything you've said. It's a confession, Geraint. You've just confessed to murder. Murders, I should say. Everything back to Coren Hall, back to the farmhouse."

He looked shocked, then angry. Then he relaxed, and sneered at me. "Now you're getting desperate, Mrs Deeson."

"Am I?" I pulled Graham's phone out of my pocket, holding it up with the back to him, so he couldn't see that it was switched off. "This has been on the entire time. Open line to DI Macrae. He's heard every word, Geraint. And he's on his way here with armed officers, to arrest you."

I smiled. Snarled, maybe.

Of course, he should have shot me then. Shot me and taken the phone and found out it was dead, and that I'd been bluffing.

But instead, he stepped towards me, holding out his hand. "Give that to me!" he shouted. "Give it me!"

Perhaps he was still wanting to avoid putting a bullet wound in me. Or perhaps he just didn't think there was any danger in getting close to a middle-aged woman.

Dunderhead.

As he took another step forward, I tossed the phone away, into the corner of the room, and his eyes tracked it, his head turned to watch it go, and his hand with the gun in it followed.

I kicked him as hard as I could between the legs.

To be honest it wasn't a very good kick. Sitting down like that, I couldn't put a lot of force into it. On the other hand, there was a lot of anger and desperation involved.

And, of course, it's a very vulnerable spot. I've always wondered why men act so tough when they keep their weakest area outside their body.

He screamed, a high-pitched wail that cut into my eardrums. He doubled up, and at the same time tried to bring the pistol round, but I grabbed his hand, forced it away. It went off, the noise even louder than his screams, terrifyingly close, but I still had his hand. He tried to pull back, but I held on, using his momentum to help me out of the chair and launching myself forward, clawing at his face.

He fired again, and I felt the heat from the muzzle on my hand as we staggered round the room together, crashing into easels and sending paint and canvases cascading to the floor.

He was shouting, incoherent with fury, punching me with his free hand before grabbing my collar and swinging me round, slamming me against a piece of furniture. Then he stepped away, wrenching his gun hand free.

I grabbed something from the table he'd thrown me against and hurled it into his face.

Glass shattered, brushes scattered, and the thick smell of turpentine filled the room.

He screamed again and fell back, clawing at his eyes. "YOOUUUU...." he shrieked, pointing the pistol at where I had been.

He fired as I dived aside.

His face and hair and clothing were soaked with turpentine, the air around him was saturated with the fumes. The flash and bang from the muzzle was instantly followed by a softer but no less deadly explosion and a flare of light.

Geraint's scream became a shriek, the terrible noise of instant agony, as his face and hair and coat blazed. He staggered backwards, beating at himself with his free hand but still firing his pistol with the other, a wild fusillade of bullets smashing through canvases and ricocheting from the ancient brickwork, but none of them coming near me as I lay flat out on the floor, and each recoil sent him further backwards until he reached the unguarded stairwell and fell into it.

I knew what was coming. Part of my mind was shrieking, "No! Not again", even as I struggled to pull my jacket up over my head to give my face and hair some sort of protection.

Geraint, blazing and screaming and shooting, crashed down to the floor below, where the petrol vapour waited. It seeped from the open tank, forced out by the pressure of its own volatility, sinking, heavier than air, to flow along the floorboards and pour down the next set of stairs like an invisible waterfall.

The old floorboards heaved under me, flames shot up through every crack, and a gout of searing brilliance burst out of the stairwell, drowning out Geraint's final screams.

It struck the ceiling and spread out in every direction, cooling to a yellow-orange incandescence. I felt my skin and hair sizzle in the heat and gasped for breath as the oxygen was sucked out of my lungs and the fire rolled down the walls. It caressed the stacked canvases and they too flared up with colours more brilliant than any the artist could have achieved.

Air was flooding in through the windows Geraint had opened. Sucked in by the combustion, feeding the flames as he'd planned, but also reaching me.

I sucked desperately at the wind, dragging life inside me, and pulling my jacket over my head as a shield against the awful heat.

The room was already filling with smoke, where it wasn't already full of fire. But, down on the floor, I could see across the room to Emily's desk and the little black fire extinguisher she had kept under there. Of course she had. Emily would have thought of that.

I scrambled across the floor and snatched it up. Knowing, as I did so, that it was futile. The initial fireball had died back, but paints and canvases all around the room were ablaze and the stairwell was a firepit. There was no escaping that way; the little CO_2 extinguisher would barely make a dent on that conflagration.

The window then. But I was three floors up, and a jump from that height could be just as fatal as the fire.

Better that than burning, though. The pain in my exposed skin convinced me of that.

I sat up, gathering my courage to dash across the room and out through the window. Perhaps I could hang from the window frame, make it less of a drop.

I saw the ladder in the corner.

I remembered the story of Murder Row.

There was a way through the attic spaces to the other houses. And the ladder suggested that there was a way up there.

There was no time to think, to plan it out. I crouched, pulling the pin out of the extinguisher's trigger. Then, on impulse, I snatched up Emily's laptop with my free hand, and ran across the room, blasting back the flames with the extinguisher, clearing a space round the stepladder.

The aluminium was already melting at the top. I cooled it with another burst of CO_2, and under my feet the floorboards were creaking and groaning. I remembered the gas canisters in the camping stove and wondered how long the fire would take to reach them, how long they would resist the heat, how big an explosion there would be.

The extinguisher spluttered and died. I dropped it on the floor and stared upwards. Above the ladder I could see a hatch in the ceiling. Closed. But it was that or the window.

Up the ladder.

Heat had gathered under the ceiling, a layer of searing hot air. I pushed through it, holding my breath, wanting to scream with the pain, hammering at the hatch. It burst open and I hurled myself up and through with tendrils of fire chasing me.

I rolled out onto the floor above. Sheets of plywood roughly laid over the beams, more paintings stacked and piled in every direction. Images that danced in the glow from the hatchway. Dead flowers, decaying rooms, hanging bodies. More images of Terry's long obsession with his terrible past.

The attic was already filling with smoke. I staggered to my feet. The boarded area extended about ten feet in either direction from the hatchway, but the open space continued beyond that, disappearing into the gloom.

There were no walls.

I walked into the darkness, bent over to avoid the low rafters as well as the smoke, a growing heat and glow from behind urging me on. At the end of the boarded section, joists continued on, while a faint daylight filtered up from below. Where the plaster had once been was an empty space – promising a way down, until I looked and saw that the floor below was missing as well. Rotted away or taken for some reason. There was no safe way down.

Stepping precariously from joist to joist, gripping the rafters for support, and still keeping a firm hold on the laptop, I kept going.

At some point I crossed a divide, and was over another house. The plaster was intact here. But it would give way if I trod on it, and falling through into the unknown didn't appeal.

The smoke was ever thicker. I was struggling to breathe, I could barely see. I had to get down again, I had to get out.

Ahead, another faint glow of daylight.

There was a hole in the plaster. Not big, about a foot across. Big enough so I could see through to the floor below; see that there was a floor, partly covered with a mound of old clothing, partly with empty bottles.

Good enough.

I perched on the joist and kicked at the edges of the hole. The old plaster crumbled away, falling in lumps onto the clothing. When it was big enough, I said a short but sincere prayer and stepped through.

I was aiming for the clothing, but landed among the bottles. Fortunately, they were plastic, but my ankle twisted painfully as one slipped out from under my foot, and I stumbled forward onto the mound of clothing.

Which sat up and roared at me.

"Wha? Wha yer doing? Wha?"

Now I was out of the smoke I could smell the stench of long-term neglect overlaid by cheap alcohol.

"You've got to get out! Fire!" I shouted.

Tried to shout. I couldn't manage more than a whisper.

A red face peered at me through a tangled mass of hair. "Wha?" he said again. At least, I thought it was a he. "WHA?" He added some other words. Swear words. Actually, only one, repeated.

"Fire!" I tried again. "Fire." Still no volume.

"Go awa'!" he shouted back. More successfully than me. "My place! Go AWAY!"

There was a distant boom. The building shook and more plaster fell from the hole I'd enlarged. The fire had reached the gas canisters, I assumed. The shaking didn't stop, and the boom was followed by a rumbling and crashing, which sounded like walls coming down.

"Wha?" he said again.

I had to get out. I didn't have time for this smelly piece of human wreckage.

"*Why bother?*" Geraint whispered in my mind. "*Why care, Sandra?*"

I stepped forward, leaned as close as possible, and whispered as loudly as I could. "What's your name?"

"Eh?" He looked puzzled. "My name? Sam. I'm Sam."

I nodded. Smiled. "Good name! My son is called Sam. I'm Sandra. But listen carefully, Sam. We've got to get out. The building's on fire. It's all coming down."

He looked round, bewildered. "It's my place."

I pushed my mouth into the mass of hair, about where I judged his ear to be. "Fire, Sam! It's on fire! Get out!"

I grabbed a handful of whatever he was wearing and pushed him towards the nearby stairs. "Go! Fire!"

The building shuddered again. Comprehension suddenly showed in Sam's eyes.

"Fire!" he said, and followed it with another stream of obscenities. Probably justified, in the circumstances.

He turned to his bedding and began searching through it.

"No time for that, we've got to go!" I tried to tell him, but he ignored me, reaching into the ragged remnants of a sleeping bag and pulling out a small rough-haired dog, who yapped sleepily at me.

Without another word, Sam lumbered towards the stairs and down. I followed, hobbling because my ankle was adding pain at every step.

The stairs lacked a banister, and in several places lacked even stairs. Sam stepped over them, which at least gave me a clue of what was coming, but I had to stop on the edge, unsure if I could get across. I could barely put enough weight on my ankle for a normal step, let alone to stretch across the hole.

Sam was nearly at the bottom, but turned around and saw my predicament. Without a word – not even a swear one – he put his dog down, came back up, and extended an arm.

"Come on, Sandra. Got to go. Fire!" he told me. He gripped my arm and with surprising strength pulled me across the gap.

I still had the laptop. But I continued to hold on to Sam with my other hand as we carried on down the stairs, and then out through another one of the council's metal doors, this one hanging half open, and finally back out into Quondam Road and the mercy of fresh air.

But not very fresh.

Thick smoke was rolling along the street, driven by the fresh breeze. Just a few houses up from where we stood, flames were pouring out from every window, while beyond them a pile of burning rubble blocked off the road.

I turned to look the other way, and saw more walls, where Quondam Road ended in a small square, the Victorian buildings staring down from every side, doorways sealed off with brick or metal.

"We can't get out!" I whispered. "Sam, we can't get out!"

He didn't say anything, but began heading down the street, away from the fire, still supporting me, and with the dog running ahead.

The dog knew where to go. So did Sam: round the corner of the square, off to the left, pushing aside some boards to enter an enclosed alley running between and beneath the buildings.

We came out on another street. This one was more open. The air was fresher. And at the end of it was another fence.

"Come on. Not far."

There were sirens in the distance. Getting louder, getting closer.

Sam was practically carrying me now. The strength seemed to be draining out of me. But he kept me upright, kept me moving, all the way up to the fence.

Like Quondam Road, the further end, with slightly more modern housing, was still occupied, and people were coming out of the houses, staring at the huge cloud of smoke, packing kids and possessions into cars and vans.

Sam pushed aside a section of fence, the barrier as porous here as elsewhere. People were looking at us. Speaking, asking questions. I couldn't understand them, couldn't manage to answer. I just wanted to sit down, or lie down, take the weight off my ankle, go to sleep.

"Safe now, Sandra," Sam said, and stepped back as other hands came to take my weight. "Got to tell the others." He disappeared, and someone was helping me across to a doorstep, sitting me down.

"We'll get an ambulance," someone was saying. I didn't know if they were talking to me, but an ambulance sounded good. An ambulance would take me to hospital. I might get to see Graham. I so wanted to see Graham.

The sirens were very close now. And then a car was in front of me, blue flashing lights. Police. A constable was out of the car, telling everyone to evacuate, to clear the buildings and leave quickly. "We're setting up shelters!" he was saying. "Go to the church hall. Saint Mark's."

There were people round him, asking questions. He was telling them something. I couldn't hear. Didn't matter. Except that I needed to talk to him. Something I needed to tell him.

Then he came over. Talking on his radio. Just like that night at the library.

"November Charlie four-two, can we get an ambulance to Manatee Street, ASAP. Woman with severe burns here."

November Charlie four-two. That was Mike Newbold's call sign.

He was leaning over me. "Ambulance is on its way; you'll be OK."

I looked up at him. "Mike?"

His eyes opened in surprise. "Who... Mrs Deeson! What are you doing here?"

I forced a smile. "Long story. Here." I pushed the laptop at him. I'd been gripping it so hard that I had trouble letting go. "Give this to DI Macrae. Tell him it's Emily's."

DAY 7: QUONDAM

He took the laptop. "Yes, OK, but…"

I didn't hear anything else. His voice faded away, along with the sirens.

EPILOGUE

I had a new phone now. I hadn't downloaded the "Daily Eloquence" app. I'd decided on a different approach: from now on, I'd wait till the end of the day and then find a word that fitted it.

Brodie snored contentedly on the sofa next to me as I stroked his fur – gently. Not for his sake but mine – my hands, along with a great many other parts of me, were still very tender. It was only my second day out of hospital, and I was still enjoying the simple pleasure of just being home.

Graham had been out a lot longer than me, of course, and had had the door replaced and the house repainted before I came back. There was no longer even a lingering smell of smoke, which was just as well. I didn't want to have the slightest whiff of that odour, ever again.

He bustled in with the local paper. "Grim headlines," he announced. "But at least it seems like something's going to be done about Delford Mills."

"A bit too late, though." My voice was still a bit croaky, and I couldn't talk for long. "Nearly two hundred years too late." I reached for the paper.

"TENTH BODY DISCOVERED IN MILLS FIRE" the headline shouted. And, underneath: "Is This the Final Tragedy in the Delford Saga?"

"I don't want to read it." I handed the newspaper back to him. "Summarize it for me, will you?"

"Well, they've pulled another body out of the rubble, but they think that everywhere's been searched now. Huge fuss over it all, of course – national scandal and so on. Big argument between government and council over who's responsible. There's a certain body of opinion suggesting that these bodies might have been dead before the fire – overdose victims and so on. Though to my mind that's still a tragedy, if of a slightly different sort. But in any case, a lot of people are pointing out that if the wind had been in the other direction, the fire would have spread into the inhabited – officially inhabited – streets, and the body count would have been far higher."

"I hope Sam got out OK."

Graham sat down next to Brodie and took over stroking duty. "Ah, that's a funny thing. According to some reports, the reason why a lot of the squatters made it out is that someone called Sam went round raising the alarm. They're calling him 'The Hero of the Mills' and saying that he deserves a medal."

"I'd be happy to give him one. I wouldn't have got out myself without him."

"Unfortunately, no one's been able to find him. He disappeared off somewhere in the confusion; no one knows where to."

"So what happens to the Mills now?"

Graham opened the paper, flicked through a few pages. "Apparently, some funds have finally been found to redevelop the whole area properly. Maybe this time…"

Brodie suddenly woke up and looked suspicious, just before the doorbell rang.

"He never goes to answer it now," I observed. "Very sensible, Brodie."

"No need to worry, though. It's probably DI Macrae. I'll get it."

Brodie followed him to the living room door, and looked round cautiously as he opened it. David Macrae came in a moment later, stopping to give Brodie a scratch behind the ears.

"Sandra, it's good to see you looking so well," he said.

"I'm still looking awful, and I know it, so spare me the flattery!"

"Well, you're not yet at your best, I'm sure. But better than you were, perhaps?"

"That's true," I conceded, and indicated a chair.

He sat down, but refused Graham's offer of tea or coffee. "I can't be staying long," he explained. "I've another murder investigation running, so things are a wee bit busy. But I wanted to see how you're doing, Sandra. And to give you this."

He took a small object from his pocket, and handed it over. A flash drive.

"That's from Emily's laptop. She'd photographed every one of Terry Naylor's paintings, it seems, and catalogued them all. We're holding on to the laptop itself, but I've been cleared to pass these to you. I understand you might have use for them?"

I nodded. "When I finally get back to work, I want to have an exhibition in his memory. And Emily's. It won't be the same as having the originals, of course, but we should still be able to give an idea of how talented he was. And perhaps we'll get some of Sir Arthur's works as well. That would sort of tell the whole story, wouldn't it?"

Macrae nodded. "The local artists."

"Indeed." I hesitated, then went ahead with my question. "I heard that you'd called off the search of Sheerside Quarry?"

He nodded. "Aye. I'm sorry, Sandra, but there's no certainty that Emily's body is even down there, and the divers tell me that conditions are terrible. Visibility at the bottom is no more than a foot or two with all the mud and silt in the water. It took them a week to find Jonathan's Porsche, and that's knowing it was there."

"OK. I understand. It was just that… well, Emily deserved better."

"That she did. We may find something yet. There's a team still going over everything we got from Geraint Templeton's house – and very interesting some of it is, as well! – so we're hoping we might be able to trace whoever was doing all the dirty work on his behalf. In which case, there's a lot of questions we'd like to ask, but Emily would be one of the first ones, I promise." He stood up. "Sorry to be rushing off so soon, but duty calls. Let me know about that exhibition. I definitely want to be there."

Graham showed him out. I sat back and closed my eyes, trying to remember Emily as I'd last seen her. "I wish I'd known what she was up to," I said as he came back in. "Perhaps I could have done something."

"Hey, no more guilt trips over things you can't help!" he admonished. "You did everything you could, and more than could have been expected, and things would have been a lot worse without you!"

He was about to sit down when the phone rang, and he got up again with a sigh. "All this butlering about is getting tiresome," he complained. "You need to recover faster!"

He went out to the hall, and came back a few minutes later with the handset, and a strange expression on his face. "It's for you," he said, handing it over.

I took it, raising an eyebrow at him, but he just shrugged.

"Hello, Sandra Deeson."

"Hello?" A familiar voice, but I couldn't quite place it for a moment. I hadn't heard it in a while. "Hello – Mum?"

The breath stopped in my throat. "Sam? SAM! Is that you?"

The voice held laughter. "Yes, Mum, it's me! Listen, I'm back in the UK just now. I was wondering…" A note of hesitancy crept in. "Would it be OK if I came home for a while?"

I didn't answer at first. I struggled to get the words out.
"Yes, yes! Come home, Sam! Come home!"
The word for the day is "Prodigal".

COMING SOON

LOCAL LEGEND

Whet your appetite with Chapter 1…

CHAPTER 1

"I'm not saying that sport is corrupt. But money and corruption go together like nuts and bolts. And there's a lot of money in sport."

Adi Varney, quoted in Adi Varney – A True Legend *by*
Graham Deeson

A lot of things start at weddings. A new life for the happy couple, obviously. New relationships among the guests, quite frequently. A fight, sometimes.

For me, June and Rob's wedding was the beginning of the end of a very long story.

I picked my place card out of the detritus of the meal, and ran my thumb over the name. Nice clear font, slightly embossed printing, and they'd spelled my name right.

"GRAHAM DEESON".

Perhaps a bit more businesslike than was right for a wedding, but on the whole I approved. Having some good contacts in the area, I'd been asked to recommend a printer who'd do a quality job at a reasonable price: I was glad to see that they hadn't let me down.

I picked up the card next to me, and checked that as well.

"SANDRA DEESON".

It had a smudge of something on it, which I carefully wiped off. And finally admitted to myself that I was bored. Weddings are OK, up to a point. I like the ceremony and I'm always ready for a free meal. But I've never been one for parties. Not the loud and crowded sort, anyway. My idea of a social occasion is a quiet meal in a good restaurant with a few friends, and the reception was well past that point.

It had taken a little while, since Rob's mates – mostly van drivers – had been wary of June's colleagues, who were all coppers. However, with a bit of alcohol to remove inhibitions, they'd come to realize that police officers were basically just people, and things had started to take off.

The live band had helped. A local group – pretty good, actually, but they were really hammering it out now, and it didn't do my ears much good.

I turned to my wife, who was deep in conversation with a young woman whom I had been introduced to earlier. David Macrae's lady, I recalled. I hadn't realized that the Detective Inspector was married – apparently she'd just moved down from Scotland, and was giving Sandra the full details.

"Sandy – I'm going for a walk, get some fresh air," I told her.

She nodded, looked around. "Where's Sam?"

"Over there by the buffet table, talking to that CSI girl. Alison, is it? Discussing something technical about photography." Our son had spent a good many years wandering the globe and in the process had discovered an interest.

Sandra peered through the crowd until she'd identified Sam, and nodded again. There was still a part of her that was afraid he'd take off again and disappear back into the world. I was almost certain that he would. "OK, love." She returned to her conversation.

I weaved between the tables, picking up odd scraps of conversation on the way. Old habit. I've had a lot of useful leads like that.

"... I kid you not, this bloke must have been seven foot tall..."

"... If you know you can't handle them, why do you keep on..."

"... I bet you've arrested every one of my mates!"

That sounded interesting, but I moved on, found an exit, and stepped out into a cool summer evening.

CHAPTER 1

The Stag is a bit of an architectural disaster. It started off as an unremarkable village inn. Then it had a big single-storey dining area added on and became a gastropub. The development of a major road network nearby suggested other possibilities to the owners, and they built a two-storey extension and made it into a hotel – or motel. Do we still use that word? Finally, as an afterthought, they put in a semi-permanent marquee at the back and advertised it as a "function room", which was where I'd just escaped from.

It wasn't the place I'd want to begin married life, but it wasn't my choice. Apparently, Rob and June had some history with the place, first date or something. And at least the catering had been OK. Especially the gateaux. I'm very fond of gateaux.

There was a wide terrace along the back of the gastro section of the pub, opened up for eating during the day but closed now it was dark. The restaurant itself was crowded and doing good business, but I ignored that, preferring the relative quiet of the lawn on the other side. It ran down to a stand of trees and some picturesque ruins a few hundred feet away. They had made a nice backdrop for the photographs earlier. I suspected that they had been placed there for just that purpose. I wondered if there were builders who specialized in fake ruins.

The original pub building at the end of the terrace was now a separate bar for guests in the hotel section that stretched off beyond it – a dreary concrete slab that should never have been given planning permission in my opinion. But nobody had asked me.

I glanced into the bar as I strolled past. It was crammed full of rustic charm – horse brasses, quaintly rusting farm implements and, of course, a stag's head. Not nearly as crowded as the restaurant, just a few people sitting here and there, nursing drinks.

And sitting on a bar stool was Adi Varney.

I nearly missed seeing him altogether. He was with two other people, half hidden by a tall, thin man in a suit. But just as I glanced that way, he was leaning back, glass to his lips, and I saw him in profile.

I stopped. And stared.

Of course it wasn't him. It couldn't be him. Not back in England, back home again. Not after all these years.

But it looked like him, just like him, and a big bubble of joy burst out of me, and even while I was still not believing it in my head my body was at the window, banging on it and shouting, "Adi! Adi! Hey – Adi – it's me!"

A middle-aged woman sitting nearby jumped, and splashed her drink. She gave me a furious look which I barely noticed.

Adi didn't respond, perhaps didn't hear me. They'd put some thick double glazing in the old windows, and the bar was on the other side of the room. He just sat there, cradling a drink and looking at something in his hand. A mobile, probably.

The thin man looked round as I continued to bang on the window. He touched Adi's shoulder and said something. Adi glanced up and saw me.

He looked puzzled. Frowning. Looked right at me – and looked away again.

Not a flicker of recognition. As if he didn't know me at all.

I stood staring through the window, not understanding. *It must be the light*, I thought. *There's a reflection on the glass or something. He can't see who it is.*

I moved along to another window, a bit closer to where Adi was, and tried again. A bit more carefully this time. No frenzied banging, just a gentle tap. Less gentle, though, as he continued to ignore me.

The other man with him looked around and frowned at me. Not a puzzled frown. More of a warning, a "back off" sort of frown. He was a big bloke, wide shoulders straining at a black leather jacket. He looked as if he was used to telling people to back off.

The thin one, an older man, was saying something to Adi, who shrugged and stood up, finishing his drink.

They all headed for the door without a glance back in my direction.

CHAPTER 1

I looked around for a way in, saw a fire door at the far end of the old pub. Of course, it was locked from the outside. I hammered on it with the heel of my hand to no effect.

Beyond the original buildings was the long concrete block of the hotel accommodation. I started running. They hadn't bothered landscaping this end of the site – it was all rough ground and scraggly bushes. Hard going for anybody, let alone someone with all my recent health problems. I was panting hard by the time I rounded the end of the building – at which point it occurred to me that it would have been quicker to go back into the marquee and out the front.

Too late. It was further to go back now, and there was at least a path this side, running down towards the hotel entrance.

I burst into the lobby, and the young man at reception jumped up in alarm – as well he might, when a panting, sweating, balding middle-aged man suddenly charged through the front door and ran at him.

"Sir? Do you need an ambulance?" It was a reasonable question, under the circumstances.

"N… N…" I gasped, and waved my hands ineffectually. "No!" I finally managed to get out, as he picked up a phone. "I'm OK." Pause and gasp again. "Really. Thank you. I'm fine."

The lad didn't appear convinced, but he put down the phone and gave me a wary look. "Was there something else I could do for you, sir?"

"Yes. I've just seen someone. In your bar. An old friend. Adi Varney?"

"Adi Varney?" He frowned, then his eyebrows shot up. "You don't mean *the* Adi Varney? Adi Varney the footballer?"

"Yes, that Adi Varney!" Was there another one? "He's in the bar – was a few minutes ago, anyway."

The receptionist shook his head, regretfully. "No, sir. You must be mistaken. That bar's for hotel guests only, and I'm pretty sure that Adi Varney isn't one of them. More's the pity – I'd love to be able to call my dad and tell him we've had Adi staying here!"

I took a longer look at him. He couldn't have been more than twenty, so he wouldn't have been around when Adi was in his heyday. But his dad would have been.

"You a Vale supporter, then?"

His face lit up. "Third generation! Used to be there for every home game – me, me dad, and me grandpa!" In his enthusiasm, a bit of local accent began to creep in. "Me ma as well, sometimes. Me dad can't get out much nowadays, so I don't go so often. And they're not doing too well just now, are they – not like the old days."

"That's a fact. Only just escaped relegation last season – and to be honest, that was better than they deserved."

We shared the sad look of loyal fans who've been let down by their club.

"You wouldn't mind just having a look at the guest list, would you? Make sure that Adi's definitely not on there?"

He shrugged. "Couldn't do any harm, I suppose." He turned to the computer, punched some keys, and studied the screen. "No, sorry. Twenty-three guests currently, none of them a Varney. But I can't see someone like him coming here in any case. He'd be at a five-star place somewhere."

The lad had a point. Adi had always been ready to enjoy whatever money could buy him. I scratched my chin, baffled.

"OK, so perhaps he came in as somebody's guest? Visiting someone who is staying here?"

"Perhaps. But I've been on all evening, and I'm pretty sure that he didn't come through here."

"But if he'd been here earlier?"

"Maybe, but if Adi Varney was in the hotel, someone would be bound to recognize him and the word would get around."

That was a thought. The bartender must have seen him.

"Could I go through to the bar and ask in there? Just to put my mind at rest?"

He hesitated. "I'm not supposed to let anyone through apart from guests…"

"Just for a few moments. I'll just look, ask a few questions – no trouble, I promise."

"OK then. For a Vale supporter!"

He nodded to a door just past the reception desk.

"Thanks." I slipped through quickly, in case he changed his mind.

The bar had filled up a little since I'd looked in from the other side – there was another entrance that came directly from the guest rooms. The one that Adi and his companions had been heading for, I decided, as I looked around and got my bearings. They certainly weren't here now. The woman I'd caused to spill her drink was, though – fortunately engrossed in something on her mobile. I stayed well clear of her as I made my way to the bar.

The barman looked up as I approached and took on a wary expression. He had obviously seen me banging on the window.

I held up my hands. "Sorry about just now. I didn't mean to cause any trouble. It was just that I thought I saw an old friend in here – someone I haven't been in touch with for years – and I was trying to get his attention."

He relaxed slightly at my explanation. "Yes, sir. I understand." He had a definite transatlantic twang.

"His name is Adi Varney."

He returned a polite but essentially blank look. "I don't know the name, sir."

"Adi Varney the football player. England international, top league goalscorer…"

"I guess you mean football as in soccer? Sorry, sir, I'm not much of a sports fan."

"Over from the States?" I hazarded a guess.

"Yes, sir. Taking a little time out from law school."

"OK, so you wouldn't know about Adi Varney. But he's a really big name round here. Ask your colleague out in reception."

The barman picked up a cloth and began wiping down the bar. Every bartender does that while they're having a conversation.

"So he's like the local superstar? And a friend of yours as well?"

"That's right. We were born in the same hospital, grew up on the same street. And Adi played for the local team for his entire career. So in these parts he's a really big deal – nearest thing we've got to a superhero! But I haven't seen him in years, not since he went out to the US himself. California. Are you from that way?"

He shook his head. "Boston. Never been further west than Chicago. I guess it must have been a surprise, seeing him again?"

"You can say that again! Listen, he was sitting just about here. Do you remember? Light brown hair, little moustache, a sort of roundish face?"

"Yeah, I remember him. Didn't hear his name, though."

"Is he staying here at the hotel?"

"I couldn't say for sure. The guy with him is though, because he had the tab charged to his room."

"The man with the black jacket?"

"No. I didn't know him either. It was Mr Lonza signing for everything."

"Lonza?" It wasn't a name that was familiar to me.

"Sure. Rocco Lonza. Hey, you think you were surprised to see your friend here? Well, it was one heck of a surprise to see Lonza, I can tell you! Never expected a guy like him to turn up in a place like this."

I still had no idea whom he was talking about, but he seemed happy to talk and I was happy to let him. Hotel staff are often a bit tight-lipped about their guests – but bar staff are the best bet for a bit of information. Especially when they are essentially just passing through.

"You know him, then?" I prompted.

"Not personally, but over in the States he's real big in business. *Some* sorts of business." He put a distinct emphasis on "some", and gave me a knowing look. "Sort of like your guy is in soccer, I guess: if you know the game, you know the name."

"What sort of business? Sports, perhaps?"

CHAPTER 1

"Sure, sports. Lot of other things as well. He's one of these wheeler-dealer guys, always got a whole lot of things going on at once, you know?"

He glanced around, then leaned forward and spoke more quietly. "Word is though that a lot of those deals are – what's the word you use over here? Dodgy?"

"You mean dodgy as in borderline illegal?"

"That's right. That sort of dodgy. Not that he's ever been convicted or anything, so don't repeat it. But they say he's connected."

"Connected?"

"Yeah! You know. Like he's connected with the Mob."

The Mob. Gangsters, organized crime, Godfathers. I looked at him, incredulous. That sort of stuff happened in films. Not in commonplace little hotel bars in England.

"You're kidding me. The Mob? Really?"

He nodded vigorously. "That's what I've heard. All that money he does his dealing with – it's Mafia money, and he's their top laundry guy."

I stared at him, then shook my head. "Well, I must be wrong then. I mean – the Mafia? That wouldn't be Adi. Couldn't be. Sorry, my mistake."

I went back out through reception, nodding to the Vale fan, who was still behind the counter.

"Any luck?" he asked.

"No, it wasn't him. Just looked very much like him, that's all."

He shook his head, sorrowfully. "Pity. It would have been something to have Adi Varney here."

"It would indeed," I agreed. "Thanks for your help, anyway."

I headed back to the marquee and the wedding reception, amazed yet again by the affection that local people still had for Adi, even after all these years. I wished it had been him. There was so much I wanted – needed – to say. But I was now quite sure that it couldn't have been. Adi, mixed up with the Mafia? One hundred per cent not.

Well, ninety-nine per cent not, anyway.
That odd one per cent was going to get me into trouble.

COLD, COLD HEART

"An intelligent, thought-provoking read, with engaging and believable characters. It gripped me from the start, and didn't let go."
Shots Magazine

MIDWINTER IN ANTARCTICA.

SIX MONTHS OF DARKNESS ARE ABOUT TO BEGIN.

Scientist Katie Flanagan has an undeserved reputation as a trouble-maker and her career has foundered. When an accident creates an opening on a remote Antarctic research base she seizes it, flying in on the last plane before the subzero temperatures make it impossible to leave.

Meanwhile patent lawyer Daniel Marchmont has been asked to undertake due diligence on a breakthrough cancer cure. But the key scientist is strangely elusive and Daniel uncovers a dark secret that leads to Antarctica.

Out on the ice a storm is gathering. As the crew lock down the station they discover a body and realize that they are trapped with a killer...

ISBN: 978 1 78264 216 9 | e-ISBN: 978 1 78264 217 6